A Deadly Kind of Paradise

Joe Greaney

First Print Edition: July 2013

For Nancy

A Deadly Kind of Paradise

One

I don't know when, exactly, it became obvious to me that I had to get out of D.C. I mean, there were a lot of things going on that I wasn't too crazy about, and I had been vaguely dissatisfied with my life in general for a long time. Years, maybe. And I think I might have made up my mind without really even knowing it long before I made the move. But Reynard getting killed was pretty much the last straw. Reynard was a good friend of mine, I met him on the very first case I ever had, right when I started with the Public Defenders Service a dozen years ago. He had lived with me for a while when he was finishing high school, and he had gone on to promote concerts and parties all around the District, all quite successfully. And then he put on a small concert up in Upper Northwest, in one of the safest neighborhoods in the city just down New Mexico Avenue from American University, and somebody put a bullet in his brain over the gate receipts. The receipts might have totaled a couple of thousand dollars at the most, and the show was a benefit for AIDS research and now he was dead and suddenly I didn't want to be in a place where this could happen. Of course everywhere is a place where this could happen, but that's not what I was thinking, how I felt, as I helped carry the coffin into the church. What I was thinking was, I need to get out of this city. And then I thought of Dickie.

A long time ago, longer ago than I really care to think about, I went to high school with Richard Du Pont Harrington . Back then I never knew Dickie's middle name, and I wouldn't have cared or thought differently about him if I had. Lots of people have important relatives. Not me, but that doesn't prove anything. And Dickie was the furthest thing from a snob. He was a lean whipcord-strong kid with long sandy hair, a lightweight wrestler and cross-country runner with a passion for martial arts and anything to do with the ocean. A shortish bandy-legged kid with a quiet self-effacing manner and a quick smile. A normal guy, a smart kid with a wry wit and a positive attitude. A good friend to have.

After graduation Dickie and I went our separate ways and we hadn't seen each other for years. But a couple of years ago my sometime girlfriend Bunny and I went on a little weekend excursion to Dewey Beach, Delaware. Bunny is Bonita Lopes, a raven-haired Portuguese-American beauty from Fall River, Massachusetts, who somehow ended up with a Spanish first name. The story on her nickname went that Bunny's younger brother couldn't pronounce "Bonita" when they were little, hence "Bunny". And now it was somewhat ironic – in the same vein as calling a big guy "Tiny". Because while Bunny could have been a bunny in any magazine she wanted to appear in, there is nothing of the rabbit in her personality. Far from it. Think polar opposite.

On a sunsplashed July afternoon in Dewey Beach there walking down the street carrying a bucket of Buffalo wings and a six-pack of Grolsch beer was Dickie. We had known each other instantly. His long hair was lightly flecked with grey, and there were a few creases in the sun-weathered face, but it was Dickie for all that.

Bunny and I had been on our way back to our hotel, and since it was only steps away, and since we had a nice little balcony overlooking the beach, we invited Dickie to come along. The delicious-smelling wings and the glistening bottles of Grolsch had nothing to do with it. Or not much, at least. As we demolished the wings and beer Dickie told us that he had been living in Dewey for several years, in a beach house he had inherited from his grandfather, and it was only then that I found out about his middle name. Du Pont is a big name in Delaware. It's been said that the Du Ponts own the whole state. It's not true, of course. Some other people own small parts here and there.

We sat on the balcony outside our hotel room and shot the breeze until the shadows began to lengthen and Dickie got up to leave. Before he left he invited us back to his house for a cookout later and we were happy to oblige.

Later Bunny and I made love with the balcony doors open, the rhythmic pounding of the waves keeping time. Or was it the other way around? And when we were done Bunny slipped into sleep, her head thrown back, her black black hair splayed out on the pillow, the barest hint of a snore rattling in her throat. I tried to nap but I wasn't tired. After a few minutes I went out and stood on the balcony and smoked a cigarette, and when that was done I went back inside. Bunny was the picture of relaxation so I left her alone and went for a walk down to the liquor store so we wouldn't arrive at Dickie's place empty-handed.

Out on the street it was busy, the pulse quickening and the traffic thickening as beach time ended and party time approached. Dewey Beach is a funky little resort town on the Atlantic coast of Delaware, about three hours east of Washington. Barely more than a mile from end to end, wedged onto the spit of sand that separates the ocean from the warm shallow waters of Rehoboth Bay, Dewey doesn't really have room to grow, so it has remained small and relatively low-key. Delaware doesn't have all that much coastline - or all that much state, for that matter - but what it does have is very nice. From Lewes in the north to Fenwick Island in the south the whole Atlantic coastline is barely twenty-five miles long, but that short stretch encompasses some of the nicer beaches and towns that you'll find, and much of the land has been preserved as parkland. Just to the south of the state line lies the resort colossus of Ocean City, Maryland, home to thirty-story beachfront condos, more bars than you can imagine and more than three hundred thousand revelers on a big weekend. Delaware's not like that. Not that you won't find a few Camaros in Dewey. Dewey has a reputation as a party spot in its own right, a reputation fueled by the big bars like the Bottle and Cork and the Starboard and the legions of young people who fill many of the rental houses to capacity every summer weekend. Dewey was one of the last places in the East where it was legal to drink on the beach, but that had changed. And in recent years the town fathers, with an eye on real estate values, have tried hard and with some success to tone things down a bit, to quiet the kids and slow the pace.

But still on this summer's Saturday night the narrow sidewalks were thick with sun-reddened twenty- and thirty-somethings, and loud music blared from the outside courtyard at the Bottle and Cork and the deck at the Starboard was jammed and the line at the counter on the liquor store was ten deep and it was a Dewey Saturday Night, Yes Sir.

When I got back to the hotel Bunny was in the shower and I sat outside and drank a beer, and watched people strolling on the darkening beach, and listened to the waves and it was fine, just fine. And the cookout at Dickie's was a blast, you couldn't believe the house, a rambling grey-shingled relic on its own quarter-mile or more of beach, the only house on the empty stretch between the north end of Dewey and the south end of the next town up, Rehoboth. The house was perched on the narrow strip of sand between the ocean and Silver Lake, and the only way to get there by road is to go through Rehoboth. The house is in neither Dewy nor Rehoboth, occupying instead a sliver of unincorporated land that separates the two. A leggy sun-bleached blond with a molasses drawl and the regal bearing that comes only with generations of money told me that Dickie's grandfather hadn't wanted to pay taxes to either town and had thwarted all attempts at annexation so successfully that in the end the towns stopped trying. One of the results of all this was that there was no law on Dickie's beach. The only police with jurisdiction over the place were the State Police, and they needed to be called in by Dickie because it was all private property. And so far Dickie had never had to call them in. So Dickie's house had water front and back and high old dunes anchored by tortured wind-blasted pines on three sides and we didn't have to worry about the neighbors or the police since there weren't any and we cranked the music up and laughed and danced and joked with Dickie and maybe twenty of his friends and it was a full moon and a cloudless night and we went skinny dipping in the ocean around midnight and Bunny and I finally dragged ourselves back to the hotel when the sky had begun to lighten again, and it was, well, it was just one of the better times I've had.

I'd been down to see Dickie, with Bunny and without, several times in the couple of years since that night, and always had fun, always felt like I had really gotten away, and Dickie had been up to D.C. a couple of times and stayed in my apartment and whenever he did he'd always extend an open invitation, he'd say come down and visit, come and stay a while, stay as long as you want, all summer if you want, there's plenty of room and why the hell would you want to stay in Washington all through the hot hazy summer anyway? And in the May of a difficult year, I took him up on it.

A difficult year. It sounds so melodramatic. I wasn't having a difficult year by the standards of a refugee or a cancer patient, but everything's relative. I had spent a dozen years working the same job, a dozen years as an investigator for the Public Defender Service in Washington, and it was getting harder and harder to go to work every day. The grind continued, the flood of tragedy and heartbreak continued, no matter what you did. There were times when you could help someone who needed it and that still felt good, but most of the time it was a never-ending trail of tears and heartbreak, of lives ruined, of victims and criminals you could barely tell apart and it was getting old. Was old. I wasn't getting anywhere. Not with work, and certainly not personally. Bunny and I just couldn't seem to move forward, couldn't seem to take the next step, and although there were times when a breakthrough appeared imminent, when it seemed like the time to make a commitment, to make a life together, had finally arrived, something would always happen and everything would blow up and it would be back to square one.

And now in the spring of the year the on-again off-again relationship was off again, and Reynard was dead, and I had time coming to me at work, and I said the hell with it. Or more like the heck with it. I deliberately didn't burn any bridges or make any permanent life-changing decisions, I just called Dickie up and asked him if it'd be cool if I came down and stayed a couple weeks, maybe a month or so, a little longer if it's all right, and he said yeah, of course, how many times have I said it's fine, and the answer was somewhere between several and a lot so I said I dunno, Dude, but if you meant it I'm on my way. He asked when and I said tomorrow morning and he said, what you do, Bro', is throw some clothes in a bag and lock the door and pick up a six-pack and get the hell on the road right now before you change your mind and I'll see you in about three hours, 'cause I'm having a party tonight and besides you don't want to think about it and change your mind, so just, like they say, do it. And he had a point because I knew that if I started thinking about it, started debating the relative merits of staying versus going, started worrying about Bunny and work and just what, exactly, I was doing in life and started thinking that it was silly to be going away without any definite plans, well, I probably would end up staying put. Paralysis by analysis, I call it. I read somewhere that it's a sign of intelligence to be able to see both sides of an issue at once, but it's more like a curse when it prevents you from doing anything at all.

And so I just did it. In half an hour I was heading outbound on New York Avenue with the radio up loud, tuned to the best station on the east coast, WRNR in Annapolis, and I was listening to the Dead and singing along to the Wheel. And a couple hours after that I was rolling down Route One in Rehoboth, running the gauntlet of the endless outlet malls, their vast parking lots empty under the orange glow of the sodium-vapor lamps, and a few minutes after that I was pulling into Dickie's driveway, the crushed-shell surface crunching beneath my wheels, and a minute or two after that I was sitting out on Dickie's deck with a cold Heineken in my hand and a sea breeze blowing through my hair and Dickie was telling me about how he was going to teach me to windsurf, and music was playing on the stereo in the high-ceilinged living room and crystalline female laughter from one of the other guests mixed with the music, all of it spilling out the open windows and the two sets of French doors into a night fraught with possibilities.

And six weeks later I was still there, with no plans to leave. After I'd been down for a couple of weeks I decided I had no desire to go back - not yet, at least. I missed Bunny, a bit, sometimes, but she seemed like she understood when I drove up to D.C. to talk to her and to Lenny, my boss at work. And I told them both that I needed some time away, some time to figure out what it was that I was doing with my life and to tell you the truth I think they both agreed completely. Maybe too completely. I was almost insulted, probably would have been insulted if I wasn't relaxed and happy for the first time in a long time. Bunny said she'd come down for a weekend soon, and Lenny said my job was there if I wanted it, and there was a young guy, an earnest young clean-cut law student from Antioch who was interning at PDS over the summer who was looking for a place to live and I sublet my apartment to him though the first of September and I packed up my CD's and some more clothes, put the rest of my personal stuff in the hall closet, secured the closet door with a padlock and a hasp I picked up at the hardware store down the street and I was set. For once I even had some money in my pocket and I was due some more from the court system for cases that I had worked on. All told about three grand in hand and another three coming, and free rent at Dickie's place so all I needed was beer and food and gas and I was in pretty good shape for a couple of months.

Imagine that. Money in the bank, and no responsibilities and a beautiful house on the beach to stay in rent-free. And it turned out that Dickie was a gourmet cook and loved to feed people and since much of the time I was the only one around that meant me. And Bunny had come down a couple of times and it had been great to be with her, we got along better than we had in years, with all the pressure off it was easy to remember why I loved her, and we laughed and had fun and made love in the big bed in the big bedroom overlooking the ocean , and it was all good. And I was learning how to windsurf, and I was outside every day, getting healthy, getting fit, and feeling really good, really sane and content for the first time in years. It was almost too good to be true.

It was, in fact, to good to be true.

Two

"Dickie?"

No answer.

"Yo, Dick!"

Still no answer. It was the end of a beautiful Dewey day, an mid-August day that had been warm and sunny without a trace of humidity, one of those days when you can smell just a hint of the approaching fall in the air and it's chilly in the shade but warm and pleasant in the sun. I had spent all afternoon at the sailing spot at New Road in the Delaware Seashore State Park on Route One just south of Dewey, trying yet again to figure out windsurfing. A steady wind had blown from the northwest across Rehoboth Bay all afternoon, and it had been a perfect day to practice. And I needed the practice. I was still terrible, but at least I had learned enough about the sport to have a glimmer of an idea about what I was trying to accomplish. And now back home, I was tired but feeling good, feeling like I had made some progress.

I had pulled the trusty rusty Impala into the drive and parked next to Dickie's truck. For some reason his driver's side door had been wide open. When I went to close it I kicked something metallic on the ground. Dickie's keys.

The front door to the house stood open too, but there was no sign of the man himself, no answer to my calls. It was already quite dark in the house, and I had felt like I was trespassing somehow as I walked from the foyer back into the living room. One of the sets of French doors leading to the deck was open, the long sheer curtains billowing ghostlike in the breeze. I stepped out onto the deck and stopped short. It was still pretty bright out here and I saw Dickie's inert form immediately. He lay on his side on a deck chair, curled up in an almost-fetal position. For some reason I feared the worst, feared that something terrible had happened, and my breath caught in my throat and my heart was pounding as I walked over to where he lay motionless. But when I leaned over him I saw the double row of empty beer bottles and the half-empty liter of Jim Beam and the overflowing ashtray on the ground on the far side of the chair, and I felt better instantly. Dickie had obviously spent the afternoon tying one on. While this was unusual, it was unlikely to be fatal. I was surprised at the cigarettes stubbed out in the ashtray, though. I never knew Dickie to smoke. And he obviously wasn't very good at it, judging by the slender white butts in the ashtray —Virginia Slims or something, some woman's brand, not the manly Marlboros like me. You got to be a real man to smoke the Cowboy Killers. Yup yup yup.

I shook Dickie lightly by the shoulder. "Hey, Dickie… Dickie, wake up, my man." He mumbled something in an irritated tone and pulled away from my grip, then shivered and curled himself into an even tighter ball. He was obviously freezing, but too drunk to do anything about moving. I thought of getting him a blanket but decided it would be better to get him up and into bed, so I shook him again and called his name a bit louder and more insistently until finally he rolled on his back and opened bleary eyes. He tried to speak, but only croaked unintelligibly. He wet his lips, cleared his throat and tried again. "Time's it?"

"Your bedtime, looks like. Seven-thirty, quarter of eight, somewhere in there. C'mon, let's get you upstairs."

"Need water."

"I'll get you some water when we get upstairs. I can't leave you here or you'll fall back asleep."

Dickie nodded sagely. "Sleep," he said solemnly. "Sleep."

"Yeah, it's a fine idea, just not out here. All right, here we go." I grabbed him by the ankles and turned his body, set his feet on the floor, then grabbed him beneath the arms and hoisted him to his feet. He was pure dead weight, it was like lifting a heavy bag of sand, but once he was on his feet his body took over and he stood under his own power, swaying gently in an imaginary breeze.

"Let's go, soldier."

Dickie nodded and mumbled "Go.". We had some trouble with the stairs but finally made it to the top and soon Dickie was sitting on the edge of his bed as I removed his shoes. "Thanks, man," he said. "Sorry."

"No problem. I've been there. What got into you, Dickie? Looks like you were hitting it pretty hard.."

"S'long story. Tell you sometime."

"Okay, here we go." I hoisted his feet up on the bed and flipped the covers from the other side over him, then went to get him a glass of water. When I returned with the water Dickie was still awake, staring at the ceiling. "Y'know what, Bill?"

"What's that, Dick?"

"Friggin' bassards always fuck things up. You know that?"

It had been my experience that he was correct, even if I had no idea which specific bassards and what particular things he was talking about, so I agreed that the friggin' bassards did indeed always fuck things up. You can't argue with the truth.

"Can't lettem get 'way with it. Friggin dirty bassards."

"Nope. Can't let them get away with it. You're absolutely right. Good night, Dick."

"'Night, man. Thanks."

"You bet. Get some sleep."

"'Kay."

I stopped by the door to switch off the light and he was already snoring. Somebody was going to be hurting in the morning, there was no doubt about that.

Back downstairs I sat on the deck, listening to the waves, feeling the pleasant ache of overtaxed muscles allowed to relax, and gradually I drifted off. It was almost midnight when I awoke shivering, and I went straight up to bed.

Dickie was up before me the next morning, stumbling around and mumbling to himself. I felt great, if hungry, and stretched out luxuriously in the crisp sheets, listening to Dickie's troubles. I doubted he needed my help, doubted that he even wanted to talk. I had felt how I was sure he felt this morning, but not for quite a while. And I'd be perfectly happy never to feel that way again. Cold sweats, tremors, the feeling that your head was about to explode, your stomach doing flips at the thought of food, yeah, I knew what he was going through. Then something glass or porcelain shattered, followed instantly by an angry bellowed curse from Dickie. Now it sounded like he could use some help so I dragged myself out of bed and crossed the room to the door.

From the door to my room you can see straight into the bathroom across the hall, and when I opened the door I saw Dickie on his knees in front of the toilet. Jagged shards of broken glass glistened under the overhead light and a splash of blood on the white tile glowed a vivid red. Before I could say anything Dickie vomited, his body hunching and shaking with the effort, and I stood and waited until he was through, trying to spare him any further embarrassment. After an eternity Dickie sighed and pushed himself up to his knees, then flushed the toilet. "Jesus," was all he said.

"Dickie, you all right?" Stupid question, I know.

"Oh, I feel fucking great. Let's go for a run on the beach."

"You're bleeding, man."

"Wonderful. Do me a favor and shoot me, willya?"

"Sit down and let me look at that foot."

"I'm okay, screw the foot."

"No."

"Fine, whatever, who gives a shit anyways." He lowered the toilet seat and pushed himself up, then sat with his foot extended. Barefoot, I walked carefully across the glass-strewn floor and took his heel in my hand. It was a long cut but not particularly deep, years of callus from walking barefoot having lent him a measure of protection.

"Stitches?" he asked.

"Nah. At least I don't think so. Peroxide, Polysporin, and a good big Band-Aid and you'll make it."

Dickie nodded but said nothing. He was looking grey and rocky, older than I had seen him. After a moment he shook his head and sighed heavily. "Jesus. What the hell did I do to myself." It was a statement, not a question.

"Burned a few brain cells, that's for sure."

"Burned more than that. Bridges. There's Band-Aids and shit in the medicine cabinet. Would you...?"

"Yeah, sure. Sit tight. Actually, rinse your foot under some water in the tub." While he did that I retrieved the necessary supplies from the well-stocked cabinet. I was willing to help him, but Dickie waved me off, saying, "You want to do me a favor, get some shoes on and grab a broom so we can clean this glass up."

I nodded and went downstairs and got the broom, and when I returned to the bathroom Dickie was no longer there. His bedroom door was closed but I could hear his muffled voice through the door. It sounded like he was on the phone and from the tone of his voice it also sounded like he was less than happy with whoever was on the other end. I swept up the glass and dumped it in the trash and since Dickie still had not reappeared I took the trash can and the broom downstairs. I made some coffee and went out to retrieve the paper from the end of the driveway, then went back in and waited for the coffee to finish brewing while I scanned the headlines.

I was on my second cup of coffee and had finished the sports, comics and the lifestyle sections –you know, the important stuff - when Dickie finally came downstairs. He still looked grey and worn but he had showered and shaved and he looked quite a bit more human. He had nicked himself shaving, and a piece of bright-red tissue was stuck to the cut. Poor Dickie was shedding some blood this morning.

But the real shocker was the suit.

Dickie's usual uniform was shorts, a tee-shirt and flip-flops, maybe a sweat shirt if it was chilly. I hadn't seen him in a tie since our prom lo these many years ago.

"Jesus, Dickie, you clean up pretty good. What's the occasion?"

He shook his head, a sour look on his face. "You don't want to know. "

"Sure I do. Coffee?"

"Yeah, thanks. I just hope I can keep it down."

"Only one way to find out."

When I handed him the mug his hands were visibly shaking, so much so that at first he was forced to hold the mug with both hands as he sipped. The coffee seemed to do him some good, and after a few sips he had lost some of his deathly pallor and was even looking around for something to eat, albeit with limited success as neither of us had been to the market for several days. He settled for some saltines, which was probably as good as anything for his unsettled stomach. Back in the day, McDonald's was my favorite hangover food. Something about the grease and the special sauce seemed to have a salubrious effect on my system. Now that I was reformed, or mostly reformed, I hadn't been to McDonald's in years. No point in it.

Dickie munched his crackers and sipped his coffee silently. Wordlessly, at least. You can't eat crackers and slurp coffee silently. I read the paper. I had already asked him what was going on and he hadn't answered. I figured that if he wanted to tell me something he would. And just then, of course, he cleared his throat and spoke. "Well, I'm off to see the wizard." I looked up, thinking that an explanation might be forthcoming but none was. He stood, took a last sip of coffee, set his mug back on the table and said, "Wish me luck. I'll need it." And then with a tight little smile, Dickie went out the door.

Three

When Dickie finally got home that night I was already asleep after another exhausting day lying around doing a whole lot of nothing, soaking up the sun and watching the world - and the girls – go by. I needed to catch up with Bunny soon. I'm not the cheating kind, but I ain't no monk. Could be a country song.

I didn't hear Dickie come home and would have slept right through if he hadn't awakened me. He touched me on the shoulder and I sat up bolt upright, startled, some sort of primal defense reflex at work, and I had him by the throat before he could get a word out. "Whoa, Jesus, whoa there, boy," he said quickly if somewhat indistinctly. "It's only me, Dickie. Take it easy."

I let him go and lay back down, my heart pounding in my chest. "For Christ's sake, Dickie."

"Sorry, man. Sorry. I just wanted to tell you something."

"I hope it's good news."

I sat up and fumbled for the cigarettes I had left on the bedside table. That I thought I had left on the bedside table. They weren't there. It's a bad habit anyway. When I was able to focus I saw that Dickie was still wearing the pants from his suit and the shirt that he had on when he left in the morning. But the tie was gone, the shirt was open at the neck, and his pants were wrinkled and either stained or just wet.

"You been in a fight?"

"Me? Nah. Just been out on the town a little, celebrating."

"Celebrating what?"

"That's what I'm trying to tell you. I made a decision. A couple of them"

"Well, congratulations. Now good night."

Dickie looked crestfallen. "Okay," I said. "A decision on what?"

"On this house. And on my will."

I pondered this. Nothing came to me. "Great. Well, see you in the morning." I fluffed my pillow and rolled over even though I knew it wasn't going to work. Worth a try.

"C'mon, man. Wake up. This is important."

"Better damn well be."

"It is. Come downstairs. I need to get something to eat. I'll tell you about it."

I grumbled but obeyed. On the bright side, I found my cigarettes on the kitchen counter where I had left them. I lit one while Dickie the gourmet chef fixed himself a bowl of Cheerios. He was having a hard time with it, too. If anything he was fading on me, the alcohol in his system catching up with him before my eyes. He sat down across from me at the kitchen table and fixed me with a baleful stare. "Thassa bad habit, you know, man," he said solemnly.

"Yeah, thanks. I know. But this particular cigarette is your fault. I should be asleep right now."

Dickie nodded and ate some cereal. He swallowed and said, "You think you'd be happier."

"Why? Happier than what?"

"Happier than you are, man. After all, I just gave you this house. Or, I mean, I'm going to."

"You what?"

"When I die, I mean. I'm putting you in the will. I die, you'll get everything."

"Uh, gee, thanks, but you look pretty healthy to me. Healthier than me, for that matter."

"Probably am. But that doesn't mean I'm going to live longer than you."

"Well, sure, you might get hit by a bus, you never know."

"'Zackly. You never friggin' know. You're 'zackly right on that one."

"Dick. There's no polite way to say this. You're out of your frigging mind. Or else you're just drunk. Either way, go to sleep."

He ignored me, saying between spoonfuls of cheerios, "It's 'cause I trust you. 'cause you appreciate this place and I know you'll take care of it if something happens to me."

"What's going to happen to you, Dick? And what about your family? Don't you think maybe your family should get your stuff in the unlikely event that something does happen to you?"

"Nah. My family's the problem. Or one of the problems, at least. I don't trust any of 'em as far as I could throw 'em."

"In your condition that's probably not very far."

Dickie smiled and nodded. "'Zackly."

That explained everything. To him, at least.

"But don't tell anybody, man. Issa secret. Okay?"

"Hey, I promise. I promise I won't tell anybody a lunatic woke me up in the middle of the night and willed his house to me."

Sarcasm was a little past Dickie at the moment. He said thanks and picked up his cereal bowl, draining the remaining milk in a gulp. "Gotta get some sleep, my man," he said. "Big day tomorrow."

"Later."

"Late."

Dickie put his bowl in the sink and made his way upstairs. I could hear him bumbling around up there as I smoked another cigarette. But by the time I went upstairs he was already snoring. Lucky him. I wasn't quite so lucky, tossing and turning until the sky began to brighten and the birds raucously awoke to the new day. Finally I gave up. I was up and rattling around the kitchen looking for something to eat when it was still well before seven. Finding the cupboard bare, I decided to go out for breakfast. I went to see if Dickie wanted to come along but I could hear him snoring still through his door so I went back down the stairs and then outside. I stood there in the sun a moment, car keys in hand, but changed my mind and instead hopped on my bike. I rode down to Dewey in the nearly empty street to Sharky's Grill and dismounted, leaning the bike against the edge of the deck without locking it. Sharky's is basically a deck built around a kitchen, seating limited to a few picnic tables and some stools which line a somewhat makeshift counter. I ordered and ate two ham, egg and cheese sandwiches on English muffins, the cholesterol special. There's free coffee with breakfast at Sharky's, so I had two cups of that too while I chatted with Sharky himself. More accurately, Sharky chatted at me. A shortish man of about fifty with preternaturally blond hair in a too-boyish Prince Valiant cut, Sharky's a born salesman, and since he never remembers me he always says the same thing, going on about how folks deserve a warm welcome, a sincere thanks, and a clean place to eat at a reasonable price as he sucks down Carlton cigarettes through some sort of filter that always makes me think of FDR. He's not wrong, of course, it's just that I've already heard it. But what the hell, for four bucks for a good breakfast it's worth it.

Breakfast finished and at least partially digested, I got back on my bike and rode down to the sailing spot to see what was going on. I pedaled the mile or so south along Route 1 slowly, enjoying the day, looking out at the marshland which lines the highway, just generally loafing along. Indolence just agrees with some people.

I nodded at the middle-aged woman attendant in the little glassed-in booth by the entrance to the spot and she nodded back and smiled, and why not? It was a perfect summer morning, the sun was out, a breeze was blowing, and there was nothing in the world to worry about. There was only a single car in the large dirt parking lot, a rusted old Subaru wagon which appeared to be held together with decals from skiing and windsurfing companies. There was a pile of windsurfing equipment on the narrow sand beach, and a beach umbrella with a ratty aluminum chair and a cooler sitting beneath it. Out on the water a lone windsurfer charged along, carving long arcs across the bay. As the person drew nearer I saw that it was a woman out there, and as she drew nearer still I saw that it was a young fit tan woman with long brown hair tied back in a pony tail. And as she pulled up to the beach and jumped of her board I saw that in addition to all of the above she was beautiful, a perfect specimen of outdoorsy American womanhood, the kind of woman you find camping in the wilderness or rock climbing in Yosemite or skiing in the backcountry or, for that matter, windsurfing by herself on a glorious summer morning. She left the board floating and jogged through the knee-deep water toward where I stood near her car with my bike, she like some new iteration of Aphrodite, this one not coy, not soft and rounded, no creamy skin here. And me like a jackass with my mouth open wide, displaying my expensive dental work to the world..

"Hey," she panted.

"Hey," I replied intelligently.

"Is there something I can help you with?"

"Help me with?" I echoed. Well, sure, I thought, there's probably a lot of things… "Uh, no, thanks," I said. " I'm all right. How are you?" God, I'm brilliant.

"I'm fine," she said and for the first time I noticed the chill in her tone.

"Is there something the matter?"

She looked around the parking lot. "You're on a bike?" she asked, somewhat less than brilliantly, if you ask me. I mean, I was sitting on the bike.

"Well, yeah, I'm on a bike. It's right here. What's the problem?"

She shook her head and smiled a little sheepishly. "Nothing, I guess. I saw you standing there and I got worried about my gear. It wouldn't be the first time someone helped themselves to my stuff. But I guess you couldn't steal much of anything on a bike. Sorry."

I smiled my best disarming smile. "Well, the bike's stolen."

She looked shocked. "It is?"

"Nah, I'm just kidding."

She looked a little uncertain.

"Really," I said. "I was just trying to be funny."

"Oh," she said.

"But I guess it didn't work."

"No," she said, stumbling slightly over her words. "I mean…yeah. I mean, I get it. A joke."

"Sort of."

We looked at each other for a long moment. A very long moment. Actually, an embarrassingly long moment. I couldn't think of a single thing to say. This is usually not a problem for me. Quite the contrary, in fact. But at least I wasn't alone in my difficulties.

Finally, I said "Ummm." This may not sound like much, but it was better than nothing. Not much better, I agree. But better. And my monosyllabic mumble did at least seem to break the logjam. The still-dripping young lady flashed a quick smile, and said "Well…"

A couple of geniuses, you're thinking. You may be right. But there was more going on in the long silence than can really be expressed, or it seemed like there was, which is good enough for me. Or was then. Next it was my turn to talk, and I actually did pretty well this time around. "Your board's floating away," I said. And it was.

She turned and spoke the words I'll never forget to my dying day: "Oh, shit. Gotta go." The board was a good hundred yards off and she splashed through the warm shallow water after it, pausing only to turn and shout, "Come by my work sometime. I tend bar at the Grand Slam, up on Highway One. I'm there every night but Wednesday and Thursday. I'll buy you a drink."

"Okay, " I shouted back. "Hey, what's your name?"

She shouted back something that sound like Jareese or something. "What?" She shouted it again, and I still couldn't understand it, but I didn't want to seem like a total idiot, so I waved like I had understood her. Jareese, or whatever her name was, waved back, and then charged off again after her departing windsurfer. I watched her go with a smile on my face. She caught up to the board, got the sail up in the air and moments later she was flashing away across the sun-dimpled waters. "Damn," I said. "I wish I could sail

Like that." Hell, I wish I could sail at all.

Four

It was five o'clock, and I was pouring myself a carefully concocted libation – Myers' Dark rum, Absolut, Fresh-squeezed orange juice, a dash of grenadine, a slice of lime, all in a frozen pint glass with enough –not too much, now- ice, when Dickie burst through the kitchen door as though the hounds of hell were right on his tail. He slammed the door shut and leaned against it heavily, panting.

I took a sip of my drink. Needed more vodka. "Everything all right?"

"Yeah, it's just, just, ah, never mind, screw it."

Well, that explained everything. "You sure everything's all right?"

Dickie pushed himself away from the door and walked, perhaps a bit unsteadily, across the kitchen towards where I was standing. "Yeah, sure, everything's fine, dude. Why?"

I poured another measure of vodka into my drink, stirred it with a finger, took a sip. Perfect. "I don't know. I mean there was that business with the will last night, and all that, and now you come crashing into the house like somebody's husband's chasing you with a shotgun. I was just curious. Drink?"

"Yeah. A drink would do me good. Can I have that one?"

I looked down at my beautiful drink glistening on the counter, frost still on the glass except near the top where beads of condensation reflected and refracted the late-afternoon sunlight streaming through the windows. "This one? " A pause, a silent sigh. "Sure, bro', here you go." I handed it over and set about constructing another. What the hell, anything for a friend. Besides, a dash of pineapple juice would make it even better. Dickie clutched my —okay, his – drink in both hands and slurped it down in big swallows. I watched him out of the corner of my eye as I worked. It sure didn't look like everything was okay. But if he didn't want to tell me about it, that was his business. I certainly wasn't going to meddle, or pry, or interfere. Not on your life. People need space and privacy in this world, need to be able to handle things their own way, at their own pace. Strict non-interference, that's my policy. "So what the fuck is going on, Dickie?" I said.

Hey, rules are made to be broken.

Dickie affected wide-eyed ignorance. He does that well, the open face framed by the long sandy hair somehow giving him a childlike air when he wants it. "With what?" he asked sweetly.

I wasn't buying it, strict non-interference policy or no. "Get serious, dude. You know damn well with what. I mean, look at you. You're a mess. So what's up?"

Dickie took another long sip of the drink and set it on the counter. "Let's just say… let's speak hypothetically, here, okay?"

"Fine. Whatever."

"Okay. Let's say there was a little prince…"

I couldn't help snorting.

Dickie looked a little indignant but continued, "There was this little prince, and he lived in a little kingdom that his uncle had given to him. It was a beautiful kingdom by the sea…"

"Jesus, Dickie."

He ignored me. "The little kingdom was beautiful and peaceful, but it was also very valuable. And there were evil forces that wanted to see the little kingdom destroyed, cut up and sold to the highest bidder. But the little prince didn't want that to happen, and he came up with a plan that would save the kingdom but he had to keep it a secret because if the evil forces knew about the plan they might launch a plan of their own first. And that plan would be very bad for the little kingdom and maybe for the little prince too. It might even be life-threatening for the little prince. So the little prince launched his plan, but it's going to take some time to complete it, and just as soon as he launched the plan there were some signs that the evil forces either found out about it or else just strongly suspected something. Either way they're not happy and the little prince might be in real danger." He paused, took a long pull from his glass, and then said, "So. You got it?"

"Yeah. I got it all right. You're losing your mind."

"No I'm not."

"Sure sounds like it."

Dickie pouted. It wasn't attractive. "Look," he said after a while. "It's all real. I just gotta be careful. Or something bad might happen. All I need is a couple of weeks and everything will be all set. They won't be able to touch me then."

"Who? The evil forces?"

He nodded, all earnestness. "Right."

"You sure you're not going wacko on me, Dick?"

"Yeah. Pretty sure, at least."

"Pretty sure? What the hell does that mean?"

"Well, it means maybe I am going wacko. I don't know. I keep thinking people are following me. And some guy was messing around my truck when I went in to East of Maui this morning." East of Maui is the local surf shop, a cool little shop on Rte. 1, on the left just as you come into Dewey from the north.

"What happened?"

I went into the shop to get a couple of things, but I forgot my wallet so I came right back out. There was a guy on his hands and knees next to the truck when I came out. He pretended he was tying his shoe but when I walked over he took off running. I yelled but he didn't stop. Dude nearly got run over on Rte. 1, he was in that much of a hurry."

"Probably wanted your wallet. Or maybe the truck."

"That what I thought, at first."

"At first? What changed your mind?"

"When he almost got hit he kind of halfway turned around and I got a look at his face. I saw the same dude on the beach a couple of days ago with a camera, taking pictures of the house."

"Oh. Well, we can't have that, can we? I hope you called the police."

"No, I thought of it but…oh, you're kidding, right? You don't believe any of this."

"I don't know what to believe, Dickie. I know it's not illegal to take pictures on the beach. A lot of people would be in jail if it was. And I know I don't believe in fairy tales."

"You don't?"

"Nope."

"But they're the truest things ever written."

Jesus. Spare us from the English Majors. "Whatever that means."

"It means that…"

I held up a hand. "Never mind. I don't really care, not right now, at least." Dickie looked a little crestfallen so I added, "Look, we can talk about that later. But right now what I'm interested in is why you think you're in danger."

"You're standing in it."

I resisted the impulse to check the soles of my shoes. "Dicky. Could we skip the riddles for right now? Would that be okay?"

"Sure. In fact, let's skip the whole damn thing. I'm sure I'm just being paranoid. How about another drink? That one was damn good. And then what do you say we go out for something to eat?"

"Okay. You ever been to the Grand Slam?"

"Up on One past the outlets? Nope."

"Well, you're going tonight."

It was after eight when we left the house and climbed into Dickie's truck for the ride up to the Grand Slam. Whatever, exactly, was bothering Dickie hadn't been a topic of discussion in the interim. We talked about a lot of things but not that. I knew that it had to do with the house and his family, but the rest of the story was not forthcoming and I left it alone, figuring he'd tell me about it when he was ready. I still think he would have done so had he had the chance.

One reason we didn't leave the house until late was that I didn't want to seem too eager to see Jareese or whatever her name was. Coming into her bar the very same day I met her was pushing it far enough. Showing up right when she started work was definitely too much. Besides, I already had a girlfriend, so I couldn't really be on the prowl. Just following up, I told myself. Just making a friend. I couldn't quite make myself believe it, but what the hell, I tried. Another reason we didn't leave the house until we did was Route One, a road I try to avoid as much as possible. In Dewey Rte. 1 is a honky-tonk hodgepodge of bars, restaurants, shops and motels. South of Dewey, at least until you get down to Bethany, it's a beautiful road as it passes through the Delaware Seashore State Park, miles of undeveloped beaches on the ocean side and sweeping views of marshland, scrub forest and Rehoboth Bay to the west. But north of Dewey Rte 1 is a mess, pure unadulterated commercial dreck as far as the eye can see. The draw is the four big outlet malls, each with dozens upon dozens of stores and parking lots fit for a stadium. All summer the traffic is thick on Rte. 1, the siren song of discount shopping in a state with no sales tax drawing relentless crowds. Mix in a sale or two (and it seems like there's always a sale or two) and it's like throwing chum on the water. And God help you if you have to get somewhere on Rte. 1 on a day when even a single raindrop falls from the sky: It's impossible. But by eight things usually begin to die down a bit and it's at least feasible to try to use the road. As we headed north traffic was still thick but moving fairly well. We drove in silence, lost in our own thoughts, nominally listening to the Top 40 schlock of one of the local FM stations, and in less than fifteen minutes we pulled into the parking lot at the Grand Slam.

The Grand Slam sits at the far northern end of the sprawl, or at what was the far northern end a year or two ago, hard by the highway on what was cropland in recent memory. There's still a cornfield – a doomed cornfield, certainly – next door and there's farmland out back, but the Grand Slam itself was lit up like the headquarters of a sign company, all neon and spotlights. The kiosk out front advertised that they had the Cardinals at the Expos and the A's at the White Sox on the big screens tonight, which hardly thrilled, but I wasn't there to watch a baseball game.

We walked into the brightly-lit barroom and I looked around for Jareese, quickly spotting her working the back corner of the square bar that dominated the room. I nudged Dicky and said, "Let's sit over there," nodding toward a couple of empty barstools near where Jareese stood chatting to a bulky blond man with a deep tan. I recognized the man as one of the lifeguards from Rehoboth beach, where he has worked for as long as I can remember and I'm sure well before that. Dicky shrugged and followed me across the room, and we made ourselves comfortable at the bar. A few minutes later Jareese walked over, smiling. She had let her long straight hair down, and with her tan and high cheekbones she resembled nothing but an Indian princess.

"Hi, guys," she said heartily. "What can I get you?" She paused and added, "Hey, didn't we meet earlier?"

"Yeah," I replied with what must have sounded like a mouth full of mush, "Down at the sailing spot. You're Jareese, right?"

She laughed. "Uh, no, actually. Denise." She stuck out a hand and I shook it. It was a nice hand in every way a hand can be nice.

"Sorry, I…"

"Oh, Don't worry about it. At least you tried. I don't know your name at all."

"Bill. Bill Flaherty. And this is Dickie Harrington."

"Hi, Dickie. Hey, I've seen you around before, haven't I? On the beach, maybe?"

"Probably so. I live down here. But I think I would have remembered you."

"Oh, stop it. Now what can I get you guys?"

We placed our orders and she walked off to make our drinks. I became aware that both Dickie and I were admiring the bounty of her retreating form. "I think she likes me," Dickie said.

"Hey! It's me she likes. She invited me up here this morning. Why do you think I dragged you all the way up here?"

"I was wondering about that. Seemed like a long way to go for a beer and a burger."

"Well she's why, Bro'. She's something else, right?"

"Yeah, she's something, all right. Healthy-looking girl. Far too good for you."

And so it went, a night out, friendly banter, gentle bickering and teasing, shameless flirting with Denise and a pact between the two of us that, no matter what happened, we would make sure that the lifeguard didn't get her, which he was clearly trying to do. We left late and happy, with promises to Denise to return soon. A fun night, especially so since the lifeguard finally gave up and left at a little past eleven, and when he was out of earshot Denise turned to us and said, "What a loser," which brightened both of our moods considerably.

Back home we listened to music out on the deck and had a nightcap, and we looked at the stars and listened, after the music went off, to the waves and the wind. It was a good night, maybe the kind of night I would pick if I got a chance to choose what to do for my last night on earth. I don't know about Dickie, though. I didn't ask him, and I don't think he knew that it actually was his last night on earth.

Five

I woke up late, the sun streaming through the windows, the day for most folks well underway. Dickie was already gone, where I didn't know but I certainly wasn't worrying about it either. I had a slight hangover, one of those little edges that can be almost enjoyable, a reminder of good times had, a little badge that lets you know you had some fun without bringing you to our knees. This being the summer of my indolence I didn't have anyplace I needed to be anytime soon, so I nuked the cold coffee that Dickie had left in the pot and read the paper and had some toast and acted pretty much like I hadn't a care in the world . Which I didn't, as far as I knew.

Later I went for a walk on the beach and had some lunch and read a mystery by John Straley, whose writing I admire, and basically hacked around and spent a whole lot of time doing a whole lot of nothing. I regret that now, of course. At the particular instant that I was reading, say, Doonesbury, I might instead have been saving Dickie's life. Had I known. And maybe I should have known, should have taken Dickie's talk of people following him and wills and fairy kingdoms by the sea more seriously. Probably I should have done so, but I didn't. It just didn't seem real, didn't seem like something that could happen to Dickie, to me – yes, to me too – not in this place at this time, not with the sun out and the beach and a chair out on the deck to sit in and a book to read or a chance to go windsurfing. This summer was about escape, about sanity, about pulling myself together and moving forward after that. It wasn't about death and intrigue and greed and jealousy and suspicion and all the bad things in the world, or at least that's what I thought then. But things change. We all know that.

I went to sleep that night still unconcerned, and awoke the same way. I was a bit surprised to see that Dickie hadn't been back but shrugged it off. The sad truth is that I figured he'd gone back to see Denise at the Grand Slam and that it had worked out for him, and I cursed him for it. In a good-natured way, of course.

It wasn't until the next day that I really became concerned and even then I chided myself for being silly, for worrying about a grown man who was probably off enjoying himself somewhere and who certainly didn't owe me a call or an explanation. But I was worried and once I started worrying it was off to the races. By five o'clock I was standing in front of the low brick police station in Rehoboth, debating madly whether I should go in an make a missing persons report. After two false starts I marched up and pulled the door open. Inside there was a small lobby area with dingy white industrial-looking tile on the floor. A low counter went across the room in front of me. Centered n the wall behind the counter was an open doorway that lead back into the rest of the building. A young woman in uniform sat behind the counter in front of the door. She was reading something and didn't look up until I cleared my throat. But when she did look up she smiled and closed the three-ring binder that she had been reading from and all I could think was that she didn't look like any of the cops I knew in D.C.. For one thing she was young and pretty, with strawberry blonde hair cut stylishly short, makeup sparsely but expertly applied, and the picture of health. Most of the cops in D.C. look like they got locked in a cave filled with doughnuts for a few months and they just escaped. She was attractive, that was for sure, but I think maybe it was the smile that threw me off the most. A wide welcoming smile that couldn't have been false, a smile that indicated genuine concern for me and a real interest in anything that might be bothering me, it really threw me for a loop.

"Can I help you?" she asked. And when I didn't answer the smile faltered a bit as she repeated herself.

I pulled myself together and said that I'd like to file a missing person report. She noted the information and clucked with concern at all the right places. I stood there awkwardly and wished that I wasn't there on business, reflecting that it probably wouldn't be good form to ask someone out on a date when you're filing a missing persons report on your friend. Not to mention Bunny of course. It probably wasn't a good idea to ask someone out on a date when you have a girlfriend either.

When we were done she promised to get the ball rolling right away and that she would make sure that someone contacted me as soon as they found anything out. I thanked her and turned to leave. After a couple of steps I stopped and turned around. "Are you really a police officer?" I asked. She smiled. "Why? Don't I look like one?"

"Well, no, now that you mention it."

"Twelve years this October."

"Damn. You don't look old enough for that."

"Well, I started when I was ten."

"That would explain it. Thanks for everything. I'm sure it's all a false alarm, but let me know if you find anything out, okay?"

"Will do. Or give me a call sometime."

I walked out of the station turning that line over in my head. Was that strictly professional, like, "Please feel free to call for a progress report"? Or was it more on the lines of Mae West, like, "Come up and see me sometime"? I couldn't decide. And I had more important things to worry about just at the moment. For instance, as I stepped out of the police station I nearly got run over by one of those three-wheel bicycles with a bench seat that will hold up to three normal people or two of the type of person who always seems to rent those things. What they were doing on the sidewalk I have no idea. Probably always ride their bikes on the sidewalk back in Podunk. I'll never know because they didn't stop to discuss it and I didn't feel like running after them. I only run when someone is chasing me. I collected myself and then drove down to Dewey.

The Dewey Police station was altogether less impressive than its counterpart in Rehoboth. It occupied the first floor of a white – formerly white, now sort of gray – clapboard structure set on a side street back towards the bay. And the counter help was less impressive than in Rehoboth as well. A short burly man of a about fifty with a grey buzz cut and a roll of fat around the back of his neck looked up as I walked in but didn't say anything. After a while I said, "Excuse me…. "

"Yeah?" Not harsh or warm. Just flat. Not interested. Now this was a cop like the cops I know. I felt much more at home than I had in Rehoboth.

"I'd like to file a missing persons report."

"Yeah?"

"Yeah." We seemed to have reached an impasse.

"So do it."

"Aren't you going to take notes?"

"You're being recorded. I need to, I'll listen to the tape."

"Oh. Okay. Well my friend Dickie's been gone for almost three days."

"What's almost three days?"

"Um. The amount of time my friend has been missing?" I felt like I was on Jeopardy.

He shook his head. I was the sorriest specimen he had ever seen, I was sure. At least since the last member of the general public that he'd seen. "No. What I mean is, when exactly has he been missing since. When the last time you saw him was."

"Oh. Today is…" I couldn't remember. I did remember that psychiatrists often ask their patients if they know what day it is if they suspect that the patient is loony. A technical term, loony.

"Thursday, Sir." Somehow he made "Sir" sound like an insult.

"Right. Thursday. Sorry. Last I saw Dickie it was Monday night, late. About midnight."

"Dickie?" He showed the first sign of interest that I'd seen. "Dickie who?"

"Dickie Harrington. You know him?"

"Yeah. We all know Dickie. I was wondering who "we" was when he continued, "Who are you to Dickie?"

"A friend. We went to High School together. I've been living in his house most of the summer."

"Huh. Nice place he's got there."

"Yeah it is. Is that important?"

He didn't answer my question. Probably just as well. Instead he mused, "Sorta been wondering about his truck."

"What about his truck?"

"Been parked down at Keybox Road for a few days. Park Rangers called and asked about it, but we just figured he was having engine trouble or something, so we asked them not to tow it. Still there, far's I know." Keybox Road is a short dirt track that runs from highway One to the beach in the state park, a couple of miles south of Dewey. All that's there is a little kiosk for the parking attendant and a small unpaved parking lot. A truck parked there for three days would be very noticeable.

"I don't mean to tell you your job, but don't you think maybe somebody ought to go down and look at it?"

He looked at me for a long time. "You don't want to tell me my job, then don't do it."

"Hey, sorry. But maybe you need a little help. Seems like it from here."

"Don't start with me, Mister."

"Too late."

He looked at me for a few seconds and then agreed. "Yeah, I guess it is at that. Hold on a minute and we'll take a ride." He tuned on his chair and yelled into the unseen offices in the back, "Riley!"

A thin blond young cop, no more than twenty-three or four, a surfer by the look of him, came running out. "Yeah, Chief?"

Chief?

"Riley, you take over the desk. Me and Mister...?"

"Flaherty. Bill Flaherty."

"Me and Mr. Flaherty here are going for a little ride. I'll be back in a while. Anything happens you call me on the radio, hear? Anything at all. Somebody gets a parking ticket, I want to hear about it. Got it?"

"Yes, sir." Riley looked a little like a puppy that had peed on the rug. I had the feeling that he looked like that a lot.

"You sure?"

"Yes. Sir," Riley said glumly. "Chief, you don't have to..."

"Riley, you just do as you're told and we'll be fine. See you in a while." The Chief turned on his heel and marched out with me on his heel. "A good kid," he said when we were outside. "A little scatterbrained. Too much time in the water, I think. Brains got waterlogged, maybe."

I couldn't think of much to do besides nod, so that's what I did. The chief stuck out his hand. "Sorry," he said. "George Hartner." We shook, and he nodded to a big white Ford Bronco with blue markings. The words "Dewey Beach Police" and below that in large letters, "Chief" were emblazoned on the door. "Hop in." If he hadn't told me that it was his car I guess I should have been able to figure it out. I climbed up into the passenger seat and with a squeal we were off. Within a couple of minutes we pulled onto the shoulder of Route One, slowed, and turned into Keybox Road and stopped. A metal gate was closed, blocking access to the lot. The Chief climbed out with a ring of keys and tried them in the padlock until one worked, then came back and drove us in. The only vehicle in the lot was Dickie's Blazer on the far side of the lot facing the high dune and the ocean beyond. And there was no doubt it was Dickie's Blazer. I'd know that truck anywhere. It was parked a little strangely, almost as though Dickie had been in a hurry. It wasn't quite straight in, and it was pulled a little bit further in than you might have expected, so that the left front tire was off the hard surface of the of the lot and in the soft sand beyond. It wasn't anything drastic; it just looked a bit odd. Which, considering that Dickie was missing and the truck had been parked here for days, was enough to give me a bad feeling, a sinking kind of sick feeling in the pit of my stomach.

The Chief and I climbed out of the Bronco and approached Dickie's truck, with me on the passenger side and he opposite. Nothing seemed particularly extraordinary at first glance. I peered in the window and the Chief did the same from the other side. The interior of the truck was a mess, but considering whose truck it was it would have been more surprising had it not been. Papers, empty soda cans and various pieces of clothing were strewn about. A navy blue and yellow rep tie, the same tie Dickie had worn with his suit a few days before, hung from the rearview mirror. And the keys were in the ignition. Which, if you were having engine trouble and you weren't worried about anyone driving off with the truck and you expected somebody to come and tow the vehicle and you weren't going to be there and they would need a key –deep breath – if all of that was the case, then it wasn't completely unreasonable that you might, possibly, leave them there in the ignition. Pretty damn doubtful, though. The sick feeling was getting worse, not better. "Key's in the ignition," I called to the Chief. He tried the door and it was unlocked, which, if you followed the scenario above…oh, forget it. I was grasping at straws. Something was definitely wrong with this picture. The chief peered in for a moment and then straightened. "Don't touch anything," he warned. "I've got to make a call." He walked back to his truck, reached in and retrieved his radio, stretching the curly cord through the window so he could stand outside. "Riley, Chief Hartner here, come in."

After a few seconds I heard a response but I was too far away to understand what was said. The Chief shook his head and spat. "I'm not checking up on you, Riley, for chrissake. Listen to me. Get Bellegarde on the radio and tell him to come down here to the parking lot at Keybox Road. Tell him to bring the crime scene kit. Then get everybody else on shift down here too as soon as they can. Then call the Troopers and tell them we have a possible – remember that word, and use it when you talk to them – a possible homicide in State jurisdiction and they should bring the mobile crime lab as soon as possible. Got it?"

Again the response was unintelligible. Hartner shook his head, exasperated. "Here, Riley. Keybox Road. Where the hell do you think I mean? Why would I tell you to send our people to Keybox and the State Troopers somewhere else? Jesus. Just do what I said, and call me on the radio when the Troopers tell you how long it will be before they get here. Out." He left the radio hanging out the window and walked closer. "Something wrong with that boy, I swear."

I had to know. "Why do think it might be a homicide?"

"Dark material on the driver's side floor. Might be dried blood. We'll know soon enough."

We stood there in silence for a few moments, the only sounds the waves beyond the dunes, a faint hum of traffic out on Route One and the hysterical laughter of a solitary black-headed gull that circled above our heads. I didn't see what was so funny. Still don't, for that matter. The chief sighed. "I always liked Dickie. Knew him since he was a boy. Knew his grandfather since I was a kid." I could tell he felt as bad as I did. Which made me feel even worse. And I didn't much care for his use of the past tense, either.

"Well," he said. "Might just as well see if we can't do something useful. Be dark in another hour, hour and a half."

I nodded, and the Chief turned and walked back to the rear of his truck. He returned with a large handful of small orange flags, and gave half of them to me. I'd been to enough crime scenes to know that the flags were to be used to mark anything we might find in a search. "Okay," said the Chief. "Let's try and be organized about this. Might as well check the parking lot before everybody gets here. Doubt we'll find anything after three days, but you never know. I'll walk the perimeter and you start sweeping back and forth. Mark anything suspicious or interesting with a flag. If the ground's too hard just lay the flag down next to whatever it is."

I started by looking under the car and then began walking back and forth, moving about six feet further out on each pass. In ten minutes I had covered most of the compact lot with no success, my little bundle of flags still intact in my sweaty hand. The chief was still making his way around the edge of the lot but he hadn't had any more success than I had. A tan Ford Crown Victoria with a tall whip antenna, the ultimate undercover cop car except for the fact that it screamed "Cop!", turned into the drive and parked next to the Chief's Bronco. The chief looked up but kept working. I covered the last bit of the lot and walked over to see who the new arrival was. The Ford's driver-side door opened as I approached, and a cloud of cigarette smoke billowed out. In the center of the cloud was a thin stoop-shouldered man with thin reddish hair in a bad comb-over. Gimlet eyes peered at me from above hollow, deeply wrinkled cheeks. A cigarette hung from the corner of his mouth. He wore a ratty houndstooth jacket and a tie that had seen better days. The tie was loosely knotted and hung askew. As I approached he turned and bent to retrieve something from the back seat of the car. Greasy pants hung loosely from his bony rear end. Not the most pleasant of sights. He stayed that way, head stuck in the car, ass towards me, until I sopped a few feet away. I tried to look nonchalant. I don't think it worked.

"Help you with somethin'?" rasped the man without turning to face me.

"No, I guess not. I was just going to introduce myself."

"Huh." He stood and pulled a large black bag from the back seat, grunting with the effort. He turned and set the bag next to the car. "But you changed your mind?" he asked, squinting against the smoke that rose from the still-lit cigarette. I hadn't seen him remove it from his mouth yet. "Why's that?"

Because I don't need to meet any more pricks, I thought, but said, "Doesn't matter. I'm Bill Flaherty." I stuck out my hand. He looked at it and said, "Don't shake hands no more. Nothin' personal. Arthritis. Sonsabitches always squeezin' my hands, hurts for a week." He started coughing, a liquid racking cough that came from deep within.

Have another cigarette, buddy.

He removed the cigarette from his mouth, eyed it with disgust, and tossed it aside. It landed, still burning, a few feet away. When the coughing fit subsided he gasped, "Fuckin' smokes gonna kill me." I didn't doubt it. He fished another twisted butt from a crumpled pack and lit it with a big silver Zippo lighter. He took a deep drag and said "Lieutenant Dave Bellegarde. Dewey Beach Police. What's goin' on here, Flaherty? And who in the hell are you?"

The sad part is, he was trying to be friendly. As I began to fill Bellegarde in, the chief walked over. "Dave," he said.

"Chief."

Sparkling conversationalists, these two. I hoped they were better at their jobs than they were at small talk. There was a long silence, and then the Chief cleared his throat. "There's some material on the driver's side floor in that truck." He jerked his head toward Dickie's vehicle.

"See what you can make of it. State Troopers're on the way if that damn Riley did what I told him to, so try not to disturb things too much. No sense pissing 'em off if we don't need to."

Bellegarde nodded, threw his cigarette on the ground, picked up his case and walked off toward Dickie's truck. He was leaning to one side, the weight of the case nearly pulling him over. I don't know what he had in there, but the word "bricks" leaps to mind.

"See here, Flaherty," said Chief Hartner. "Why don't you go on home? Hell, maybe ol' Dickie's there right now drinkin' a beer and wishing he had somebody to tell his story to. We'll have plenty of help here in the next few minutes, and we need to keep things on a professional level, if you know what I mean. Okay? Thanks for your help, and we'll keep you posted."

I can tell when I'm not wanted. I said "Call me, please," and when the chief nodded I turned to go. No car. I turned to ask the Chief for a ride but he was already walking away from me toward where Bellegarde was working so I said the hell with it and went shank's mare. Maybe the walk would do me good. Doubtful, but possible.

Six

Of course Dickie hadn't been home when I got there. The house was silent as a tomb, an analogy that made me feel distinctly uneasy. I turned the TV on, loud, in an effort to drive away the chilly emptiness, but it wasn't working. There were echoes in the house that I had never noticed before and I kept hearing noises, or at least thinking that I did so, and each time I heard something I would use the remote to mute the TV and there would be nothing there except for the silence. It was not a comfortable evening. I mixed myself a drink and took a sip but I didn't want it. In a move that was rather uncharacteristic of me I poured it down the sink. There's a first time for everything, I guess.

I t was late when the Chief called, almost midnight, but I was still wide awake. The shrill ring of the phone, which was on the table right behind the couch where I was sitting, made me jump about a foot in the air, which isn't easy from the seated position. When I landed I grabbed the phone, hoping to hear Dickie's voice but knowing I wouldn't.

"Mr. Flaherty?" the Chief asked

"Speaking."

"This is Chief Hartner."

"Yeah. Hey, Chief. What's up? What'd you find out?"

"Well…I'm sorry to say that the material on the floor in the truck was definitely human blood. Blood and, uh, other stuff. You wouldn't happen to know Dickie's blood type by any chance, would you?"

"No, not off the top of my head, sorry."

"It was a long shot. Don't worry about it, we'll find it out somehow. You happen to know his doctor?"

"No. I don't think he's been to one since I've been here."

"If you wanted to do me a favor…"

"Yeah?"

"Well, I hate to ask, but…"

"Don't be coy, Chief. What do you need?"

"Well, maybe you could kind of look around wherever he keeps his mail, bills and so forth. See if you see a bill or a statement from a doctor's office. I can't really just barge in there myself, not without some backup from the court, and it's…"

"I got it, Chief. No problem. What number should I call if I find something out?"

He gave me his pager number and then said, "Do you happen to know how to reach any of Dickie's family?"

That didn't sound promising. "No. I know his Dad's still alive, though. He was just taking about him the other day. I'm not sure about his Mom, he didn't mention her. And there's a brother somewhere. Maybe he has an address book around here someplace. I'll look around."

The chief thanked me and we hung up. I never would have expected to be looking for Dickie's blood type and next of kin, not in a million years. But life's funny like that sometimes. Not ha-ha funny. But a lot of the time it seems to me that all of life is just a wait for the other shoe to drop. Bad shit happens, then everything calms down for a while, then bad shit happens again. Repeat as necessary, then die.

But what are you gonna do?

I went upstairs and opened the door to the spare bedroom that Dickie used for an office. I knew he was no neat freak, but this was ridiculous. Books and papers were strewn everywhere, drawers were open with their contents spilling out, even the small trash can by the desk was on its side, with trash flowing out onto the nearly-obscured floor. So, the guy was a slob. Big deal. This, as it turned out, was not the correct attitude. But I had never been in the office before and Dickie kept the door closed, so who knew? The great investigator shrugged, waded in, and went to work.

I quickly found an address book in the top middle desk drawer, and in the book found an entry under Mom and Dad that gave an address and number in Marco Island, Florida. I found a piece of typing paper and noted the address. I knew that Dickie's brother's name was Robert, and under Bobby I found a long list of addresses in various locales around the country, each neatly crossed out in turn. The final and I presumed current one was apparently an apartment or a condo in Key West because it gave both a street address and a unit number. I wrote that down below the parents' address.

I had known Bobby a bit back when we were in school. He was a couple of years older, a slender dark boy with long straight jet-black hair, sideburns, and an ever-present pair of Ray-Ban Wayfarers. He was kind of a mystery. He seemed smart enough and good-looking enough to do well, to be whatever he wanted to be. He was a good athlete but preferred to sneak off into the woods behind the school to smoke pot with a couple of friends. Not that I'm against that, but there's a limit. He was usually so cynical and sarcastic and at times downright unpleasant that he was hard to get to know and harder to like. He was too cool for school, and certainly too cool for a couple of younger scrubs like Dickie and me. Just the same I had looked up to him after a fashion. He was a rebel, or at least acted like one, and I fancied myself one too. He didn't buy into all the pressure and hype that's part of the program at a high-level prep school, the need to excel just to get by. So he went the other way, scraping along, doing everything he could to distance himself from his surroundings and his classmates, declaring victory in the game he was playing and ignoring the game that his classmates were playing. But still he was a pain in the ass, and in the more than twenty years that had passed since I had spoken with him I don't think I had thought of him once, not even while I had been living here with his brother. Check that. Now that I thought of it I remembered an afternoon early in the summer. Dickie had been cleaning the accumulated debris out of his wallet, sitting at the kitchen table. He had pulled everything out of the wallet and it was all spread out in front of him. And there in one of the little piles had been a picture of Bobby. I don't suppose it was all that recent, and still Bobby looked older than he should have, his face deeply lined and going towards jowly, the hair still long but going to gray. I remembered asking Dickie how he was doing and Dickie said, "Bobby is a royal pain in my ass," and then Dickie had taken the picture by the corner and expertly flipped it into the trash. So I had thought of Bobby once, but that was all.

I sat there in Dickie's office with the address book opened to Bobby's address, lost in thought. On a whim I picked up the phone and dialed. It was well after midnight, but the address was in Key West and midnight is prime time down there. Hell, midnight is when prime time starts in Key West. The phone rang four or five times and I was about to hang up when somebody picked up and said, "Pizza Hut". I could hear music and the buzz of several indistinct voices in the background.

"Oh, sorry, I must taken have dialed a wrong…"

"Aw, man," said the person on the other end in a lazy drawl that sounded like it had been made even lazier by a liberal measure of alcohol. "I'm just kiddin'. Keep your shirt on. Who you lookin' for?"

"Robert Harrington."

"Robert? My, my, my. Hold on, my man."

Without taking the phone away from his mouth the man yelled, "Yo, Bobby, man. Telephone." I winced and pulled the phone away from my ear. Guy had a set of pipes.

The next thing I heard was the same voice, but much fainter. Apparently he had taken the phone away from his mouth and he probably thought that I couldn't hear him. He said, "Dunno, man. Some damn Yankee lookin' for Robert Harrington."

There was a pause, then sounds of a telephone being fumbled around, and then, "H'lo?"

Even after all this time I recognized the voice. It was deeper, tobacco raspy and whiskey-tinged, but it was Bobby. "Bobby," I said.

"Yeah. Who's this? And what're you doin' in my brother's house?"

How....? Oh. Caller ID. A wonderful invention if you don't like telemarketers, which I don't. Also good against bill collectors, I hear. "This is Bill Flaherty. Remember me? Dickie's friend from high school?"

There was a moment of silence, then Bobby said, "Yeah, I remember you, man. Hold on, I'm gonna take the phone in another room where I can hear you, man. Gotta party goin' on down here, man. Fuckin' people getting' crazy. Hold on."

The next thing I heard was Bobby yelling angrily, "Get the fuck out. I don't give a shit about your clothes, bitch. Get the fuck out." A moment later Bobby came on the line. "Sorry, man. People fuckin' in my bed. B'lieve that shit? People no better'n damn dogs, man." He broke into a prolonged coughing fit that seemed liable to turn his lungs inside out. The coughing subsided and Bobby wheezed, "Least they could do is invite me. Shit. So what's up with l'il Billy, man? An' why you callin' me from my bro's place?"

"I've been staying here most of the summer with Dickie. He's not down there, is he?"

"Dickie? Here'n Key West? Fuck no. Why? He missing?"

"Uh, yeah, sort of ."

"Whassat mean, 'sort of'"?

"I guess it means, yeah, he's missing. Been gone about three, four days. I was kinda hoping he was with you."

"Nope. Me'n Dickie don't hang, my man. Don't get along."

"Well, I'm sorry to have bothered you. I'm sure he's okay."

"Aw, Don' say that, man."

"Say what?"

"Say he's okay like that. "

"Why not."

"'Cause maybe he's dead."

"Oh, I…"

"An' if he is, maybe I got some of that jack he got comin' my way. Can you say, 'next of kin', baby?"

"Well, I…"

"'Course you can. Next of Kin. Ain't hard to say an' sounds good when you say it. Thanks for the news, bro. Now we really gon' party tonight. Late."

He hung up, and I sat there holding the phone for a moment. Well, I thought, at least he's taking it well. I set the phone back on the hook and leaned back in the old captain's chair that served as Dickie's desk chair. The address book was open on the desk in front of me. I closed it and set it on the corner where I would be able to find it the next day if I needed it.. Dickie's computer was on a side table next to the desk and for one reason or another, maybe morbid curiosity, maybe just to get the sound of Bobby's voice out of my head, I turned it on.

While the computer booted up I swung around on the chair and surveyed the room. It really was a shambles. Too much of a shambles. I got up and cleared a path to the door, stacking books back into piles and replacing and filling the trash can. I pushed papers back into the folders from which they jutted and closed file cabinet and desk drawers. A couple of minutes work made a big difference. There was a stack of bills on a small table near the door and among them I found one from a doctor's office about ten miles north, in Lewes. A Dr. Lewis Gerard, General Practitioner. Sounded like Dickie's doctor to me. The envelope was unopened, so I noted the name and address on the paper with the other addresses. When I was done I sat back down and got on the computer, opening the word processing program.

I'm no computer genius. I'm not a luddite either, but I just haven't had the time or inclination to really get to be very proficient at much besides typing and solitaire. I'm pretty good at solitaire, though. And I'm smart enough to know that a word processing program without a single file in it is not normal. The program was completely blank. Even if you weren't a writer, even if you hated computers, even if you couldn't type a lick, there should be something. Normal curiosity would lead you to mess around with the program at least a little bit, would result in at least something being created that would end up being saved by the computer. And I knew that Dickie used this computer with some frequency. I had heard him in here working, had heard the muted click of the keyboard late at night. I didn't know what he had been working on, but he sure as hell had been working on something. And now there was nothing. I skipped around the different programs. Nothing in the spreadsheet program, nothing in email, nothing anywhere that I could find.

This, I thought, is what you might call a clue.

Pretty smart, huh?

I don't really know why I did what I did next, but I'm glad I did it. There were a couple of fresh boxes of diskettes sitting on the windowsill beyond the computer, and I decided to make a copy of everything that was on the computer. I had heard that nothing really gets erased on a computer, that the information just goes somewhere else and can be recovered if you know how to do it. Maybe whoever had erased this stuff, and I was sure that it had been erased, I had no doubt of that, maybe they didn't know that you can recover erased files. Or maybe they were much smarter than me and they knew a way to get rid of things completely. Either way it wouldn't hurt to have a backup copy. I know about three commands in DOS. But one of them is the copy command and so I exited Windows, went out to DOS and started copying the hard drive onto the new floppies. It wasn't a new computer, didn't have a lot of bells and whistles or a huge memory, so it didn't take too long. While the computer was grinding away I sat there and thought. About Dickie, certainly. About what might have happened to him, why someone might have hurt or kidnapped or killed him, why someone would come in the house and erase his computer files. The answer to those questions was at this point rather brief: Hell if I know. And that wasn't getting me very far. I thought too about how I had probably – admit it, definitely- screwed up by cleaning up the office. There might have been some pattern to what was on the floor, in what files were open and what was left alone, that might have helped an investigator determine what exactly was the object of the search. Too late for that now, thanks to me. And only a year ago when the Public Defender Service offices back in DC had been ransacked I had helped figure out what was going on in exactly that way, by finding a pattern in the destruction. Here it was a year later and I just cleaned the damn place up without even thinking. A year older. Wiser? Maybe not.

When the copying was done I put the diskettes back in the box from which I had taken them. I turned Dickie's little copier on and made a copy of the sheet of paper with the addresses written on it, then put that in the box with the diskettes. Again without really knowing why, with nothing driving me except a feeling, I took the box out to my car, wrapped it in an old paint-splattered dropcloth and stowed it in my trunk, then locked the trunk for the first time in years. I went back inside and stared at the TV for a while. When I was sufficiently anesthetized I went to bed.

In the morning I drove over to the Dewey police station. As I drove I realized how hungry I was and that I hadn't eaten dinner the night before. It wouldn't be good for the great investigator to faint from hunger on the job, so I stopped for a couple of takeout ham, egg and cheese sandwiches and a bucket of coffee at the Sunrise, which is right on Route One more or less in the center of town. Pretty good chow pretty cheap pretty quick. Not the highest recommendation, I guess, but not the worst.

I parked in front of the station house, loaded up the first sandwich with salt, pepper and Tabasco from the bottle I always keep in the glove compartment and began eating my breakfast behind the wheel while listening to the news radio station from up in Wilmington. Apparently not much was happening in Delaware today. There was no mention of Dickie but I would have been surprised if there had been. A team from Seaford had made it to the Little League World Series. They were scheduled to play a team from Arkansas, and the winner would play the winner of the Taiwan-Philippines match. And get thrashed, of course. Ho hum. The weather forecast had just begun when a voice that came from over my left shoulder said, "Where's mine?" It was Chief Hartner. Not smiling, but not notably grim, either.

I turned the radio off and then dug in the paper bag on the passenger seat and retrieved the second sandwich, "Right here if you want it. I'm not going to eat it." I was lying, but my mother taught me to share.

"You sure?"

"Positive."

"Well, all right, then. Don't have to beg to get me to eat."

I handed him the sandwich. He glanced over his shoulder at the station house door, and I said, "Why don't you just hop in? Eat your breakfast in peace."

He nodded. "Not a bad idea." He walked around the car and climbed in.

I said, "Sorry, but I only have the one cup of coffee."

"That's all right. Have any more coffee and I'll have to spend the rest of the day in the bathroom getting rid of it."

This was an image I didn't care to ponder. Before I could change the subject the Chief asked, "Salt and Pepper?"

"In the bag."

He reached into the bag and said, "You know, I think I'll just run inside for a minute and grab the Tabasco from my desk."

Anybody who'll eat Tabasco for breakfast can't be all bad. My own sandwich had plenty of it. "Here you go," I said through a mouthful of food, handing him the bottle.

The Chief took the bottle, looked at it for a moment with a hint of a smile on his face and said, "Anybody who'll eat Tabasco for breakfast can't be all bad."

"You think so?"

"I know it for a fact.."

We ate in silence for a minute or two. I took a sip of my coffee and said, "Got that information you were looking for on Dickie – his doctor, at least I think it's his doctor- and his folks. Got an address for his brother, too, in case you need it." The Chief swallowed and said thanks. I debated what to say about Dickie's office and decided it was best to just come out with it, despite the fact that I had screwed up. I described how messy the office had been and how I had cleaned it up. The Chief's eyes narrowed but he held his tongue. I told him how everything on the computer had been erased and his eyes widened again.

"You sure about that?" he asked.

"Sure I'm sure."

"Computers are damn tricky machines," he said meaning "you probably just looked in the wrong places because you're a dumbass".

I let it slide. But I didn't mention the box in my trunk either. Let him make his own copies. The Chief finished his sandwich, licked grease and Tabasco from his fingers and said, "Damn, that was good, and thanks for it."

"You're welcome."

"I don't suppose you'd mind coming inside, answering a couple of questions, would you? Just routine, you know. Nail things down a bit, make sure we got our bases covered."

I hadn't had a real plan for the morning, had just intended to see what I could see. But I definitely hadn't planned on spending the morning in the Dewey Beach Police station. "Aw, Chief, c'mon. Do I have to?"

The chief pulled a pack of Winstons from his inside jacket pocket and a lighter from his pants pocket, lit a cigarette, exhaled, put the pack and the lighter away, took another drag and asked, through a blue cloud, "Mind if I smoke?"

"Just open the window."

He did so and said, "Well, I don't know that you 'have' to, no. You're not under arrest, not yet, anyways."

"Not yet!"

"Now, don't go getting all excited. All I mean to say is we don't have anything to arrest you for right now…"

"Chief, for chrissakes…"

"…and we want to keep it that way, and I'm sure you do, too. So if you were just to come on inside, we could get a statement, and I'm sure that would eliminate you as a suspect, and then we could all move on. Just easier for everybody, way I look at it."

A thought occurred to me. This is rare enough that I try to take notice when it happens. "Chief, let me ask you a question."

"Shoot."

"Okay. Now Dickie's house isn't in Dewey – or Rehoboth, for that matter. It's state jurisdiction, as I understand it. And Keybox Road, where the truck was, that's in the State park, so that's State jurisdiction, too. So, what are you investigating? Seems like if I'm going to give a statement to anybody it should be the State

Troopers or whoever else investigates things statewide, I don't know what they call themselves."

The Chief nodded. "Delaware Bureau of Investigations. DBI."

"I should have guessed that. But without being a pain in the ass, I mean, aren't I right?"

"Well, yes and no. You're right about Dickie's place and all, and about Keybox road, too. No real question about that. And I wouldn't worry about the DBI, I'm pretty sure a visit from them is in your immediate future. But you see," he paused, and folded his hands in front of his face almost as if praying. When he spoke again it was in a low voice, icy and calm. "You see, while the house is one way and the truck's the other, we found the body right here in Dewey, so that puts me in charge." He paused for a fraction of a second and his voice tightened. "So, you gonna come in and give us a statement or not?"

I managed to choke out, "Yes, Sir."

The body. Shit. Shit, shit, shit.

I spent a couple of hours in the station answering questions over and over and then answering them over and over all over again. I went through the whole thing three times, first with Lieutenant Bellegarde, who I decided really was a prick, then with a jovial fat man with bright red cheeks who identified himself as Officer Charlie. I wasn't sure whether Charlie was his first or last name and I didn't really care. Finally Chief Hartner came in with a man he identified as Agent Smith of the Delaware Bureau of Investigations. Chief Hartner began by explaining that, although the body had been found in Dewey Beach, and as such the case was without question –without question, he repeated- in the town's jurisdiction, the State had an interest due to the circumstances and the town was happy to accommodate them. It seemed this speech was more for Agent's Smith's benefit that for mine. By the irked look on Agent Smith's broad Nordic face and the arch of one blond eyebrow I could tell Agent Smith thought the same thing I did. The Chief led the questioning, Agent Smith taking notes and making little humming noises deep in his throat apparently at random. I detailed my actions since Dickie's disappearance at length and in detail, answered questions about how I came to be living in Dickie's house, about how Dickie and I got along, about Dickie's relationship with any- and everybody else, was asked to speculate on what might have happened, and even endured some rather indelicate questions regarding my sexual preferences and about whether Dickie and I had been lovers. This last was a little much and I wasn't shy about saying so.

Agent Smith didn't speak until the last. Fresh out of questions, the Chief turned to him and asked if he had anything else to ask or add. Agent Smith continued writing for what seemed like a long time. For what was a long time. The Chief cleared his throat and started to repeat himself when the Agent looked up. "I heard you, Chief. I think you've pretty much covered it, in your way." Agent Smith turned to me. I could see the Chief, behind him, mouthing "In my way?" with a look on his face that clearly said, "Prick." Smith said, "Mr. Flaherty."

"Yes?"

"Unfortunately, we don't have anything to hold you on at this time. But you are the primary suspect in a capital murder case. You know you're dirty and I know you're dirty."

"Wait just a goddamned minute...!"

"Save it. I really don't give a rat's ass about anything you've got to say. We've seen these things before and we'll see it again. You two had a little spat, things got out of hand, and you end up killing Mr. Harrington. And because you think you're so cute and smart, you think you should get away with it. Well, you've got another think coming, Mister. We prosecute murders in this State. And we fry muderders." By now he was getting red in the face and his voice was rising with every word. Flecks of foamy spittle had collected in the corners of his mouth. "You make damn sure," he continued, "real damn sure, that you don't go anywhere or I'll have a warrant out for you so fast it'll make your head spin. Got it?"

This was too much for me. I mean, find out Dickie's dead, then discover that you're a suspect, that's bad enough. But this jerk...I stood. And without knowing what I was going to say, began to talk. "That's the stupidest thing I ever heard, you ignorant self-important asshole. You got things exactly, exactly ass-backwards. You want to arrest me, go right ahead. Otherwise stay out of my face. This interview is over." I stood, adrenaline and rage making me lightheaded. I put a hand on the edge of the table to steady myself and then walked a bit unsteadily to the door. Behind me I heard someone shuffling papers and not much else.

I was in my car by the time the Chief caught up with me. "Hey, hold on a minute," he said, leaning to the window and speaking rather softly. He held up a hand, walked around in front of the car and climbed in the passenger seat. "Drive," he said.

"Where?"

"Doesn't matter. South."

I drove south. We worked our way through the Dewey traffic and had passed the sailing spot at New Road before either of us spoke. It was the Chief who broke the silence. "Sorry about that," he said.

I took my eyes off the road for a moment and looked over at him, but I didn't say anything. Mainly because I didn't have anything to say.

"Goddamn guy's an ass," he appended.

I still couldn't think of anything to say. "No shit," was the best I could come up with, so that's what I said.

"I don't know if it'll be any consolation, but I got a couple of things to say. First, I don't consider you a suspect in whatever happened. I don't know why, exactly, and I might have to change my mind later, and I probably shouldn't be telling you this, but I just don't think you had anything to do with whatever went on. Second, we don't know what went on. Things are pretty strange. I told you we determined it was human blood in Dickie's truck, and I told you we found his body. But there's no obvious wound on the body. It had been in the water for a couple of days, and the crabs and whatnot…well, never mind, we'll just have to wait for forensics on that. But to me, from what I could see, I don't see how it's possible that all that blood came from Dickie. Not to mention the brain material."

"The what?"

"Brain material. You know, brains."

"Jesus. Where'd you find that?"

"In the truck. On the seat and the back window. Consistent with a suicide except there's no bullet in the vehicle and no bullet holes. But the bullet could have stayed in the body, so…so who knows?"

We were approaching the sleek soaring bridge that spans the Indian River Inlet, the only point where Rehoboth Bay connects to the ocean. The campground by the base of the bridge was full of massive beige and silver RV's and as we began to climb I could see fishermen standing shoulder to shoulder along the rock groin that lines the waterway. A large white sportfisherman bucked its way out the channel against the incoming tide, followed by a flock of wheeling gulls. A man stood in the back of the boat, near the fighting chairs, pouring the contents of a bucket into the water. Probably old bait, judging by the way the gulls fought over it. Or it could have been just about anything else. Gulls are not very particular.

At the apex of the bridge you can see for miles down the beach. I always want to stop to take in the view but with the speeding traffic that would be suicide. Suicide… if someone had committed suicide in Dickie's truck, what would that mean? And without a body, how do you tell suicide from homicide? Clearly somebody besides Dickie was dead, but who it might be was anyone's guess. The only thing that was certain was that the two events were related. They had to be.

"So," I said, "so you think somebody killed Dickie, dumped his body in the ocean, and then killed themself?"

"Don't know. But we found Dickie's body –well, we didn't find it, it was found- in the bay, not in the ocean. On the little beach right behind Coconuts, lying on the sand." Coconuts is a popular waterfront restaurant and bar near the south end of Dewey. "Manager said he had just closed the place for the night and he was sitting on the little pier back there having a drink when he noticed the body at the edge of the water. About three o'clock in the morning." The chief looked at his watch. " Maybe six, seven hours ago."

I noticed for the first time how tired the Chief looked, his eyes framed by dark bags and lined with red. He must have been up all night. "But none of that's the point," the Chief continued. " The point is I know you and Dickie were friends, and I'd rather have you working with us than against us. Never mind that asshole Smith, I'll handle him. But don't run off or it'll look bad and it'll be a lot harder to keep Smith under control. And I may need help with more questions." He paused and repeated. "So stick around, okay?"

"Yeah. No problem. I'm not going anywhere until I, until you –somebody- figures out what the hell happened, and why."

"Don't go sticking your nose in everything. I know you're an investigator…"

"How do you know that?"

"I'm a cop. It's my job to know stuff like that. I know you're an investigator, but you're not a cop, and it's not your job. Just sit back and let us handle it. And we will handle it."

"I can't do that. I need to poke around, Chief. I have to. Put yourself in my shoes and you'll know I have to."

He sighed. "I don't see how I can stop you, short of arresting you. But – hear me, now – but whatever you do, don't make my job any harder. Poke around, okay. But if I find that you've destroyed evidence, that you've scared or tampered with witnesses, that you've done

A Deadly Kind of Paradise

anything at all that prevents me from doing my job, and that includes withholding evidence, you're gonna end up locked up and quick. You with me on this?"

It was all I could ask. "I'm with you, Chief. Don't worry about me."

"That's another thing."

"What is?"

"Worrying about you. Look at what we know: Dickie ends up dead. And somebody ends up dead in Dickie's truck. Now a reasonable person might guess that whoever killed Dickie took his truck and then committed suicide. Question is, what happened to the body? Seagulls didn't carry it off. So either whoever it was who died in the truck killed himself and then somebody carried of the body for some reason, or else there's a murderer running around. Maybe a double murderer – could have killed both Dickie and the person in the truck. So watch yourself. Stay out in the sunshine. And make damn sure you tell me right away if you come up with something, anything at all. Got it?"

"Got it."

"Good. Let's go back."

I turned the Impala around in the parking lot of the first store we came to, a liquor store with a big sign at the edge of the road that said, "Absolutely No Turns". The Chief didn't object. I'm not sure if he even noticed.

A few minutes later I dropped him in front of the Police Station. He climbed out and walked around to my window. "Remember what I said, now," was all he said before turning and walking off wearily, the weight of the world obviously on his shoulders. I watched him for a moment and then turned the car around and left.

At the light that guards the intersection with Route One I stopped and let the car idle. Where to now? I sat there through two changes of the light and might still be sitting there if it hadn't been for the blaring impatient horn of the car behind me, a red Jeep with four shirtless young men all wearing stylish sunglasses and sporting buzz cuts and tattoos. They were yelling and gesturing and it seemed the better part of valor to get moving. I turned left, toward home. Toward Dickie's house, at least. I couldn't think of anywhere else to go.

There was a car in the driveway when I pulled up, a dusty dull-green Suburban with Delaware tags. The split rear doors stood open, revealing a pile of various tools and other unidentified equipment. I parked, climbed out and stood there for a moment, but no one appeared. I called out, but there was no answer. I tried the front door but it was locked, so it didn't seem that anyone had gone in the house that way, so I walked around the house with must have appeared to any unseen onlooker as almost-comic (okay, comic) stealth, placing one foot carefully in front of the next, staying close to the house and peering around corners before rounding them. I had reached the back of the house a minute or two later and I had just bent to look around the corner when a man came walking quickly around the corner and slammed right into me. I don't know who was more startled, but it was close. We both shouted and jumped back . I recovered first. He, a short balding round red-faced man of about sixty dressed in work clothes and heavy boots, looked like he might not recover at all. He was standing there gasping, holding his heart. For a moment I was convinced he was having a heart attack. "Are you okay?" I asked, forgetting all about asking him why he was there and what he was doing.

"Yeah, but Jesus Christ, boy, you like to scared the piss right out of me."

"Sorry about that, but if its any consolation the feeling was mutual."

He just looked at me with a blank expression so I said, "You scared the shit out of me, too." And he smiled. I had a feeling I wasn't dealing with the brightest bulb on the tree. "What," I asked, "Are you doing here? This is private property."

"Oh, don't you worry none, we won't be long. We's just surveyin'."

"Surveying? For what? And who's 'we'?"

"We's me an' Jerry. He's back 'round the corner. I'm working for him. An' as to why we're surveyin', don't know. Property lines, I guess. Some question, or somethin'. I just do what they tell me, Mister. I don't know nothin'."

I figured he was telling the truth there, so I didn't push it. "Where's this Jerry?"

He jerked his head to the left and back. "Round the corner. Down by the dune. I was gettin' the transit, an he's probably wonderin' what happened to me. Maybe you should go on and talk to Jerry."

"I'll do that." I turned to walk off.

The man called after me, "Tell him I'll be right along, would you, Mister?"

I nodded and waved without looking back. Jerry was where the man had said he would be, and looked a bit peevish. Actually Jerry looked like he spent a lot of time feeling peevish. He was maybe thirty or thirty-five, slim, with a thin face whose hollowness was emphasized by the scraggly beard he wore. He had long curly hair that he wore tied back in a bushy pony tail, and wore designer work clothes – expensive Timberland boots, just-so Levi's, a tight t-shirt with an abstract whale print on the front and most likely some environmental slogan on the back, round blue John Lennon-style sunglasses, a North Face windbreaker, a heavy clunky silver watch that could have doubled as a hammer in a pinch and which probably had a compass built in, a faded red bandanna trailing out of a back pocket. He looked at me with a complete lack of interest as I approached and made a show of looking at his watch and sighing. Now I hate to make snap judgements –okay, maybe 'hate' is a bit strong since I do it all the time – but some people just beg to be classified. They want you to do it. They put on uniforms and wear badges and adapt attitudes that are so clear that they might as well be wearing signs. In a way it's hard to avoid, because you are what you are and even if, like me, you try to avoid stereotyping yourself you sometimes end up playing that role – the role of the mystery man, or of the man who would have people think he doesn't care about appearances, which of course are types themselves. But anyway. But anyway this guy wanted you to see that he was a hip artsy outdoorsy environmental type, a Sierra Club or more likely Earth First member, a vegan Phish fan with an IQ higher than yours. And of course mine.

I really hate guys like that, and I wasn't about to start making exceptions now. "Is there something I can help you with?" I asked, perhaps a bit archly. I try to keep a low profile, to conceal how I feel about people and things as much as possible because it allows more room for maneuvering later if you need it. But sometimes I fail.

"No. Or yes. You can please leave us alone. We have work to do."

Well, at least he wasn't wasting my time with banal pleasantries. I smiled a broad and obviously completely false smile, then shook my head and gave a little 'aw, shucks,' chuckle. "Sorry, Jerry," I said. "I guess I wasn't very clear. Let me rephrase that. You're on private property. Get the fuck off before I call the cops. Or kick your ass, whichever you'd prefer."

He pursed his lips and looked at his watch again. And sighed again. "We're surveying," he said. "We have a legal right to be here. So why don't you just go away like a good little man?"

Little? I'm six-two and go about two-thirty. I had the guy by an inch or more and a good forty pounds. And probably thirty IQ points. At least. "Hey, you wanna compare SAT scores?" I asked. It was the best I could come up with on short notice.

"Excuse me?"

"Never mind. Who hired you?"

"No one 'hired' me. I'm here on behalf of the Foundation...oh, there you are. What in God's name took you so long?" This to his panting assistant, the round-faced man I had literally run before, who had reappeared carrying a metal tripod with what looks like a small telescope attached to the top, a transit.

"Sorry, Jerry. First this guy," meaning me, "scared the bejeezus out of me, then the damn transit was stuck in the truck, then some cop was asking me all kinds of questions."

"Cop?" Jerry raised an eyebrow. "Is he still here?"

"No, he took off."

"Too bad. We could have used him. To clear out the riff-raff." He shot me a look.

"I get it, Jerry. Touché. Bravo. What Foundation are you here 'on behalf of', Jerry?"

"I don't see that it's any of your business, Mr.....?"

"Flaherty."

"Mr. Flaherty, but it's SOS."

"SOS?"

"Save Our Shores."

"That's cute. Never heard of it."

"I'm not surprised by that," he said, clearly but wordlessly appending "since you're a moron." I heard it, at least. "Now," he continued, "Are you going to let us do our work?"

"Not until you explain why you're here."

Jerry was getting exasperated. He sighed yet again and rolled his eyes theatrically. "And then you'll leave us alone?"

"Maybe."

"Really, this is supposed to be confidential, but, we were contacted by the property owner in regards to the Foundation acquiring development rights to this property."

"Dickie was going to give the place away?"

"Hardly. When we acquire property the owner is generally compensated through a combination of cash and tax relief. The value of the two together usually meets and occasionally even exceeds the current market value of the property."

"How can it exceed the value?"

"It's complicated," he said, meaning I wouldn't understand. "Now may we continue? We do have work to do."

"You're wasting your time. Dickie was murdered. They found his body last night."

"Oh, that's terrible," Jerry said, sounding as if he meant it. "But it really doesn't change anything. He changed his will months ago. We were just here to determine the square footage, and we still need to do that. So if you don't mind…"

Actually I did mind, but it didn't seem like there was anything I could do about it. I turned to go. "Knock yourself out." Something occurred to me and I stopped and turned back. "Since Dickie's gone, who'll get the money and all?"

"I have no idea. Some family member, I would guess."

I nodded. It stood to reason. And I could think of a family member who would be mighty happy to discover that he'd had a windfall like this. I doubted Robert would be crying in his beer.

Seven

I spent the better part of a half an hour watching my new friend Jerry and his unnamed assistant from an upstairs window. They worked steadily and quickly, and for some reason it irked me that he seemed to know what he was doing. While I watched them I debated what to do. I thought about calling the Chief but wondered what exactly I would tell him and what it would accomplish. I had a suspect, Robert, and a motive, good old greed, but it was a very long shot. And I knew that Robert had been in Florida yesterday, which while it didn't prove anything made it doubtful that he had been here in Dewey in the past couple of days. I didn't want to be running to the chief every five minutes like some little kid with a secret, but there was no real reason not to tell him either and that's what I finally decided to do. I figured the chief might want Robert's address and phone number so I walked down the hall to Dickie's office to retrieve the address book I had left on the desk. I opened the door, stopped short and stood there for a moment, taking it in. I had foolishly cleaned the office the day before, but what I had done paled in comparison to what I was looking at from the doorway. The place was spotless. More than spotless, it was completely empty. There wasn't a book or a piece of paper in sight. The computer was gone, as were the diskettes, even the trash can. The desk and chair were still there, but that was it. I walked over to the desk and opened each drawer in turn and they were as empty as the day they were made. The place even looked like it had been swept. Whoever had emptied the place had been admirably thorough, and standing there I felt a chill run down my spine. Either someone had been in the house last night while I slept or they had been in and out in the few hours I had been away, in which case they must have been watching me, the house or both. Either way I hadn't noticed what was going on, which made me feel distinctly uneasy as I considered what else might have been going on under my nose. I quickly went downstairs and out to the car and a few minutes later I was back at the Police station. I parked and walked in. Young Officer Ryan was sitting behind the front counter, his back to the door, drumming on a low file cabinet using a couple of pencils for drumsticks. He wasn't bad. I cleared my throat discretely and he spun around quickly, guiltily trying to palm the pencils. But he dropped one and it rolled under the counter. He bent to retrieve it and banged his head as he tried to sit back up. When he finally managed to say "May I help you?" It looked for a moment as though he might cry.

"I was looking for the Chief, but I gather he's not around."

Ryan looked at me for a moment, obviously trying to figure out how I knew the Chief wasn't there. I said, "I just didn't think you'd be practicing your drumming if the chief was around."

With a quick shy smile he nodded his assent. "Got me there."

"You in a band?"

Another quick smile. "Yeah, sort of. We're working on some things, trying to get an act together."

"Aren't we all?"

"Huh?"

"Never mind. You expect the Chief anytime soon?"

"He had to go up to Georgetown." The county seat, about twenty miles to the west. "Something about some records. Said he'd be a couple hours and he only left like twenty minutes ago. I can get him on the radio, if you want."

"Nah, that's okay. Just tell him I came by and was looking for him. I'll try back later on."

He bobbed his head. "Will do."

The drumming started back up before the door closed behind me.

I sat in the car for a couple of minutes with the motor running. For a long time I had been perfectly happy doing nothing. Now I couldn't figure out what to do and it was driving me crazy. Go figure. Finally I went back to the house. The surveyors were gone, strips of fluorescent pink ribbon hanging from various branches the only evidence that they had been there. I didn't feel like going inside, and I didn't feel like sitting in the car, so I started walking up the beach towards Dewey. I had only gone a couple of hundred yards when I noticed a man standing atop a dune. He was well within Dickie's property and I'm a curious soul, so I climbed up to where he was standing. He had been looking out toward Silver

Lake, which lies just behind the beach there, but turned as I approached.

"Hello, there," I said from perhaps twenty yards off. "Is there something I can help you with?"

He was a short solid man of perhaps sixty with erect military posture and a completely hairless head upon which the sun reflected brilliantly. "No...," he said slowly. "No, I'm all right. Is there something I can do for you?"

"Uh, no, thanks. You know you're on private property, right?"

"Hell yeah I know it."

"So...maybe you should leave? You're trespassing, and it's bad for the dunes to walk on them."

He snorted. "It's not going to hurt the dunes to stand here for a few minutes. And I'm sure as hell not trespassing. This is my land."

"Yours? It belongs to Dickie Harrington." Belonged, I thought.

"Nope. That land there," he waved an arm to his right. "And that land over there," he repeated the gesture, this time to the left. "That's all Dickie's. But this here in the middle, it's mine. Been in the family a hundred years. Dickie's Grandad wanted to buy it, but mine didn't want to sell."

"Well, sorry, then. That's news to me."

He nodded affably. "Don't worry about it. Look over there to the right and you can see where the surveyors marked the corners, and again over here on the left."

I looked where he indicated and it was obvious that he was right about the boundaries.

"Heard there were surveying down here so I just walked over to take a look where they were putting the corners. Seems right, as far as I can tell. But it's been a while since I checked on it. Damn shame."

"What is?"

"This piece of property. Really be worth something if Dickie would grant me an easement to get to it. I might get four or five lots out of it, and that'd be worth something. You price waterfront property lately? Way things are, all it's good for is seagulls."

"How much would it be worth?"

"Oh, I don't know. Couple million, probably. Way things are going, maybe more. I don't like to think about it or I end up crying in my beer."

I could appreciate that. Two or three million dollars just sitting there and no way to get it, that could depress you. "Dickie wouldn't grant you an easement, huh?"

"Nah. Nor sell me one. I even had a backer lined up, a builder I gave an option to, but no dice. Could have given cash for the easement. Can't say as I blame Dickie too much though, really. Plenty of money and he likes things the way they are. But a couple of million dollars would really give me a jumpstart on the bills."

"I would guess so. My names Bill Flaherty, by the way." I stuck out a hand and he shook it.

"Pleased to meet you, Bill. Lou Nickerson. You're a friend of Dickie's, I gather."

"Yeah. From high school. I've been staying in Dickie's house most of the summer." For some reason I didn't feel like breaking the news about Dickie's death. I don't know why.

"Well you picked a good summer for it. Can't remember a summer where the weather stayed this nice this long. Could use some rain, but you can't have everything."

"Nope."

We stood there for a few minutes more, taking in the view. There was a fair crowd up at Poodle Beach and a lighter one down in Dewey and no one in between except for a couple of kids in baggies skimboarding out in front of us. Behind us the waters of Silver Lake shimmered like a million little mirrors in the breeze. A distant siren —maybe out on Route One- moaned and warbled plaintively and somewhere a dog howled in response. I suddenly realized that I wasn't feeling very good at all. Somehow I had been keeping it in, had managed to avoid thinking about what had happened, about Dickie, about would happen now, but all at once the dam broke inside me. I didn't cry, I don't think you would have noticed anything, any radical change looking at me, but a change had come. And it was time for me to go. I turned to Mr. Nickerson, who was looking at me a little strangely, and said, "Well, I better get going." Despite myself my voice broke on the final word, and I silently cursed my weakness as I turned to go.

"Hey," Nickerson called out before I had taken five steps. "Is everything all right?"

"Uh, not really. Look, I gotta go. See you around." He made no move to follow me and when I looked back a few seconds later he was still standing there on the dune looking out to sea. I don't know what he was thinking about. I don't know what I was thinking about either.

I walked back to the house and sat on the front step. I've never felt more at a loss in my life. Even when my father died there were things to do, roles to play, words to say. As tough as that was, and it was very damn tough, it was possible to keep going, to keep putting one foot in front of the other because you had to, there was no choice. There was Mom to think about, and my brothers and sisters and details that needed tending to and all of that put a false but somehow comforting sort of blanket over things, kept me from thinking too much about what it all meant and by the time things had slowed down enough to really sit and think enough time had gone by that already the emotions were dulled. But sitting there on Dickie's front stoop I was just at sea. I didn't want to go in the house. I didn't want to stay out here in the yard. I might have gone home to D.C. but the renter was still in my place and would be for a couple of more weeks. I might have liked to go see Bunny, but I hadn't called her in a couple of weeks and somehow calling her now just because I needed a hug or whatever seemed like a cheap way out, like I would be using her somehow. And I didn't want that. I've been pretty confused about Bunny, about where or even whether we might go together, but I didn't want to show up on her doorstep like some damn orphan, I knew that much.

And I thought about calling Ted, my friend Theodore Lynam, III. Ted and I go back. We worked together – maybe we still work together if I go ever go back- for almost a dozen years. And Ted and I have been through some shit together, some shit that would curl your hair, out there on the streets in D.C.. But I hadn't called Ted all summer and I didn't feel like burdening him with my problems. Ted had known Dickie a bit, he'd met him more than once, but it wasn't like they were friends, and what kind of a friend would I be to ignore him all summer and then call him up all weepy and distraught out of the blue, looking for him to throw me a rope when I hadn't had the courtesy to so much as drop him a line? It was a shame too, because I missed Ted. Missed him, truth be told, more than I missed Bunny, for some reason. I wondered why I hadn't invited him to the beach all summer. Dickie wouldn't have cared, would have been all for it, actually. But it was hard to imagine Ted sitting on a beach. Does Armani make swim trunks? If they do, then maybe Ted would go to the beach. Not otherwise. That's Ted.

I sat there for a long time, an hour or more, and I might have stayed longer if the sun hadn't shifted so that I was in the shade and it got chilly. Finally I stood and sighed and stretched out my aching back and said to the world, "Shit." Which was about as eloquent as I could be, right then.

And I walked over to the car and got in and turned it on and started driving and somehow the car steered itself to Dewey Beach Liquors and I was inside with a bottle of Absolut in my hand and then back outside in the car twisting the top off – actually I was sort of frantically ripping at the damn plastic wrapper that they put over the top of Absolut bottles with my fingernails, painfully splitting the nail on my right index finger in the process-before I really even thought about it. And when I got the plastic off, at last, and I had twisted the top off and I had taken a very large damn swig out of the bottle and I was still sitting there in the car in the little dirt parking lot in front of the liquor store, then I said to the world, "Shit." Which was still all I could think of.

Details become a bit hazy from that point. I drank some vodka and drove around for a while. I was on my way down to Ocean City, having convinced myself that the bright lights and loud music of the overblown resort city were just what I needed when I convinced myself that I was a moron and turned around. Which just might prove that I'm not a moron. I ended up back in front of Dickie's house and thankfully I parked the car. I walked down the beach in the twilight and stashed the vodka by the little shack near Chesapeake street where they keep the rental chairs and umbrellas and then walked up Chesapeake and then down Route 1A, sometimes known as Bayard Street and sometimes known as King George Street and nobody seems to know the real name because there are no street signs for some obscure reason, but it runs along the water and then behind Silver Lake and connects Dewey and Rehoboth, and when I had walked the few blocks down into Dewey I went into the Starboard and then, and then I began to drink.

And then things get really hazy. I remember being at the bar talking to a slutty blonde with gigantic breasts and I remember a thin hard-looking guy with a buzz cut, a goatee and two earrings in one ear being very unhappy about it. I remember dancing with some girl who if she was eighteen her birthday was yesterday, and I remember that I was still sitting at the bar when the place closed and that I had some idea that I had a right to stay there and I was trying to make the bouncers understand me as they dragged me to the street. I remember being quite frustrated about that. And I remember remembering about the vodka I stashed on the beach and that I went hunting for it.

The next thing I remember is waking in the dunes in a sweat with the sun beating down on me and a desert in my mouth and an empty Absolut bottle lying next to me and a little girl, maybe five or six looking down at me and asking what I was doing before her horrified mother came running up and dragged her away.

I was hurting. But then I deserved it, and I couldn't complain. Hell, I didn't have anyone to complain to. I got up, which was quite a bit harder than it sounds, and brushed a fair portion of the sand off me and set off down the beach staggering back to Dickie's house. When after a month or so I was finally there I patted my pants pockets and discovered that I didn't have my keys, which wasn't making my day, but then I walked over to my car and there they were in the ignition. Brilliant.

Tucked under the windshield wiper was a note from Chief Hartner stating that he had heard that I had been looking for him at the station and that I should give him a call when I got the chance. Which last phrase I took to be the operative one, and went inside. I drank a gallon of water and ate some stale Froot Loops without milk. It wasn't bothering me, just then, that the house was empty and that I had no real right to be there now that Dickie was gone. And besides, nobody had told me to leave yet, either. He had told me to stay as long as I wanted, after all. He probably hadn't meant that I should stay after his death, but he hadn't made that clear. I walked out onto the deck, squinting against the sun, and saw that I had never cleaned up Dickie's beer bottles, ashtray or whiskey bottle from the other day. I picked up the beer bottles and threw them out. I dumped the ashtray in the trash. And then I picked up the whiskey bottle, held it up against the sun, and saw that it was half full. For some stupid self-destructive reason I twisted off the top and took a swig. Half an hour later it was gone, and so was I. After I finished the whiskey I started doing shots of Grand Marnier, nothing cheap about me, until that was gone too. And when I could barely see straight I somehow made my way upstairs and to bed.

I slept until the day was almost gone, probably would have slept the clock around except for the fact that the bed was moving or I was and I wanted to sleep and I tried to make it stop, tried to will the motion, commotion, earthquake, whatever it was, to stop but it wouldn't and finally I was sufficiently conscious to recognize my name. "Bill," someone said, and I knew it was my name but I really wanted to sleep so I rolled away from the sound but whoever it was grabbed me by the shoulder and rolled me back over and said, "William Flaherty, wake up, for God's sake." And I still didn't want to, still would have rather slept, but now I was awake so I opened my eyes at last.

"Ted," I said. "What the fuck are you doing here?"

"What the fuck do you mean what the fuck am I doing here?"

I looked at him for a while. "What is that, a riddle? I'm not in the mood for riddles, Ted"

"It's not a riddle, exactly, William. Actually it's more like a palindrome."

"What?" But then I recognized the Monty Python reference and said, "Oh." Ted. Theodore Lynam, III, Esq. The man himself. Slim dapper elegant Ted, the rich boy from Philly, the tough guy in the Armani suit, my best friend and a royal pain in the ass to boot. I sat up not without effort and when I had succeeded said, "So why are you here, Ted?"

"You're not kidding?"

"Do I look like I'm in the mood for kidding?"

"Well, no. You look like you're ready for a weekend in detox and a month at Betty Ford, since you asked."

"Ha fucking ha."

"You're really serious?"

"Ted. Tell me why you're here or don't. I don't care. But I'm not playing twenty questions, and that's final."

"I'm here because you called me and asked me to come. I gather you don't remember."

"Oh yeah, now I remember."

"Malarkey."

"Malarkey?"

"Would you prefer that I say 'Bullshit?'"

"I'd prefer that you say 'Goodbye', actually. Or at least good night." Ted looked a bit aggrieved. I held up a hand. "Don't mind me, Ted, I'm out of it." I swung my legs to the floor and stood. This wasn't a good idea. I sat back down. "Did I say why I wanted you to come down?"

"Actually, yes. Or sort of. In fact you were rather eloquent and quite persuasive despite the fact that you were slurring and making no sense at all."

"How can you be eloquent and persuasive while you're making no sense?"

"I think it's an Irish thing."

"You might be right." I looked at my wrist. "Shit. I lost my watch. I probably got frigging rolled."

"Your watch is on the bedside table."

"Oh. Thanks. " I wondered why I had taken my watch off, but I had no idea. It must have seemed like a good idea at the time. Like a lot of things.

"And your wallet was on the stairs. I put it over there." He inclined his head toward the dresser that stood just inside the door.

"Your keys were on the floor inside the front door. I left them downstairs on the table in the foyer. Your shoes are outside by the front door. And there's a tee-shirt and a pair of jeans on the steps."

"Jesus. What'd I do – explode?"

"Apparently."

I digested this for a while, tried to will memory to return. Unfortunately this is not possible. I might remember what happened or I might not, but nothing I did was going to make me remember a damn thing.

Ted said, "There's coffee. And I got some deli stuff, we could have a sandwich or something."

"How long've you been here, Ted?"

"About four hours."

"Four hours? Jesus. Why didn't you wake me up?"

"I tried, William. When I got here and both times the Police came by, but what can I say? You were out."

"I guess so. Police, were here, huh?"

"A Chief Hartner came twice, first with several other officers and then later on his own. The first time they were here for over an hour, looking around. Looking for clues."

"They find any?"

"Not that I'm aware of, but they really didn't say."

"Were they in my room?"

"Oh, yeah. Several times."

"Jesus. I guess I really was out. I hope I wasn't doing anything embarrassing in my sleep."

"Snoring to beat the band, but nothing else I know of."

"What'd Hartner have to say?"

"Not much. Asked you to call him when you're able."

"That might be a while."

Ted didn't respond. I stood again, making it to my feet this time, and stretched. Actually I didn't feel too bad, considering what I'd done to myself.. I walked over to the dresser and pulled a pair of shorts out of the bottom drawer. In the mirror over the dresser I caught a glimpse of Ted eyeing me somewhat appraisingly. He wasn't leering, but he did seem to be evaluating my naked self somewhat like a cowboy judging horseflesh. Ted's a good and dear friend, I've known him for years, partied with him, worked with him, we've been at each other's places dozens of times. I've never known Ted to be romantically linked to anyone, male or female. It was almost as though he was asexual, and that was how I had come to think of him. The look I had caught in the mirror almost made me reconsider that position. Not that I cared. I think. Suddenly self-conscious I pulled on the shorts and a tee-shirt and turned around. Whatever the look on Ted's face had been, it was now gone, replaced by that look of bland amusement which is so typical of the Ted I know. Maybe I was crazy. Hell, probably.

Downstairs in the kitchen I drank another gallon of water and then had a corned beef and Swiss sandwich on good crusty pumpernickel with plenty of mustard and about half a raw onion. Ted didn't eat, but he never eats much. I explained what had been going on as I ate my sandwich. Ted kept silent until I had finished and when I had, he said, "You know what I think?"

"No, Ted. What do you think?"

"I think it's a damn shame about your friend. I think it's strange about the other —murder, suicide, whatever – and about the office being cleaned. I think it's strange, and it's a shame, and it sucks, but most of all I think you should leave it alone. Leave it to the professionals…"

"I am a professional."

"A professional defense investigator. And you know as well as I do that that is a vastly different thing than being a police investigator. At the risk of boring you, what we do is try to create reasonable doubt in the Police's case. We start where they stop, we try to poke holes in things, not prove them. "

"And your point might be that…?"

"That you should stay out of it. People have died. For all we know, more people might die before it's all over. I mean, if you feel like investigating something, come back to work. They could use you. Especially now that…well, the place has been damn busy. Summer in the city, and all that. And not to be crass, but what do you stand to gain here? What's your motivation? Pride? Anger? Simple curiosity? Some sort of Celtic tribal loyalty?"

"Yes."

"Yes what? All of the above?"

"Correct."

Ted knows me. He sighed. He gave up.

"So," he said, far too brightly, "how's your summer been?"

"Pretty good, until lately."

"Hadn't heard much from you."

"Sorry. I'm not big on talking on the phone. Thanks for coming, by the way."

"You're welcome. Bunny was asking about you the other day."

It was my turn to sigh. I did so. "I need to call her."

For a moment it looked like Ted was going to add something but he bit his lip instead. We sat there for a while in silence. Finally Ted asked, "Is there anything to drink in this house?" Ted likes to drink. A lot. I've never seen him obviously drunk, but I've seen him pack it away many a time.

"There was some Absolut and some Myers' dark in the cabinet next to the sink. Juice and some soda in the fridge. Help yourself. I need to call Hartner."

Ted nodded and I got up to find the phone. Cordless phones are nice but I seem to spend a lot of time looking for them when I need them. I ended up having to press the "page" button three times as I gradually narrowed my search field. I finally found the phone between the cushions of the couch in the living room. I dialed the number the Chief had left me and he answered on the second ring. Judging by the static and the noise in the background it must have been his cell phone. "Hartner," was the curt answer.

"Chief, it's Bill Flaherty."

"Back among the living, eh?"

"Yeah. I kind of overdid it last night."

"I heard. Hell, I saw."

"You saw?"

"I was by the house a couple of times today, and I was outside the Starboard at closing last night. Looked like you were feeling no pain."

"Well, I made up for it later. Don't you sleep?"

"Sometimes. Not well. You came to see me yesterday at the station?"

"Yeah, I…" I paused, unsure of what to say. "Maybe you could swing by Dickie's place?"

"Sure. I can be there in five minutes if that works."

"Give me ten. I need a shower in the worst way."

"See you in ten." There was click and the line went dead. I looked in on Ted, who seemed happy enough with a large glass of clear liquid and a magazine. I told him I was going to take a shower and that the Chief was coming and he nodded. "I'll be here," he said without looking up. "Take your time."

And so I did. The hot water felt good, felt like absolution, like it cleansed more deeply than mere water possibly could. I kept turning it hotter and by the end I had it on pure hot, and it stung like hell but still felt good. Being something of a masochist I turned it all the way to cold and stood there as long as I could take it before jumping out into the steam-choked room, slipping and nearly breaking my neck on the condensation-slick tile floor. Getting dressed I looked out the window and saw the Chief's Bronco parked in the drive, and when I came downstairs he and Ted were chatting like old friends at the kitchen table. By the way the conversation came to a screeching halt I knew what the topic of conversation had been. There was a brief awkward lull and then Ted said, "The Chief was just telling me about the case. Sounds intriguing."

"Intriguing? Dickie getting killed is intriguing?"

"Well," Ted stammered, "I'm sure that's the wrong word. Mysterious. Interesting…never mind. All I meant to say was…"

"Forget it, Ted. I know what you meant. I'm just on edge. Sorry."

Ted nodded, clearly relieved at not having to say anything more. He took a large gulp of his drink and rose to refill his glass. I looked at the Chief, who was sitting there looking particularly inscrutable, and asked, "How's it going, Chief?" It wasn't eloquent, but what the hell.

"Okay. You?"

It looked like we were going to have a laconic contest. I was in. "Okay."

"Good."

"So…"

"Yeah?"

Damn. He won. I sat down across the table from him. Ted finished making his drink, glanced our way and wandered off toward the back deck. The very soul of discretion, Ted. Usually. "So, Chief, thanks for coming by."

"Welcome."

Somebody needed to tell the guy that he'd already won the contest. "I came up with a couple of interesting things…." I told him about Robert, and about the surveyors from SOS, and he listened intently. When I mentioned Lou Nickerson the shadow of a smile crept across the Chief's weatherbeaten face but he refrained from speaking. But when I told him about Dickie's office his eyes grew first wide, then dark.

He raised a hand. "Hold on a minute. Somebody else cleaned that room after you did?"

"That's what I'm saying. I straightened it up. I didn't clean it out."

"And you knew about this…when?"

"Uh. Yesterday. Yesterday afternoon."

"Why'n hell didn't you tell me about this?"

"I am telling you about it."

"Yeah. Now. So, let me get this straight. First you mess around with what appears to be evidence. It occurs to you that you've screwed up – and you had – so you finally tell me about it. . Then you discover that person or persons unknown have removed said evidence from the premises, but you don't tell anyone, giving this person or persons at least twenty-four extra hours in which to escape, destroy the evidence or whatever it is they intend to accomplish. And your reason for not telling anyone about all of this appears to be that you felt like getting drunk. Well done. Goddamn well done, Flaherty. Shit."

He punctuated this last word with a fist pounded on the table. He wasn't happy. And neither was I because he was right. I had no excuse except that I hadn't felt like dealing with what was in front of me. I had started off with the best of intentions and somehow I had gotten sidetracked, sidetracked to the point that I had probably caused real harm. Good job.

The chief pushed his chair away from the table and stood. He was not a tall man but he towered over me. "Anything else?" he asked.

I shook my head.

"Not that it will do any good, but we're going to come back and look over that room again, dust for fingerprints. We'll need a set of yours. You can either wait here for the technician or come down to the station."

"I'll wait here."

"Fine. Stay out of that room. Also don't touch any doorknobs, doorframes or windows until they're done dusting. If you must touch something use a tissue and be careful. No, check that. My people will be here in a few minutes. Just don't touch anything until then." He looked at his watch. "I have to go meet your friend Agent Smith. Jesus, if you thought that guy was an ass before…" His voice trailed off and he shook his head. "Well, what's done is done. But do me a favor and don't try to help any more, okay?"

I nodded. "Chief, I'm sorry."

"You know," he said, "I'd have to agree with that." And he turned on his heel and left, stopping only to retrieve a handkerchief from his jacket pocket before touching the doorknob.

Eight

Lieutenant Bellegarde, looking even more cadaverous than earlier, and two other Dewey Beach Police officers were in the house along with a fingerprint technician from the State Police. They were busy with their dusting and collecting and had set up bright lights throughout the house, with thick electric cables snaking everywhere. The normal quiet of the place had been replaced by the buzz of men working and the crackle of police radios and I had been in the way despite my best efforts to stay out of it, so I joined Ted on the deck after they took a sample of my fingerprints.

We were watching the ocean as the light began to change with the approach of evening. There must have been a storm somewhere out to sea as the waves had built substantially during the day. And now a stiff land breeze was building, shearing the tops from the rollers as they crested and came ashore, white veils of foam ripped from their crests and tossed back into the troughs behind. The waves broke almost on the beach, coming down with a hollow thump and a grinding roar as they spent their energy climbing toward the dunes. It wasn't surfing weather – the shore break would pound you into bloody

A DEADLY KIND OF PARADISE

pulp before you could even get up on the board, and no one was in the water as far as I could see in either direction. A flock of perhaps twenty terns skittered along the beach, daintily keeping their feet dry right at the knife's edge of sea and sand, darting down toward the ocean as the waves receded only to rush back up as the next came in. There were hundreds of seagulls on the beach, hunkered down against the wind, their feathers ruffling in the gusts as they waited for something edible to come along. A lone crow flew low above the beach from right to left, trying to get to Rehoboth for some urgent appointment but having a hard time of it, stalling sometimes despite frantic wingbeats and hovering in place for long seconds until the gust passed and progress was again possible. Ted sipped his drink and stared moodily out at the broad vista, his only acknowledgement of my presence a subdued grunt as I had joined him at the railing.

"Stormy weather," he said at last.

"Looks like something's brewing," I agreed.

Seconds passed in silence and then Ted looked at the drink in his hand. "I'm going for a refill. Get you something?"

I took a quick inventory: upset stomach, shaky hands, lightheadedness, slight headache. Did a quick analysis: Hangover. Two cures: Time or more alcohol. Said: "Sure."

"What do you want?"

"Whatever you're having."

Ted inclined his head the merest fraction and wordlessly withdrew. A couple of minutes later he reappeared bearing two water glasses filled with ice and clear liquid and handed me one. I sipped. Straight vodka on the rocks. In for a dime, I thought, and took another sip, a healthy one, if you can use that term in reference to poison. I suppressed the urge to gag and after a few seconds took another sip. It went down easier.

Ted cleared his throat and said, "I was serious, before."

"Serious about what?"

"About you coming back to DC. It's time you came home, time you went back to work."

"Why are you so bound and determined to get me back to DC?"

"It's not...I'm not bound and determined, it's just that, well, there's a time, and it seems like this is it. You can't stay here forever, and with everything, I just think you'd be better off. I'm just trying to help."

"I don't know, Ted. Not yet. I don't even have my place back until the first of September. And to tell you the truth I'm not sure if I ever want to go back."

"No? Are you going to spend the rest of your life here? In Dewey Beach?" He almost sneered the name of the town.

"I didn't say that. Maybe I'll move out West, teach skiing. Or go back to Boston. But what's wrong with Dewey? I like it here."

"There's nothing...wrong with it. There's the ocean, and the beach, but...well, it's hardly cosmopolitan."

"What does a women's magazine have to do with this?"

"Very funny. You know exactly what I mean."

"I know that you wouldn't be happy here. There's no museums, and the only theater is at the Midway Multiplex. But...well, I don't know. I think I could take it pretty well, if I ever patch things up with Chief Hartner."

"A good question in its own right."

"I'm not too worried. I screwed up but it wasn't intentional. He knows that, and he strikes me as fair. Not tolerant, particularly, but fair."

"But you have to go back. You're the best they've got. PDS needs you. And…well, you should be there, not here. People need you."

"What people?"

"People. Just…people."

Ted wasn't making a lot of sense. Or at least I couldn't make much sense out of what he was saying. I hoped he wasn't trying to tell me he was the one who needed me, that would be a bit awkward. We sat there in silence for a while, the only sounds the waves breaking on the beach and the wind whistling hollowly through the eaves. Finally Ted heaved a troubled sigh and then stood. "I don't suppose you'd join me for a drink?"

I looked at the drink in my hand. "I am joining you for a drink, Ted."

"I mean, would you care to go out for a drink?"

"Geez, Ted, I…okay. What the hell. But I better check and see if these guys need us to be here first."

Ted nodded and turned back to face the ocean and I went inside. Bellegarde appeared happy, or as happy as he seemed to get, at the news that we were leaving, and agreed to lock the place behind them. His only request was that I send Ted in to get fingerprinted before we left and I said I would do so.

The Rehoboth boardwalk starts just a couple of hundred yards north of Dickie's house and a few minutes later Ted and I were climbing up the stairs from the beach to the mile-long boardwalk. Here the boardwalk was empty except for a Mutt-and-Jeff couple walking our way hand in hand. As we approached them the taller one, a graying distinctly professorial type despite the bikini bathing suit and tanktop, called out in a well-modulated baritone, "Well, look who it is! Hi, Theodore, how are you?"

Theodore?

"Good, Doctor, how are you?" Ted replied easily.

"Never better. This is James, Theodore. A very special friend of mine."

"Hi, Theodore," James said. He was a little coy for my taste, but what the hell, it's a free country. And I wasn't dating him.

The Doctor, smiling, said, "Aren't you going to introduce your friend, Theodore?"

"I'm sorry. This is Bill Flaherty. He's…". For a second I was sure he was going to say, "straight," but instead he said "a coworker, or at least he was. He's living down here for the summer."

"Oh, how nice for you, Bill. Isn't it grand?"

"Uh, yeah. Grand." For some reason the words didn't come out very well and the three of them looked at me a little strangely for a moment. "Grand," I repeated inanely.

"Well, Doctor, we're off for a drink or two. Nice seeing you again."

"Nice seeing you, Theodore," said the good Doctor in a voice rife with overtones that I really didn't want to think about. "Look me up in Washington sometime."

Ted and I continued on our way north to the center of Rehoboth. "Who the heck was that?" I asked after a reasonable amount of time had passed with no comment from the abnormally quiet Mr. Lynam.

"Oh, he's just a friend of mine from D.C. He's a history professor at George Washington". I didn't seem to be right about much lately so I took some solace in the fact that I had pegged the man as a professor from the start. You take your victories where you find them. Ted left it there and I didn't pursue it and we walked on in silence.

Even though it was windy it was a nice evening for a stroll, and as we approached the center of town people were nearly shoulder to shoulder on the wide wooden walkway. The word "eclectic" was coined for Rehoboth. Surging along the boardwalk as the overhead sodium-vapor lights blinked on was a throng as diverse as America itself, as diverse as is usual in Rehoboth. Redneck tourists, fresh from God knows where in the hinterlands, with their John Deere baseball caps and their "I'm With Stupid" t-shirts, the thin hollow-cheeked husbands and huge ponderous wives both painted a fiery red by the sun; pierced sunken-eyed teens in black with Metallica or Marilyn Manson t-shirts; yuppie preppie families with the moms in Ann Klein tennis garb or perhaps a print sundress from Talbot's, long straight hair tied back with a bow, the dads in Bermuda shorts, Docksiders and striped pastel button-down shirts folded back precisely at the wrist, a sweater draped over the shoulders, the arms tied loosely around their necks, the kids, embarrassed, a few paces behind; large extended black families moving together slowly, talking and laughing; a few ragged homeless people, their possessions piled high in shopping carts hidden in the shadows a few feet off the boardwalk; scruffy local kids trying to perfect insouciant swaggers but not quite making it work; half a dozen bikers on a bench wearing sunglasses despite the hour, bandannas tied just so, leathers artfully ripped and sleeves removed to expose clichéd tattoos; a group of Latino guys carrying fishing poles and buckets of bait; and through it all, the recurrent theme on which all of the others were mere variations, the gays.

Rehoboth has become something of a gay Mecca, and that's fine with me. Really. Maybe I wasn't too comfortable with the thought that my best friend might be gay, and maybe I needed to do some soul-searching on why that might be, but in general I really couldn't care less what people do, any people, as long as they leave me alone, and that's never been a problem in Rehoboth. To me, a large gay population means one thing: Good restaurants. It also means interesting shops, but I'm no shopper. I get vertigo in malls. I've never deliberately gone shopping for recreational reasons in my life. But I have spent a few mornings walking around Rehoboth looking in windows and from what I can tell from the sidewalk it looks like quite a few of the shops might be worthwhile. And as for the restaurants, well, I'm enough of a sybarite to appreciate a good meal and good service, and you can get both many places in Rehoboth. It's an exaggeration, but not too much of one, to say that in Dewey a good meal is a good cheese steak and fries that aren't too greasy. You can get those in Rehoboth, and much else besides.

We walked slowly up the boardwalk, threading our way through the throngs. Kids squealed in delighted terror on the rides at Funland, miniature golfers studied their lies, and the endemic unmistakable smell of grease, cotton candy, salt air and sunburn lotion filled the air. Rehoboth has good restaurants, but they're not on the boardwalk. The boardwalk is honky-tonk America at its finest, arcades and pizza joints and tee-shirt shops and bars and all the rest, swirling with people of every description, and all conveniently located just steps from the mighty Atlantic. There were a couple of open stools at a bar a little further on so we sat and ordered drinks and turned to look out through the large open doors at the crowds moving past just steps away. I sipped at my Bud bottle and Ted charged fearlessly through his Tanqueray and tonic as though he hadn't had a drink in a month. Ted likes to drink. A lot. Everybody needs a hobby, I suppose, but sometimes I worry about Ted's persistent pursuit of liquid recreation.

After a while, after he had his second drink in hand, Ted turned to me and said, a bit of a tremor noticeable in his voice, "Bill, there's something I need to tell you."

Uh-oh, I thought. Here we go. Ted comes out of the closet. I didn't want to hear it, I really didn't. He was my best friend. And as open-minded as I like to think I am, I wasn't sure what would happen to us once he came out. Would we still be able to hang out, watch the tube, have a drink, go out for dinner? Would I feel like he was coming on to me if he stopped by to say hi like he had a thousand times before? I really didn't want to hear it, but it didn't look like I was going to get a choice in the matter. "What's that, Ted?" I asked, keeping my voice as flat and unemotional as possible.

He took a sip of his drink. Actually he drank most of it in a gulp. He looked down at the ground, and in a barely audible mumble said, "I, uh, I'm really sorry. Really sorry, Bill…but, uh….I …"

If he was going to come out he might as well do it and get it over with. So with more conviction than I really felt I said, "Ted. You're my friend. Nothing's going to change that. Whatever you have to say, just say it."

Ted looked up from his drink, his eyes red and brimming. "I'm really sorry, Bill." He said.

"About what, for God's sake? What can you say that will change how I feel about you? Spit it out, man."

"I, uh…I slept with Bunny. "

I nearly choked on my beer.

"What!?"

"I'm sorry, William, I really am. I never meant it to happen, and neither did Bunny. The first time, it was almost an accident…"

"The first time! Jesus, how many times have there been?"

"Um, not many. Just twice."

"Twice! Are you shitting me? You're shitting me. Ted, tell me you're shitting me."

Ted shook his head woefully and upended his drink, then said, "I'm sorry, William. I don't know what to say."

"Neither do I, for God's sake. What the fuck should I say, Ted? 'That's okay, just don't let it happen again?' or maybe, 'Thanks for keeping her warmed up, old chum?' Jesus. Ted, this blows. This blows big time. I really should hurt you now, you know. Get me another beer and a shot of Jim Beam. I'll be back." I got up and stumbled out onto the boardwalk, bumping into a guy who looked like he was auditioning for the part of Beast in "Beauty and the Beast". He growled. I went around him and down the boardwalk in search of cigarettes and fresh air. Which is kind of funny, if you think about it. At that moment, I wasn't thinking about it. Bunny and Ted. Holy shit. Ted and Bunny. Holy shit.

I stepped into the blinding fluorescent brightness of a small shop just down the boardwalk and bought a pack of Marlboro Reds in the box, cowboy killers, from a person behind the counter who appeared to have some sort of severe skin disease. What the hell, I was probably looking a little strange myself. I ripped the cellophane from the package and let it flutter to the floor and fumbled with a match until I got the damn thing lit.

"No smoking in the store, sir," said the mutant behind the counter. I stepped a foot to my left, off the store's linoleum and onto the wood of the boardwalk and that seemed to satisfy her. Or him, it was hard to say. Bunny and Ted. Ted and Bunny. My mind was like one of those stupid Nascar races – going around and around in circles really fast but not getting anywhere. I sucked down the butt and then ground it out on the wood planking. Out of pure pettiness I blew the last lung full of smoke into the little shop and marched back to the bar to confront Ted. Or tried to march. It had been a while since I'd had a cigarette and I was very damn dizzy indeed as I walked back the way I'd come. Ted was still at the bar, looking morose, swirling his drink with a straw and looking down at nothing in particular. My beer and my shot stood on the bar awaiting my return. I sat down on my stool rather more heavily than I had intended and said, inventively, "Hey." Ted replied in kind.

And then we sat there, not talking, for quite a while. I had no idea what to say. I had always known that Ted and Bunny were fond of each other – not quite this fond, but fond – and there was no reason they shouldn't be so. Bunny is smart, beautiful, athletic and driven. Ted is smart, reasonably good-looking, wealthy, suave, courageous and altruistic to a fault. They'd been around each other for years. But I'd always been there too. And then I had left, which was beginning to seem pretty crucial to this whole thing. If I hadn't left...no. If I hadn't run away, then none of this would have happened. I ran away, from my job, from my girlfriend, from my life, basically, and now I was surprised to find out that things changed in my absence. I had had some damn idea that I could step out but that everything would remain in stasis like some sort of diorama in a museum until I felt like coming back and reanimating everyone. That this was foolish had now been proven conclusively. The question was, what now? The answer was..."Another round, please," this to the bartender who was making a rare foray to our end of the bar. With a wave I indicated that he get one for Ted, too.

"Thanks," Ted mumbled after the bartender had walked off.

"You're welcome," I mumbled in reply.

"Look," we said in unison and then both stopped. "You go," said Ted.

"No, you. I got something to say, but I want to hear what you have to say, first"

Ted took a deep breath and said, "All I have to say, Billy, is that I'm really sorry. And Bunny is too. We never meant it to happen, it just did. It's so tawdry I can hardly stand it. I was going to come down here...or at least call, and then you called last night, and asked me to come down, and well, I had to tell you. I know I already said this, but I'm really sorry. I was just trying to help..."

"Help!?"

"Well…Bunny was so sad, and she was lonely, I mean…you never even called her for weeks and weeks, and I don't know, I was trying to cheer her up…"

"Cheer her up?"

Ted winced. "Bad choice of words, I know. All I did was invite her over for dinner, and my plan was to cheer her up, to get her to buck up, you know, keep the faith, that you'd be back, that you just needed some space, and she got all teary and, well, one thing led to another."

"That explains the first time."

Ted looked like he was about to be sick. He squirmed on his stool and was about to say something when the bartender brought our drinks. He took the price of them from the pile of bills on the bar in front of Ted and then went off to make change. When he was gone, Ted said, "All I can say is I'm sorry. We made love again…it was, I guess, to see if it was the right thing, to see if …to see what the real truth was, I guess. The real truth turned out to be that I couldn't take the way it was, the….I guess the betrayal is what I'm saying. It wasn't good, that second time. What we did was wrong, but when Bunny and I were together…hell, man, you know, I love her too, you know that, right? I mean, you've always known that, haven't you?"

I guess I did.

"So, I'm leaving. It's the only thing I can do."

"Leaving? Leaving where? Here?"

"No. Leaving D.C.. I quit PDS this morning, and I'm going from here to Philly, to see my Mom and Dad. My Dad lined me up job in San Francisco with Merck in the legal department out there. So I'm going from Philly out to San Francisco. I'm not going back to Washington."

Ted's Dad is the head of the legal department at Merck and could certainly get Ted a job if he wanted to – in fact he'd been trying to get Ted to take a job with Merck for years. Ted's about a semester short of graduating from law school and has been since I met him. He told me once that he just woke up one day knowing he didn't want to be a lawyer and never set foot on that campus again.

"Oh, that's great, Ted. Just fucking great. Good solution. Good solution, you fucking moron. Just run away. Yeah, that's the ticket. Just run away. That'll fix everything, won't it? You know what, Ted? You're an asshole. A big fucking asshole. Just run away. Jesus."

Ted was looking a bit stunned. Splotches of color had appeared high on his cheeks. "Well, look who's talking about running away. Mister High-And-Mighty, Mister 'I'll just live at the beach now, you all just stay here and wait for me, maybe I'll come back', Mister 'I don't care if I break my girlfriend's heart', Mister frigging... mister."

At least he was calling me Mister. And at least we had accomplished something: Now we were both pissed. I'm surprised no one said anything about the steam coming out of our ears. We sat there, stewing in our juices, for what seemed like a long time. For what was a long time. Ted's point was valid, it was what I'd been thinking myself: If I hadn't left D.C., none of this would have happened. If I hadn't been so oblivious, so self-centered and such a damn head case, it would be a different world. Yeah, and if pigs could fly... "Ted."

"What?" he snapped.

"Don't leave D.C."

"Why the hell not?"

"'Cause I don't want you to. Man, you're my best friend."

"Some friend. You turn your back and I jump in the sack with your girlfriend. It's inexcusable. It's no way to act. I have to leave. I deserve to be punished for my actions."

"Uh, don't you think that's a bit melodramatic?"

Ted looked at me sharply. "No I don't. There's right and wrong in this world, William. Right and wrong. This was wrong, there's no way around it. And as you say, once was one thing. That was bad enough, but then to go back and do it again…"

"Ted, stop it. We've covered that. Look. I blame you, sure. And I blame Bunny, too, that's for damn sure. And I don't know, right now, what I'm going to do about her. But the real blame belongs on me. That's all there is to it. My actions led directly to this situation. Change my actions, this situation doesn't exist."

Ted pursed his lips and shook his head vigorously. "You're absolutely wrong, William. That's situational ethics, which I don't believe in. No. Sleeping with your best friend's girlfriend is wrong. Period. End of story. You're right that this wouldn't have happened if you were still in D.C, but so what? Does that excuse my conduct? Does that make everything okay? I think not, William. It's all my fault, and that's all there is to it."

"What about Bunny?"

"What about her?"

"Well, if we accept your theory, than she's equally to blame, isn't she?"

"Oh, come on, William. She's a woman."

"So?"

"So she's weak and easily led."

Again I nearly choked on my beer. "Bunny? Are you nuts? You are nuts. Bunny is the strongest, most determined person I've ever met. Weak and easily led? That's a good one."

Ted didn't reply, staring moodily at what little remained of his drink. I ordered another round, and when it came we started in again, each playing –playing's the wrong word – each playing the martyr, each so eager for some reason to shoulder the blame that we couldn't let it alone. And we stayed there, at the bar, on the boardwalk, far into the night. And by closing time I was thoroughly inebriated for the third time in twenty-four hours. A new record. Wheee. Go team go.

Nine

In the morning I was hurting and Ted was gone. There was no note, no way to tell if he had left for San Francisco or simply gone out for a cup of coffee. Morose and melancholy, I lounged restlessly, which is a trick in itself. For perhaps the millionth time since I had left home twenty years before I thought of moving back to Boston. This is a favorite mind game of mine, a thing I do when things are not right in my world. Go back to Boston, stay with Mom for a while, get a job, start anew in the land where I was born and where I belong, if I belong anywhere. I never do it, though. I just turn it over and over like some well-polished worry stone, rubbing it and shining it in my mind, thinking of how good it would be to be away from the hot southern summers and the gray slush of Washington winters, to be back where people think right and talk right, to cruise the coast of Maine in a sailboat eating lobster rolls in every port, ski the mountains of Vermont and New Hampshire in winter, walk down Commonwealth Avenue on a crisp fall day, just…just be there. But it's not going to happen. It would smack too much of defeat, would make all the advice that I've received and ignored correct after all this time. It's too bad in a way, but pride has its price.

I didn't do much that morning. Moped. Recovered. Sat in the sun. Worried about Ted, thought a hundred times of calling Bunny. Actually went out to the car and sat behind the wheel for a couple of minutes, keys in hand, thinking that I would drive up to see her and see what could be salvaged or whether in fact it should be, before shaking my head and climbing back out, disgusted with myself for being, in effect, me.

"Well, fuck," I said to no one when I was back in the house. "What now?" There was no answer. Finally the oppressive silence and my restlessness drove me out of the house. The first place I went was to the Police Station in Dewey, mainly because I couldn't think of anywhere else to go. Officer Riley once again sat behind the front desk, looking very businesslike this time. He spoke and dispelled that impression. "Hey, Dude," he said, "What's up?"

"Uh, nothing," I replied, adding "Dude," so as to not be rude. "Is the Chief…"

Before I could finish a voice growled from a back room, "Back here, Flaherty. Come."

So I lifted the hinged countertop that served as a gate and went back. A short hallway ran straight back from the reception area and the Chief was in the first room on the right, a small cluttered office dominated by a portrait of Ronald Reagan. The Chief sat at a battered wooden desk in a battered wooden chair. He was leaning back in the chair and had his feet on the desk. He looked tired. He said, "Jesus, I'm tired," so I guess my intuition was on the mark yet again. I amaze myself sometimes.

"Maybe you should sleep sometimes."

"Maybe so." He set his feet on the floor, rubbed his eyes and then stood. "Time enough for that when I'm dead, I guess. What brings you down here? Screw something else up?"

"Just…just hoping for an update. Wondering if there's anything I can do to help out…"

"Don't you think you've done enough helping?"

"Well, technically, I guess you could say I haven't helped at all, so no, I guess I would have to say no."

The Chief sighed and sat back down, rubbing his temples. "Jesus," he murmured. "Why me?"

Before I could think of an answer for him he looked up and said, "The only thing you can do to help is stay the hell out of the way. As far as the update you requested, there's nothing new. I'll let you know if we come up with anything. Thanks, and now goodbye. I've got work to do."

I've been brushed off before, but seldom as effectively as that. I got up and walked out. There wasn't anything else to do. I glared at Riley as I passed him, mentally daring him to call me Dude but he held his tongue. I was so mad I was shaking. Well, that might not have been why I was shaking, considering what I'd done to myself over the past couple of days, but I was mad. Really. Back outside I fumbled for a cigarette and once I had found one I lit it and stood there in the lot in front of the station smoking. And steaming. So, the chief didn't want me involved. Hell, he didn't even want me around. But my friend was dead, not his. And unless he arrested me there was nothing he could do to stop me from trying to figure out what had happened. And that was exactly what I was going to do. I hopped back in the car and drove off. I had the impression someone was watching from a window in the station, but I really didn't really care. Chief Hartner could watch me all he wanted.

My first stop was the Kmart our on Route One. If you're going to be an investigator you need a few tools. I picked up a couple of notepads, some pens, an inexpensive camera and some film and a little backpack to carry it all around in. Then I drove a little further up the highway to the Radio Shack over by the old Super Fresh store and picked up a small tape recorder which set me back a bit more than I had expected. That went into the backpack with the rest of the stuff and I was all set. But for what? I sat in the Chevy out in front of Radio Shack for a while, trying to figure out my next move. Finally I decided to get some lunch. An army can't march on an empty stomach. This one can't, at least.

In addition to all of the Outlets, Route One is Fast Food Central. As a rule I try to stay away from that stuff but when in Rome…plus, as I said, there's some ingredient in McDonald's food that seems to help with hangovers. What exactly is "special sause", anyways? I pulled the car into the lot, intending to go through the drive-thru, but the line was too long so I went inside. A couple of minutes later I was working my way through a Quarter-Pounder (with cheese, of course) a large fries and a Coke, with a Big Mac still wrapped and waiting on the tray. It wasn't pretty.

"That stuff'll kill you after a while, you know," said a female voice, and I looked up to see the smiling face of Denise the windsurfing bartender, looking casually spectacular in cutoffs and a plain blue tee-shirt, her hair swept back and a pair of funky shades perched upon her head. Two little kids, a boy and a girl of five or six hovered a step behind her, looking out shyly. Both clutched brightly printed Happy Meal bags. I nearly inhaled a French fry. When I had recovered I said, "It might not take that long."

"So why are you eating it?"

"Hungry," I replied cogently before managing to spit out, "Well, what are you doing in here, then?"

She nodded at the little ones. "Lego in the happy meals. They gotta have it."

I focused on the kids. "Cute kids."

"Thanks," she smiled.

"Yours?" I asked, hoping the answer was no. Kids generally come with a Daddy.

"No," she laughed. "My sister's. This one's Erin and this one's Brian. I'm watching them while my Sis hits the outlets. They're in town for a ten days. Right guys?"

"Right!" They choroused.

"And we're going to the beach, right?"

"I want to go to a store that sells Pokemon," said the boy.

I said, "Pokemon's from the Devil, Brian, didn't you know that?"

A flicker of uncertainty crossed the child's open face and Denise ruffed his hair.

"He's just kidding, Brian," she said, before adding *sotto voce* "even if he's right."

"Why don't you sit down?"

"We were going to take it to go, but why not?" She seated the two youngsters at the next booth and, after some admonishments in regards to their behavior and the effect it might have on their continued possession of the Lego trinkets in their bags, slid into my booth, sitting across from me. She brushed a stray strand of hair away from eyes, looked up and smiled. "So…" she said. "How are you?"

It was an interesting question, and one that I would have been willing to explore with her at length. At long length. All of a sudden Dickie and Bunny and Ted and Chief Hartner and everybody else were very far away, or maybe I was, drifting away on the deep dark waters of her eyes, of her smile, of her, well, everything. But the spell only lasted a moment. "And how's your friend, what's his name? Richie?"

"Dickie," I said. "It was Dickie."

Ten

It ended up being a long lunch despite repeated desper-
ate pleas of boredom from the two kids. And parting
was with a warm hug and a heartfelt promise to call later,
news or no. As I watched the kids tow her out the door
I was left with the feeling that maybe something good
could come out of all of this, that maybe the future held
some promise after all.

And now here I was in the goddamn car again, sitting
in the McDonald's parking lot, trying to figure out what
to do. Again.

Ted had been right: I was a defense investigator, not
a criminal investigator. My strength was poking holes in
cases, not in making them. Poking holes in cases is fairly
straightforward- you take the facts as they are presented
and double check everything. If you find discrepancies
you try to add them up and see what they amount to.
You try to see if there is another reason the police want
your guy off the street, or if there's laziness in their case
and there often is. I've said it before: as far as the police
are concerned, it often doesn't matter if your client did
what he's alleged to have done, because the cops figure
that even if he didn't do this crime he probably did

something else, so who cares? Lock 'em up, they say, and we'll all be better off. Of course they're often right about that, but my job is – was? – to be the advocate of one particular person accused of one particular crime, not to be society's guardian angel. And the police should have the same focus, should be trying to arrest and convict the person who actually did the crime, not to roam around like a bunch of blue-clad vigilantes. All of which gets me exactly no closer to figuring out what happened to Dickie.

Even if some of my skills were transferable to the type on investigation I was trying to do, the restrictions that Chief Hartner had placed on me made things doubly difficult. I had at least an idea of what I would do if I could, which was to start interviewing people, people like Lou Nickerson and Dickie's brother Robert, anybody I could think of who might for some reason want Dickie out of the way. Actually, those were the only two I could think of, but maybe there were more. If I was to interview everybody who knew Dickie to see if he might have told them something, anything, that might lead somewhere. If I had access to the forensics that might give me an angle, an avenue to follow. But I wasn't about to get a forensics report from Hartner and certainly not from Agent Smith of the Delaware Bureau of Investigations, who I was sure would like nothing better than to throw me into a holding cell with three guys named Bubba. And If I started going around interviewing people I was likely to end up in a cell for interfering in an investigation and that wouldn't do anybody any good. Particularly me: I hate jail cells.

"Think, Goddammit!" I shouted, to the consternation of the fragile-looking white-haired lady climbing into the ancient Crown Victoria parked next to me. She fumbled with her keys and climbed quickly behind the wheel, locking her door immediately. I offered a weak smile and a wave as she pulled away but she stared straight ahead. Some people have no sense of humor. I gave the woman a few seconds so that she wouldn't think I was following her and then drove out of the lot and out onto Route One heading back toward Dewey. I decided to go back to Keybox Road and scout around. I doubted that I would find anything as obvious as a pistol or a body lying around, but thought that maybe if I just spent some time walking around something would come to me. What the hell, it was better than sitting in the parking lot at McDonalds with the stench of grease hovering over me like some sort of toxic cloud.

Traffic was heavy on One, more stop than go, and after I had passed the last of the outlets I could see that a fire engine and a couple of police cars were stopped, lights flashing, atop the bridge that crosses the Intracoastal. An accident, maybe. Or a heart attack or a jumper, there was no way to tell. Although if it was a jumper it was a pretty stupid one because the fall wouldn't be enough to kill you unless you landed on a passing boat, which would be a pretty good trick in itself. Whatever it was it must have just happened because even though both lanes were blocked traffic was still moving a bit as the cars packed in more tightly together. I was right by the exit for Route 1B, which leads into Rehoboth, so I took it planning to take the back way through town down to Dewey and then on to Keybox. As I approached the center of Rehoboth it occurred to me that I hadn't gotten the mail since before Dickie had disappeared. Not that I was expecting anything, but you never know. The investigator's creed: You never know.

I must have been doing something right because there was a parking spot right out in front of the Post Office that still had a couple of minutes left on the meter. You don't want to park illegally in Rehoboth. Take my word for it, they're good at what they do. Maybe they're not quite as efficient as DC, but no one is. I ran up the short flight of stairs and slid through the closing door behind a woman who was leaving, and nearly ran right into the attractive young Rehoboth Police woman to whom I had given the missing person report on Dickie a lifetime or so ago.

"Whoa, there, big fella," she said with a smile.

How did she know?

"Sorry, Ma'am, I…"

"Ma'am?"

"I mean, Miss…"

"Miss?" At least she was still smiling. "Try 'Officer', or maybe Becky."

"Okay, Officer, um, Becky. Sorry about that."

"No problem. I was sorry to hear about your friend."

"Oh. You remember, huh? Yeah it was pretty rough. Is pretty rough."

"I bet. I can't imagine, really. Are you doing okay?"

Good question. "Yeah, I guess so. Things are pretty strange right now. I'll get through it."

"Well, if you ever need a shoulder to cry on," she paused, chewed a lip. "Here, hold on a second." She took a silver business card holder from a shirt pocket, took a card out and wrote her number on the back. "Give me a call sometime if you want to. We could go out for a drink or something. You know, just to talk, or…well, whatever."

She handed me the card. I looked down briefly at the number scrawled on the back and then tucked it in my pocket. "Thanks. I just might do that."

"If you want to. Well, I gotta go."

"Bye."

I watched her through the glass door as she went down the stairs. She must get her uniforms tailored, I thought. No way does standard issue fit like that. I kicked myself for my insipid response. Why would I say, "I just might do that?" Why wouldn't I just say, "I'll do that." Or "How about tonight?" I never cease to amaze myself. And speaking of amazing, I hadn't been on a date with anyone but Bunny in years, and hadn't even seen her in over a month, and now on the same day the two best-looking women in town wanted me to call them. What a life.

I retrieved the mail from the overstuffed box and went through it as I walked back to the car. Not much for me – my cell phone bill, the electric bill for my place in DC, which I had agreed to pay, and a couple of pieces of junk mail. Dickie had a lot more stuff, and I wondering what to do with it when the logo on one of the envelopes caught my eye. It read "Morgan, Jenkins and Taft, Attorneys at Law" and had a Lewes address. It was a slim envelope and I turned it over a couple of times as if that might help me to discern the contents. It didn't. Dickie had said that he was going to see his lawyers and then there had been that incident where he woke me up and told me that he had willed me the house. Maybe he really did it, I thought. Wouldn't that be something. Of course it also gave me a motive for killing him, if you thought about it, which is exactly what I was doing. And...and if Dickie had been killed over the house or the will, and I was now the one who owned the house, that might put me in danger. Just what I needed.

I drove back to the house and went inside. I dropped all of the mail on the small table in the foyer except for the letter from the lawyers, which I had decided to steam open. Hartner would kill me if he found out, so he just couldn't find out. A few minutes later I extracted what tuned out to be a bill from the slightly soggy envelope. The bill was the firm's letterhead and showed charges for executing a new will, with a note at the bottom asking Dickie to stop by and review the documents when he was able. The note was signed by Gerry. A glance at the letterhead showed that this was probably Gerald Morgan, Senior Partner. I put the bill back in the envelope, resealed it, and put the envelope with the rest of the mail in the foyer. It looked like a trip to Lewes was in the cards.

Eleven

"I'd like to speak with Daniel Morgan, please."

The severe-looking grey-haired receptionist peered up at me over the wire-rimmed glasses perched on the end of her nose. You could tell just by looking at her that she was not a happy person. Of course her demeanor might have been affected by mine. I was not a particularly happy person right then either. Alcohol poisoning will do that to you. "And you might be?"

I might be the Pope, I thought, but I'm not. "William Flaherty."

She retrieved a gold-engraved leather-bound appointment book from a shelf, spread it open on the desk in front of her and made a point of studying it at length. Eventually she said, "And did you have an appointment, Mr. Flaherty?"

"No ma'am," I said, without asking why she had to ask since she had the book right in front of her, knowing that it was just her way of establishing dominance, of showing me that she was the important one in the room and that I was nothing but an annoyance. Hell, she was probably right. "But it will only take a minute. It's in reference to Dickie Harrington."

She looked at me closely and said, "What about Mr. Harrington?"

"I understand he was a client of Mr. Morgan's."

"And what's your interest in that relationship? Assuming you are correct."

"I'd really rather discuss it with Mr. Morgan, if you don't mind." I lowered my voice and leaned closer. "Confidentiality, you know. Can't be too careful."

She looked doubtful so I said, "Of course if Mr. Morgan's not interested…" I let my voice trail off, mainly because I had no idea what I would say next. But the air of mystery worked as I had hoped it might and she picked up the phone from her desk and pushed a button on the keypad. "Yes, Mr. Morgan. It's Earlene. There's a gentleman out here by the name of Flannery,"

"Flaherty."

"Excuse me, by the name of Flaherty, who wishes to speak to you in reference to Mr. Harrington. Yes. Very good. I'll ask him to wait." She hung the phone up and looked up at me.

"I heard," I said before she could speak. "Thanks." I cooled my heels in the lobby reading a three-year-old copy of the Journal of the American Bar Association. It was fascinating in a kind of completely dry, dull and dated kind of way. I was deep into a passionate repudiation of tort reform when Earlene's phone rang and when she hung up she said, "You may go back. Mr. Morgan's waiting for you. Second office on the left."

I almost said thanks but decided it really wasn't worth the effort. Morgan met me at his office door. A big man of about fifty or fifty-five, white hair perfectly coifed, he wore an expensive suit and looked like a caricature of a politician. He smiled broadly and extended a hand. We shook and he squeezed the life out of my hand while looking me intently in the eye, giving the impression that I was the most important person in the world to him. If he wasn't a politician, he was missing his calling.

"A pleasure, Mr. Flaherty. Please have a seat." He clapped me on the back and ushered me to a chair, then went around his desk and sat. "So, Mr. Flaherty, what can I do for you? I understand you're here in regards to something about Dickie Harrington? I just tried to reach Dickie but I guess he was out."

Obviously he hadn't heard. "That's right. I, I'm not sure quite how to break this to you, but Dickie...Dickie passed away."

Either the shock was genuine or Mr. Morgan was a very accomplished actor. I didn't have any reason to think he would be acting so I assumed the shock was real.

He said, "Passed away? But he was just here a few days ago. He seemed fine. "

"He was, then."

"But...well, what happened? This is terrible. I've known Dickie and his family for years. What was it, an accident? Heart attack?"

"No...somebody killed him."

"On purpose? Murder? Why haven't I heard anything about this?"

"I don't know. It only happened – it was only discovered to have happened- a couple of days ago. I'm not sure when he died, exactly. The police have been keeping the whole thing low-profile while they investigate. The news is bound to get out sooner or later, though."

"I…I would imagine so. Has anyone informed Dr. or Mrs. Harrington?"

"I'm not sure. I haven't spoken to them."

"There's no mistake, is there? You're positive it's Dickie?"

"No, there's no mistake. I wish there was, but there isn't."

Morgan got up from behind his desk and walked across the room to a dark-stained antique armoire and opened the door to reveal a row of bottles. "I need a drink," he said. "Join me?"

"No, thanks. I'm trying to cut down."

"Suit yourself. Soda?"

"I'll take a Coke if you've got one."

He opened the small refrigerator that occupied the bottom half of the armoire and pulled out a can of Coke, poured himself a healthy measure of Scotch and then carried both beverages back across the room. He handed me the Coke and then went back behind the desk. He took a large sip, closed his eyes and leaned back in his chair. "So," he said. "What brings you here? Just delivering the news?"

"No. I'm looking for some information."

"Are you with the police?"

"Not exactly."

"Not exactly? What does that mean?"

"It means…it means no, I'm not with the police."

"Who are you with?"

"Nobody. I just want to get to the bottom of things. Dickie was my friend, and…well, I'm an investigator, I think I might be able to help."

"Oh. An investigator. You're a private eye?"

"Ah, no. A defense investigator. For the courts in D.C. More like a public eye."

He eyed me strangely over the rim of his crystal tumbler as he took another sip of his drink. He set the glass down carefully on a coaster and said, "A defense investigator from D.C.. How…unusual. Well, what sort of information are you interested in? And if I may ask, why?"

"The 'why' is easy: I already said Dickie was a friend of mine. I've known him since high school. I've been living in his house all summer. And now somebody killed him. I want to help the police in any way I can. It's the least I can do."

"Do the police need your help? "

"I don't know. Maybe not. It's hard to say. It can't hurt, the way I look at it."

"Do they know you're here?"

"No."

"If they knew you were here looking into Dickie's affairs, would they approve?"

"Um, no. Probably not."

He arched a silver eyebrow. "Probably?"

"Okay, they wouldn't approve."

"And why is that?"

"Well, Chief Hartner and I –he's the police chief in…"

"I know Chief Hartner very well."

"Chief Hartner and I sort of got off on the wrong foot."

"Hmm." He swirled the scotch in his glass and took another sip. "Am I to presume that the Chief has told you to mind your own business and let him mind his?"

"Something like that." I was feeling a little sheepish. Baaa.

"Huh." Morgan picked up his drink and drained it, leaned forward, placed his elbows on the desk and regarded me for long seconds over his folded hands. For a moment I thought he was smiling.

"Huh," He said again. It wasn't very enlightening.

"Look," I said. "All I'm trying to…"

He held out a hand. He had two fat gold rings and a nice watch. I'm not crazy about jewelry on men, but I didn't feel a need to tell him that just then. "Hold on, hold on, now. I'm thinking this through. Tell me if I've got this straight. You come here, against what I gather to be the express wishes of Chief Hartner, and expect me to reveal privileged details of my relationship with Dickie – stop me if I'm going wrong – details which, generously, may or may not be germane to the matter of Dickie's passing. Were Chief Hartner to find out about your inquiries he would be upset at you for pursuing them and at me for assisting without first clearing things with him. Leaving aside the ethical matter of privileged communication with a client - Dickie, in this case - and I assure you that it's not an insubstantial issue, leaving that aside, what would be my motivation?"

"Well, I…"

He interrupted. "Let's look at outcomes. Possibility number one is that I give you nothing and you go away. I kind of like that one. It's simple, and there's no downside for me. Possibility number two is I help you but you fail to accomplish anything of significance. It gets out that I helped you and suddenly I get in trouble with the bar, with Chief Hartner and with my other clients, who would have good reason to doubt my ability to keep a secret. I'm not too fond of this scenario, as you can imagine."

"But…"

He raised his voice a notch and talked right over me. "Another possibility is that I help you, you figure out the case before Chief Hartner, which embarrasses him in front of the good people of Sussex county, and it somehow comes to light that my assistance was crucial to cracking the case, helping me in my triumphant sweep back into office in the next elections."

I knew he was a politician.

"Clearly there are other scenarios," he continued. "But, to tell you the truth, I'm not very fond of the Chief, and I do want to be reelected and for some reason I trust you. Plus, you've got another interest in this, don't you?"

"I'm not sure what you're talking about."

"Oh, Mr. Flaherty," he beamed. "Your name isn't all that common. Do you think I'd just forget it?"

"I have no idea what you're talking about."

"Surely Dickie mentioned…his will?"

"Oh. The will."

"Of course, the will."

"To tell you the truth, I wasn't sure whether Dickie was pulling my leg. He only told me about it a couple of days before he, before he disappeared. He really wrote me into his will?"

"He most certainly did."

"To…to what extant?"

"To nearly the greatest extent possible. There a couple of bequests, but the lion's share is yours."

"And what's the lion's share worth?"

"Oh, today, maybe five million or so. It's appreciating rapidly though, so that's probably conservative. The way things are going it could be worth twice that by the time we clear probate, which will take a while, especially under the circumstances. Let's just say that you won't have any difficulty paying my fees."

"Your fees?"

"My fees. I think it would be a good idea to throw the iron cloak of privilege over this little exchange of ideas, don't you?"

I could see his point, and I said as much. "But I don't have much money."

"Oh, but you will. I'm not worried. We'll just set up an account and give you a small bill while you're here. Give us a check and we're all set. Fair enough?"

"I guess so."

"Good." He rose. "How about that drink?"

"I think I could use one."

"Excellent." He picked up the phone and after a moment he said, "Earlene, I'll be with Mr. Flaherty for a while. Take messages, please." He hung the phone up and said, "Scotch all right?"

"Fine."

Twelve

When I walked out of Morgan's office an hour later it was with a slight buzz, the conviction that Dickie had been killed because of his house and a strong feeling that I was on track to find out who had done it.. Not bad for an hour's work.

Over several excellent single-malt Scotches Morgan had showed me a copy of the will and it was there in black and white: I was either going to be rich or house-poor in the not-so-distant future. But more interesting than that –don't get me wrong, I found sudden wealth rather interesting – were the previous iterations of the will. Dickie had re-written his will twice in six months. Up until the previous March, Dickie's will had been pretty straightforward, giving most everything to his family and a limited amount to a couple of charities. But in March he had changed the document drastically, and the new beneficiary was the Save Our Shores Foundation, the outfit on whose behalf that guy Jerry and his bumpkin minion had been surveying the property.

That version of the will was in effect for almost six months, during which time no one at Morgan's office talked with Dickie at all. And then a few days ago

Dickie had come into the office, obviously upset about
something, and had insisted on changing his will right
away. Morgan said that there had been two versions of
the will drawn up on that day, with the first essentially
returning things to where they had been before the
change in March – giving everything to his family – and
the second giving everything to me. As Morgan told it,
they had drawn up the first draft and given it to Dickie
for review. Dickie left the office and took it with him,
only to return a couple of hours later asking for the
changes. Despite being a bit bewildered by the changes
they had made them and Dickie signed the new version
on the spot, had it notarized and then left. That was the
last time they had seen Dickie.

I wondered why Dickie had cut the SOS Foundation
out. And I wondered why he had cut his family out on
two separate occasions. The only way to find out was
to ask. Morgan said he had no idea. And I had already
spoken with Robert, and he clearly wasn't going to give
me anything, especially when he found out that he wasn't
in the will and that I was. That might steam him just a
bit. I was sure that Hartner would be less than pleased if
I called Dickie's parents to ask them, and that he would
find out if I did. So that left the SOS Foundation. Clearly
a visit to SOS was in order. It was nearly five but I decided
to give them a call as I left Morgan's office. Earlene was
still guarding the lobby doing her rather impressive
gargoyle impression. I stopped, smiled my most charming
and disarming smile and asked if she happened to know
where the Foundation was based. Earlene was neither
charmed nor disarmed; rather, she sniffed and wrinkled
her nose, letting me know quite efficiently that she both

smelled and disapproved of the alcohol on my breath. Icily she said, "Annapolis," before turning imperiously back to her computer. The computer was at an angle to me but I could still see a wedge of the screen. "Black ten on the red jack, Earlene," I said. She stiffened but said nothing, and I laughed my way out the door.

It was nearly five o'clock when I got back in the car. I pulled out of the parking lot and took the next turn, looking for a place to park. Morgan's office was in a busy commercial strip fronting route 9, but just a block behind the all the dreary dreck was farmland. I pulled over under a large shade tree and called directory assistance on my cell phone. And a couple of minutes later a comely female voice said into my ear, "Save Our Shores, how may I direct your call?"

"To, um, I'm just looking for some general information on your organization."

"Please hold."

A series of clicks followed, then a man's voice came on the line. "This is Bob Feingold. How can I help you?"

I fished through my handy-dandy detective kit for a notebook and found one. No pen, though. Shit. "Uh, Hi, Mr. Feingold…"

"Bob."

"Okay, Bob, this is…" It occurred to em that using my own name might not be a great idea. "This is, um, Steve Carter, and I was interested in getting some general information on your organization. Can you help me with that?"

"I think so. Are you interested in becoming a member?"

"Well, I don't know. I mean, maybe, but I don't know what you do. That's why I called. Maybe you could give me, like, a thumbnail on what you all do. How it works."

"How what works?"

"Everything. What your programs are."

"Are you with the press?"

"No. Why?"

"No reason." I doubted that. "It just sounded like you might be a reporter."

"Well, I'm not. Definitely not."

There was a long silence on the line, then my new friend Bob said, "Hmmm. Okay...well, SOS is a charitable foundation dedicated to the preservation of waterfront property. Mainly oceanfront, but also some lake and river property as well. Development pressure is so intense across the country that shoreline is disappearing at an unbelievable rate..."

"Disappearing?" This seemed unlikely. I mean, I know erosion can be a problem, but...

"Well, maybe disappearing is the wrong word. Undeveloped shoreline is disappearing. In other words, it's getting developed. And if we don't do something, there will be no natural shoreline left. This would be a disaster for many many species of plants and animals, of course, but we believe it would be a disaster for people as well. Imagine never being able to walk along a deserted beach, never being able to canoe through a quiet marsh, never being able, even, to get to the water because private property leaves no public access points. That, in a nutshell, is what we are all about."

"How do you get the property? Donation?"

"Well, we get a significant portion that way, but we buy most of it. Sometimes at fair market rates, sometimes at discounted rates from people who want to preserve their property but who can't afford to just give it away despite the tax advantages inherent in such donations."

"Where do you get the money to buy the land? I mean, isn't it expensive?"

"Are you sure you're not a reporter?"

"I am definitely not a reporter or journalist of any kind. I'm just looking for information. Trying to get information so I can make up my mind."

"About what? If I may ask"

"Look, I don't really feel like going into details right now. I'm sorry, but I have my reasons. Could you answer my question, please?"

"Your...? Oh, yes. Well, since you asked, we're a membership organization. We look for people, likeminded people, and we try to convince them to join us, and to help us achieve our goals."

"How do you find these people?"

"Why?" Bob was getting exasperated. I don't really blame him. In fact I was getting a bit exasperated too. I had no clear idea of why I was asking the questions I was asking. But I had to start somewhere. In my mind there was no doubt that there was a link between SOS and Dickie's death. Not necessarily a direct link, but a link nonetheless.

"Bob," I said trying to spread a little oil on the water, "Look...I've come into some property. It's nice, and I don't want it to get spoiled, but truthfully I could use money more than the property. But if I sold it to a developer that would be directly against the wishes of the person who, um, willed it to me. I'm exploring my options and I'm trying to make an informed decision, that's all. So if I'm bothering you I apologize. Maybe I should call back and speak to someone else."

"No, no, that won't be necessary,' Bob quickly replied. " I quite understand your position , now. What were we discussing again?"

"I asked how you guys find your members."

"Oh, right. Direct mail, mostly. Sometimes we run ads in various publications. We've done a TV spot but it hasn't aired yet as far as I'm aware."

"And your members are the only support you have? All your money comes from them?"

"No, not all. A significant portion, but not all. We solicit wealthy people directly and that often pays off, particularly when they have a direct interest."

"What do you mean?"

"Well, say that you're rich and you own Parcel A. Parcel B next door comes up for sale and you would prefer it remain as is. You might buy parcel B, give it to us, and take the tax break. You get a deduction, we get the property and everybody's happy."

"Except the developers."

"Right. But any time I make a developer unhappy I count it as a mitzvah. A good deed."

"I know what a mitzvah is, Bob. Anything else?"

"Anything else what?"

"Are there any other sources of support for your activities?"

"I swear you sound like a reporter."

"Bob, we went over this already."

Bob sighed. "We get a limited amount of support from various corporations and foundations, particularly when it suits their needs. We got quite a lot of money from Exxon after the Valdez disaster, for instance. It gives them something to point to. In a way it's a shame that they trade on our name for public relations purposes, but we rationalize. After all, the oil had already been spilled. Nothing was going to change that. So if they feel that giving us money helps them and we can use that money to preserve some other piece of shoreline, well…" He let it hang there. After a few seconds he said, "So when can we come see your property?"

"I don't know, Bob. I need to think about all of this and figure out what I want to do. I don't want to waste anyone's time if it's not going to happen."

"Well, if we saw the property we could at least figure out if we'd be interested in working with you. We're not indiscriminate; we only have a limited amount of money available."

"I'll think about it, Bob. I'll get back to you."

"Feel free to call anytime. Might I ask where the property is located?"

"You just did."

"What? I'm sorry, I don't…"

"Never mind. I'd just really rather not discuss specifics just now, if you don't mind. I don't need you people hounding me."

Bob was shocked. "Oh! We would never do that, Mister, um…"

"Flaherty." Shit!

"Flaherty? I thought you said…well, never mind. Just call me whenever you're ready and we'll set something up. Should I send you some literature in the meantime?"

I wouldn't have minded seeing it, but I didn't want to give out the address of Dickie's house. "Nah, that's okay. Do you have a website?"

"We certainly do. Saveourshores dot org. It's quite good."

"I'll check it out. Thanks."

I hung up before he could say anything else. A trip to Annapolis looked to be in the offing. I glanced at my watch and saw that it was almost quarter past five. Poor old Bob had been working overtime to answer my questions. Non-profit organizations such as charities and foundations are one of the last bastions of the nine-to-five America your parents grew up in. Everybody else (present company excluded, of course) works harder and longer with each passing year but, insulated from the vagaries of the marketplace by their special status, the non-profits just keep ticking along like it's still 1955.

I still hadn't made it down to Keybox Road, so that's where I headed. I drove back down to Dewey, bucking the traffic all the way. It wouldn't be so bad if there wasn't a light in front of every shopping center. It seems like you never make it through on the green and I've wondered if they do it so that you'll decide that you might as well go in and shop since you can't get anywhere anyways. By the time I crossed the bridge over the Intracoastal I was so happy to be out of the traffic that I never noticed the cop behind me as I gave the car some gas. He noticed me, though. And I did finally notice him when he turned his lights and siren on. I glanced quickly at the speedometer and saw that I was doing over fifty in a thirty-five zone. I used some bad language and pulled to the curb. I was really wishing I had a breath mint when the uniformed officer walked up to the window. I wasn't drunk by any means but the Scotches I had had with Morgan would reek and would certainly show up on a breathalyzer if it came to that. I was looking straight ahead as the officer approached the car, trying not to breath too much. The last thing I needed was a DWI. I probably should have thought of that earlier.

The officer spoke. "Oh, hey, Dude. It's you."

Of course it's me, I thought. Who else would I be? "Hey, Officer Riley. How are you today?"

"I'm doing great, man. How about you? In kind of a hurry, huh?"

"Uh, yeah. I mean no. I'm not in a hurry. I just wasn't paying attention. I guess I was just happy to be out of that traffic."

"Sucks, doesn't it?"

"Yeah. It definitely does."

"I mean, they shoulda put all those stores out in the boonies somewhere. What's the deal with putting them here, where it's already crowded?"

I was feeling a little strange having a conversation about the traffic with a cop who had pulled me over. Even if it was Riley. I should have told him that the surf was up and that's why I had been in a rush. His lights were still on behind me, but he was standing there just passing the time of day. I said, "Uh, well, I guess they wanted to put the stores where the people are."

"I guess, but it still blows. Hey, how's it going with your case?"

JOE GREANEY

"My case?"

"You know what I mean. Your case you're working on. About your friend."

"I…I don't have a case. Chief Hartner told me to stay out of it, so that's what I'm doing."

He laughed. "Yeah, right, bro'. Don't shit a shitter, dude. I know you're looking into things."

"How do you know that?"

He tapped a forefinger on his temple. "Always thinkin'. I don't miss much, dude. Look I gotta get going. Take it a little slower, okay, my man?"

"Yeah. Sorry. I'll do that."

"Cool. Later."

He went back to his car and drove off with a squeal. I heaved a very large sigh of relief, put the Impala in drive and pulled out cautiously. And slowly. How had Riley known that I was still looking into things? It wasn't like I'd done a whole hell of a lot. Really, the only thing I had done was talk to Morgan. Maybe Morgan told Hartner, trying to keep his bases covered. But it hadn't been an hour since I'd left Morgan's office. What were the chances that Morgan could have called Hartner, and Hartner told Riley, and Riley pulled me over and told me, all in less than an hour? Slim. I had to put Riley's guess down to instinct or dumb luck. But if Riley knew I had been poking around then there was no doubt in my mind that Hartner did too. Well, I thought, he knew where to find me.

I passed Dewey Beach Liquors. You'd have to be an idiot to stop at a liquor store two minutes after getting pulled over and nearly getting caught for DWI, I thought. So I drove right past the store. Then I promptly pulled a

U-turn and went back. Who says I'm not an idiot? Not me, certainly. I bought a six of Bud cans and set off for Keybox Road. I told myself that I'd be careful driving and that there was no reason I couldn't sit at the beach and have a beer. No reason except that it's illegal, and who really cares about that. Okay, the police care, but who else?

The kid in the parking kiosk was locking up for the day and waved me in without paying the parking fee. I parked near where Dickie's truck had been and got out, leaving the beers in the car. There was no real reason to push my luck. The parking attendant was walking across the lot to where a old Jeep Wagoneer with an improbable amount of rust was parked.

"Excuse me," I called, and the attendant turned around. I had thought it was a guy when I pulled in but now realized it was a slim young woman of maybe eighteen with close-cropped hair and a boyish figure. She stopped, turned and said, "Yeah?" She was quite attractive in her way but the silver stud in her tongue didn't do much for me. Neither did the black eye. It was a few days old and turning yellow, but it looked like somebody had socked her a good one. She had put some type of makeup over it but it was still obvious.

"I was just wondering, do you remember a blue Blazer that was parked over there," I pointed. "For three days last week?"

"You mean Dickie's truck?"

"Uh, yeah. Dickie's truck."

"Yeah, I remember. Bummer about Dickie. He was a cool old dude."

Dickie was three months older than me. But hey, three months is a long time. A lot can happen in three months. "Did you see him when he came in and parked?"

"What are you, a cop?" There was an edge there.

"No. A friend of Dickie's. I'm just trying to figure out what happened. The cops don't seem too interested." This wasn't true, of course, but I was trying to pick up on the edge I'd heard in her voice, trying to make a connection.

She laughed briefly and mirthlessly. "They wouldn't be. Too busy hassling kids and making sure no one has any fun in this godforsaken town to worry about a little old murder."

I didn't agree with her assessment of Dewey but knew that when you're a teenager whatever place you're from is, by definition, godforsaken. That's just the way it goes. But I didn't doubt her judgement about the police. I'm sure they have a reputation with the kids. In a party town like Dewey they'd have to be tough just to keep a lid on things. I said, "Yeah, well, cops aren't exactly known for being a good time. Must be something that happened to them when they were kids, made them so uptight." Maybe, I thought, that's laying it on a little too thick.

"Too true, man," she said, proving that if anything I wasn't laying it on thick enough. "Too damn true. So what about Dickie's truck?"

"Were you here when he came in? I'm trying to find out if he was alone."

She shook her head. "The truck was here when I came in in the morning. But I had the day off the day before, so I didn't see him come in."

"Do you know who worked the day before?"

"Yeah. Darla. It's only me'n Darla here, unless somebody gets sick or something. We switch off. We did, at least."

"Do you know Darla's last name? Or where I can find her?"

"It's Darla Peterson, and no.."

"I'm sorry?"

"Me too, man. That bitch was supposed to work last all weekend, Friday, Saturday and Sunday, but she's gone. Left a message on my machine asking me to cover, said she's gonna make it up to me, but I'm startin' to doubt it."

"Why's that?"

"I went by her trailer yesterday, tell her a favor's a favor but this is uncool, and it seemed like nobody lived there anymore. Just felt that way. Like, spooky, you know?"

I've always thought trailers were spooky, but I nodded anyway. "Where's her trailer?"

She looked at me like I was stupid. Maybe I am. "Trailer park."

"I figured. But where's the trailer park?"

"Oh. Down back of Bethany. You know where Holt's Landing is?"

As a matter of fact I did. It's a small state park on the south end of the bay where people go windsurfing if the wind if from the east or northeast. I'd been there a couple of times and recalled seeing a small trailer park set in the middle of some cornfields down there. I asked her if that was the right park and she nodded, then told me which trailer it was. "Look," she said at last, "Good luck, and all, but I gotta go. My mom's got my kid an' my old man'll kill me if I don't get home."

"Kill you?"

She laughed and scuffed the dirt with the toe of her boot. "Think I'm lyin'? Shit."

Judging by the black eye I had no doubt she was telling the truth. Why a woman would stay with a man who hits her is simply beyond me. I like to think that I have a handle on things, that I think more about what happens in this life than most people. Maybe that's just vanity, I don't know. Certainly if I'm smart I don't act very smart a lot of the time. But at least I usually know what's going on, have a fair idea of what motivates people, what makes them work. It's a skill, I guess, acquired or at least honed in my years investigating cases on the streets in D.C.. You can't last very long in that job, on those streets, if you can't figure out what's going to happen next, if you don't have an idea whether the guy walking toward you on the dark sidewalk is friend or foe or couldn't care less. So I'm pretty good at understanding people, at understanding where they're coming from and why. But how a man could hit a woman and how she could stay around long enough for it to happen a second time are two things I'll never understand.

I realized that there had been a long period of silence. "You have a kid?"

"Yeah, why?"

"How old are you?"

"Eighteen. Why?"

"Just wondering. Thanks for your help."

"No prob, " she said, and walked off. I watched her go. Eighteen, a kid, an old man who hits her and a dead-end job as a summer parking lot attendant, making maybe eight bucks an hour. Ain't life grand. "Hey," I called as she was climbing in her car. She looked up. "What's your name.

"Jeanie Black. Why?"

"Just wondering. Thanks again."

She nodded and started the car. A few seconds later I was alone in the lot. I walked back to the Impala, reached through the open window and grabbed a beer from the paper bag on the seat. It was still cold. I opened it, took a long swallow and set the can back on the floor of the car. The lot was empty except for my car. I did a lap of the lot, casting back and forth along the fringes where clumps of sea oats grew tall. There was plenty of trash around, empty cans and cigarette wrappers, a cup from Burger King, a pizza box, assorted detritus that somebody really ought to clean up someday, but nothing that seemed to have any bearing on anything. What the hell, I thought, it was a long shot.

I gave up after a few minutes, grabbed my beer and climbed the dune for the view, avoiding the sea grass that keeps the dune together. It was a wide ocean view from the top, moderate rollers crashing on an empty beach, an orange freighter steaming northwards a couple of miles offshore, a plume of black smoke trailing behind. Off to my left I could see the grey shingled bulk of the bathhouse and concession stand in the state park. Sunlight flashed off the windshield of a moving car, probably someone going home after a relaxing day by the sea. Beyond the bathhouse I could see the two tall concrete cylinders of the World War II-era towers in which observers spent the war peering out to sea looking for German submarines and an invasion that never came.

The dune where I sat was very irregular, carved by the wind and waves into a series of small hills separated by tiny valleys. In one of these valleys I saw a flash of color and I climbed down after a few minutes to see what it was. After scrambling down the slope I knelt in the sand. What I had seen was some sort of rubbery orange material. I brushed some sand away and revealed more of the material and a pie-plate sized piece of broken asphalt which appeared to have been used as a weight to keep whatever it was in place. I tossed the heavy chunk of asphalt to the side and pulled on the material. A moment later I held what turned out to be a lifejacket of the type used by water-skiers and windsurfers. . I turned it over. Inside by the neck was written "R. Harrington". Below that was Dickie's phone number.

Dickie was a very good windsurfer and a strong swimmer, but if he had been sailing on the ocean by himself he probably would have worn his lifejacket just to be safe. I stood there holding it for a quite a while, not really focusing on what I held. If Dickie had been windsurfing in the ocean, how had his body gotten into the bay? And where was the rest of his stuff? I realized that I had no idea whether Dickie's windsurfing gear was in the garage back at the house and resolved to check when I got home.

"What'cha got there?" boomed a familiar voice from above and behind me. The voice was familiar but I was startled nonetheless. I was starting to think that maybe I startled easily.

"Hey, Chief. Lifejacket. It's Dickie's."

"Where'd that come from?"

"Right here. I just found it a minute ago."

The chief absorbed this silently. He knew as well as I did that someone should have found it when his people searched the area. "You sure it's his?"

"Yeah. It's got his name in it."

The chief nodded and half-walked, half-slid down the dune to join me, holding out his hand for the lifejacket when he reached my side. I gave it to him and he turned it over in his hands, holding it delicately by the edges, looking at it intently. Finally he muttered, "Now how in hell…?"

I shrugged and took a sip of my beer. The Chief raised an eyebrow but didn't say anything. We stood there by the dune in silence, listening to the wind and the waves, or at least I did. I don't know what the chief was doing, exactly. After a minute or two I walked back to where I had found the lifejacket and dropped to my knees.

"What are you doing?"

I looked up. "Well, I thought I'd dig a hole. See if anything else might be here."

"I've got a shovel in the truck. Be right back." I nodded and sat on the sand. There wasn't much point in digging with my bare hands if the chief had a shovel. In less than a minute he was back with one of those folding entrenching tools they use in the Army. Or at least they used to use them. Probably now they have some sort of laser-guided digital version that costs a thousand bucks but doesn't work.

The chief was winded, so I reached out and relieved him of the shovel. He stood bent over at the waist with his hands on his knees while I dug. It didn't take long. Less than a foot below the surface the shovel hit something.

I cleared some sand away and saw that it was a sheet of clear plastic with bright markings. I had seen it before.

"What in the world…?" muttered the Chief.

"It's a sail from a windsurfer. I think it's Dickie's."

"Huh. Well, let's get it out of there."

Which was easier said than done. We pulled on an exposed edge but it wouldn't budge so we went about digging it out. As we dug I told the Chief about how the lifejacket had been weighted down and then covered with sand, as though it was a marker of some sort. Now it was clear that it was marking the location of this sail and anything else that might be buried along with it.

The sail was rolled up, but even when it was fully exposed it was heavy and hard to move. Finally and with effort we got the thing out of the hole. The chief and I studied the cigar-shaped package as we took a moment to catch our breath. It was impossible to see through the multiple layers of plastic, hard use and salt water having turned the clear material hazy. But judging from the size of it and the ungodly odor it wasn't hard to guess what was inside.

"Who do you think it is?" I asked.

The chief straightened and brushed the sweat from his forehead with the back of his hand. "If I had to guess I'd say it's whoever got shot in Dickie's truck." He paused. But I don't have to guess. You wait here, I'm gonna go call this in. Don't touch anything."

"Don't worry about it. I've got kind of a thing about dead bodies."

I kept a vigil a few feel upwind of the body until the chief returned, and then both of us spent a quiet few minutes with the deceased. It was getting dark in the lee of the dune when the wail of sirens could at last be heard over the wind and waves, and a few minutes after that the crime scene machine was in high gear. Yellow tape marked off the area and generator-powered spotlights pushed back the night. Nearly a dozen officers from at least three jurisdictions paced around, taking pictures and generally trying to look busy. One officer was videotaping everything and another was dusting the smooth plastic of the sail for prints. When he had finished one side a couple of other officers helped him roll the macabre bundle over and he went to work again.

The Chief and I stood off to the side, watching the proceedings. Eventually a pair of officers brought a stretcher down the dune. They rolled the sail and its contents onto the stretcher and struggled back up the sandy slope with the help of a couple of the other men. A decision had been made to keep the body wrapped in the sail until they got to the morgue in Georgetown, in hopes of avoiding any loss or contamination of evidence. The stretcher was loaded in the back of an ambulance which departed with its lights on but without a siren. There was no particular rush at that point.

It was almost nine o'clock by the time the whole thing was over, and the Chief and I were the last two left in the lot. We leaned against the hood of my car and drank warm beer from the can, the sodium-vapor lamp over the parking attendant's booth casting everything in a harsh yellowish light. "Hell of a thing," said the Chief at last.

I really couldn't argue. "Yup. Just keeps getting more fucked up."

We sipped our beers. A tangled ball of yellow crime-scene tape blew by like some sort of apocalyptic tumbleweed. The chief said, "How'd you happen to be down here?"

"Just thought I'd come look around. See what I could see."

"I guess I'm glad you did."

"You guess?"

"Well, I'd be lyin' to you if I said I didn't have a lot of questions."

"What kind of questions?"

"Just questions. What brought you down here, how you noticed the lifejacket, why you seem to be sticking your nose in when I distinctly recall telling you not to. Questions."

I nodded. "Well, I don't have much in the way of answers. Sorry. I came down here on a hunch...more of a feeling, really. Like I should come down here, but without really thinking about why. I just happened to notice the lifejacket when I was sitting there. What can I say?"

"How about you investigating the case? What about that?"

"Look, Chief. It's a free country, right? I haven't done a damn thing to hurt any investigation that you might —or might not – be carrying on."

"What's that supposed to mean? Might or might not?"

"Whatever you want it to mean, Chief. I don't know what's going on. No one's keeping me in the loop. So maybe you're busting your ass or maybe you're not, I don't know. I do know that I found that lifejacket and everything else just by sitting on my butt for five minutes while I drank a beer, so offhand I'd have to say you're not exactly knocking my socks off."

The Chief glared at me but said nothing. He drained his beer, crumpled the can and threw it on the ground, them stomped off. When he was almost to his truck he stopped and turned. "I don't answer to you, Flaherty," he said. "And I guess you don't answer to me either. I wish I had a good reason to arrest you, but I can't think of one. But so help me God, if I find out you've been holding out on me..."

I shook my head. "Just go find out who killed Dickie, okay? I really don't need any threats right now. Oh, and Chief?" I added as he turned away. He stopped and looked back.

"Yeah?"

"You really shouldn't litter."

He didn't respond, climbing instead into his truck and roaring off with a spray of sand and gravel. I walked over and picked up his empty can, and then threw it in the trash can by the booth. Man, I hate a litterbug.

Thirteen

It was no real surprise that the house was dark and cold when I got home. I walked around turning on lights until it felt a little less desolate, and then I turned on the TV. Regis Philbin was asking some fat guy from Vegas if it was his final answer, and the sweat on the guy's upper lip reflected the stage lights like a mirror. I went into the kitchen and looked for something to eat without success, settling finally on a can of soup and some stale saltines. If I was going to keep living here I needed to stock the fridge. And, I discovered a few minutes later, the bar. First there was nothing to eat in the house and now there was nothing to drink. This was no way to live. I went to bed and slept the sleep of the dead. If I dreamed I don't remember it.

I was awakened by the phone. It was light out but I had no idea what time it was. I mumbled, "Hello?"

"Bill?"

Bunny. I sat up in bad and cleared my throat as discreetly as I could manage. For some reason I didn't want her to know that I'd been asleep. "Hey, Bunny. What's up?"

"Oh," she said. "Not too much." I could hear a slight tremolo in her voice. "Is Ted still there?"

"Ted?" I don't know what I expected her to say, but I have to admit that that wasn't it.

"Yeah, Ted. You remember Ted, right?" The tremolo was gone. Now she sounded like she could bite a nail in half.

Hey, if she wanted to be all business, I could be all business. "Ted left yesterday morning. At least he was gone when I got up. He didn't say goodbye. I don't know where he is. He said something about going to San Francisco."

"San Francisco? What are you talking about?"

"Ted and I went out the night before last." I was really impressing myself with how cool I was being. Suave, even. I was sure I was impressing her with how adult I was being, how civilized. "We had…an interesting conversation. In the course of that conversation he mentioned that he might move to San Francisco."

"Why?"

"He felt…I don't know, he felt it was what he had to do, that it was a like a question of honor."

"What?! For God's sake. What the hell is the matter with you idiots? I swear I'm never dating again. Bunch of fucking adolescent idiots. Christ!"

Somehow I got the feeling she wasn't quite as impressed with me as I had thought. "Um," I replied wittily.

"If that asshole shows back up tell him he missed court yesterday. And that because of him my client is currently in jail when he should be home with his family, including his sick daughter, who is now in the hospital because she got so upset at her Daddy being dragged away that she went into hysterics and had to be sedated. What the fuck is wrong with you two? What is this honor bullshit? Some sort of stupid-ass chivalry on my account? I can't believe this shit. San Francisco? Shit!"

She slammed the phone down so hard it made my ear hurt. Well, I thought. Well, well, well. And that's about as far as I got. But I hadn't had any coffee yet, so cut me some slack.

There was very little chance of going back to sleep after that pleasant little exchange so I went downstairs and made some coffee. It was just past eight o'clock when I slumped in a chair with a mug from the freshly-brewed pot. I wished I had a newspaper. But I didn't wish hard enough to actually go out to the end of the driveway and get one. I took a sip of coffee and thought about my wake-up call. It wasn't like Ted to miss court. Unless he was really hung over. And even then he would make sure to get someone to fill in for him, or at the very least try to get a continuance. In fact I had never known Ted to just blow off a responsibility in all the years I had known him. There's a first time for everything, I guess, but this seemed an unlikely time for this one.

I was sitting there pondering Ted's disappearance when the phone rang again. It was Chief Hartner. "Thanks a lot, asshole," he said. This was not starting out to be my day.

"What'd I do?"

"You could have told me you didn't talk to Dickie's parents. Shit!"

"What? What are you talking about?"

"Why didn't you tell me you never spoke to Dickie's parents?"

"Why the hell would I have talked to Dickie's parents? You told me to stay out of the way of your investigation."

"Out of the investigation, yes. But it never occurred to me that you wouldn't have called them and told them what happened."

"But, well…it never occurred to me that you wouldn't have, either. I mean, you're the policeman. Isn't it your job to inform the next of kin?"

"Yeah, sometimes, but not when the deceased's friend, who happens to be living in the deceased's house, and who knows what happened, and who also knows the parents, is right there to pick up the phone and inform them. I mean, come on, Flaherty, that's common decency."

He had a point, I suppose. But I thought I did too. "Look, all I know is that you told me to stay the hell out of the way, and that's what I did. What happened, anyway?"

"Oh, I called down there. I got the word last night that Dickie's body was going to be released, and I wanted to find out what funeral home I should have it sent to."

"Oh, shit."

"Oh, shit, fucking-A right. I call down, Mrs. Harrington answers the phone – she's gotta be closing in on eighty – and I say good morning, Mrs. Harrington, this is Chief Hartner, and I'm sorry to bother you this early, but what arrangements have you made for Dickie's body?"

"Ouch."

"Yeah. Ouch. Needless to say, it didn't go well. At least she didn't have a heart attack while we were on the phone. She might have had one since, though. Or Mr.

Harrington, Christ, he's old as the hills, too. Who knows what'll happen."

"Well, that sucks. I'm sorry. But I thought you had it handled. I definitely would have made the call if I had known."

There was silence on the line. Finally the Chief said, "Yeah, I guess I know that. The whole thing just pissed me off, and you were the only one handy. This just sucks all around."

I couldn't argue with that. "Did they have any idea what they were going to do? With Dickie, I mean?"

"No. They're going to get back to me."

"Maybe I should call, see if they need help."

The Chief sighed. "Yeah. You do that. I don't see how even you could fuck things up any worse than they already are."

"Gee, thanks for the vote of confidence. Does the fact that the body's been released mean the autopsy's all done?" I knew it did, but I was trying to get to the next question. Hartner saved me the trouble of asking it.

"Yeah. He drowned. Some bruising on the head and shoulders consistent with blunt force, but nothing conclusive, could have happened a bit earlier or maybe his windsailing board thing hit him. It wasn't enough to kill him. Might have stunned him. If it was the board thingie, though, and he swallowed some water...I dunno. It could have been enough to do it, I guess. Hell, really I don't know."

"Wouldn't that be a kick in the ass if it was an accident."

"Yeah. I don't know what to make of it at all. No clue. And then there's the guy we found last night. Shit if I know." He sighed again and I almost felt sorry for him.

Almost. "Anyways," he continued, "you're going to call down to Florida and follow up, right?"

"Yeah. Think I should do it right now?"

"I'd wait an hour or two. Use your judgement. Assuming you have any."

Screw you too, I thought. "Okay. I'll let you know what happens."

We hung up and I sat there for a minute thinking of what I would say to Dickie's parents. I had known them both, a long time ago. I'd seen them at school and at sporting events, and I could picture the two of them clearly, a thin patrician couple, he always in a jacket and tie, she favoring simple dresses, maybe a single strand of pearls. They probably looked pretty much the same now as they had then, since they must have been nearly sixty when we graduated.

I was wondering what I would say to them when the phone rang again. I didn't want any part of it, not after the last two calls. I looked at the phone like it might explode, and for all I knew it could have. I don't think I've ever gotten three phone calls before eight-thirty in the morning on the same day. The phone rang and rang and on about the tenth ring I gave up and answered it. It was Dickie's brother Robert. Good ole Bobby his ownself.

"Hey, boy," he said.

"Hey."

"So you wasn't shittin' about Dickie, now, was you?"

I don't know where he gets off talking like some hillbilly with a mouth full of mush. Sure, he's lived in the south for years, but the guy's from the Boston suburbs like me, and like me he went to an expensive prep school and to college. It's none of my business, I guess, but right then it irked me. "No, I wasn't shittin' you none," I drawled back. Probably wasn't the politest thing I've ever done, especially considering the guy just found out his brother was dead, but what's done is done. Or so I've heard.

When Bobby spoke again the drawl was gone. Apparently I got through to him. "I'll be there by tonight. I expect you to be out of the house by the time I get there."

"What? Why?"

"Why? Because it's my house now, not yours. And I don't need any snot-nosed punks underfoot while I'm taking care of business."

It was obvious that it had been a long time since Bobby had seen me. I haven't been a snot-nosed punk for years. It was also obvious that he was laboring under a bit of a misconception regarding the disposition of Dickie's estate, but it hardly seemed the time to tell him, considering he hadn't even known that his brother was dead for more than a half hour. "Whatever you say, Robert." There was no way I was leaving, but I could tell him that later.

"Bobby."

"Whatever. Is that why you called, just to evict me?"

"That, and to see what happened to my brother."

"Maybe you should have done it in the other order."

A long pause. "Maybe you're right." Another pause. "So you're not going to tell me?"

"Not everyone's an asshole like you, Robert."

"Bobby."

Calling him Robert clearly rankled, but he didn't seem to mind the asshole part. Probably knew it was true. I told him the story as far as I knew it myself. I left a few things out, like the fact that I considered him a suspect, and that I was looking into things, and that he had been cut out of the will, and…okay, I didn't tell him much. But it seemed to satisfy him. He had, I thought, a rather curious lack of curiosity. It was hard to tell if he was even listening to what I told him.

When I had finished he thanked me. He had the mush back in his mouth but I let it go. And after we hung up I called Chief Hartner. His mood hadn't improved to any noticeable extent. "What the hell do you want?"

"I was just calling to let you know that Dickie's brother Robert will be in town tonight."

"And that means exactly what to me?"

"Whatever you want it to mean. I just thought you might want to know."

"Okay, so now I know. If you can tell me why I care you might get my interest."

"Are you sure you're investigating this case?"

"Maybe I am and maybe I'm not. If it was an accident there's not a hell of a lot to investigate. And I got another body to worry about, so I don't know what I'm doing about Dickie right now. But one thing I do know is that you're not investigating it. Am I right? I better be right."

"Well, somebody sure as shit needs to be investigating. If you're just gonna throw up your hands and say it was an accident, which is total bullshit, then I guess it better be me. I sure can't be interfering with an investigation if there is no investigation, can I? I mean I call, as a favor, just to let you know that one of your suspects is going to be in town and all I get is a ration of shit. You need to think about what you're trying to accomplish here, Chief."

"Don't you dare tell me my business, boy."

"I'm not your boy," I said, adding, perhaps a bit unwisely, "Why don't you just go screw yourself, old man." And then I hung up, which was also perhaps less than completely well-advised. "So what," I said to a large spider that was making its way across the counter. "So fucking what." The spider had no answer, so I killed it with the bottom of my coffee mug. Sorry, dude.

Dude. The word reverberated. It made me think of young Officer Riley, of course, but there was something else there, too. Before I could follow the thought the phone rang again. I was well and heartily sick of the phone by now. I answered on the first ring. "What?" I snapped.

Hartner again. "Don't you ever hang up on me again…"

I hung up. What else could I do?

At least the phone stopped ringing. I sat at the table for a few minutes more letting the adrenaline and the coffee fight it out to see who was in charge, and then I went up stairs to get dressed. First I stopped in the bathroom. I guess the coffee won.

I was pulling my least-dirty tee-shirt over my head when the knock came on the door. "Knock" is a rather inadequate description of the noise that came from downstairs. Good thing they built these old houses right. In a new house the door would probably have come right off the hinges. I knew who it was, and I wasn't in any hurry to see him, so I lit a cigarette and took a few leisurely drags before descending the stairs. What the hell, it might do the Chief some good to have to wait a few minutes, give him a chance to reflect, cool his heels a little.

Either that or just piss him off more.

Opening the door it was quite clear that the latter was the case. The first word that comes to mind is "apoplectic." I wouldn't have been at all surprised if the Chief had had a stroke right then and there. His face was bright red, and veins throbbed on both temples. He looked a little like the square-jawed crew-cut Sergeant Carter on the old "Jim Nabors Show," yelling at Gomer Pyle about some hare-brained screw-up. But that was in black and white. This was living color. And surround-sound stereo, too.

There were no formalities, merely a litany of semi-comprehensible rantings which ended up with, "Where in the hell do you get off hanging up on me?"

"Unless you're going to arrest me, and we both know you're not, you're going to need to speak to me in a civil tone of voice. I'm not your boy, and I'm not your dog. I asked you a couple of perfectly reasonable questions and you blew up and started screaming at me. I don't need that, and I won't take it, either. You want to come in or are you just going to stand out there?"

"I'll come in," he mumbled, considerably deflated.

I led him back to the kitchen. "Coffee?"

"Thanks," he said. "Black." He sat at the kitchen table. I poured us both a cup and sat across from him. Neither one of said anything for a while. We both sort of looked at the floor and the walls, as though we were waiting for someone to come along and tell us what to say, like a couple sitting in a marriage counselor's waiting room.

"Look," I said. "I believe you want to find out what happened with Dickie…"

"Oh, gee," he said, acid in every syllable, "Thanks for the vote of confidence."

"You're welcome."

He looked up at me suspiciously but decided to let it go. "What'd you mean about Dickie's brother Robert being a suspect?"

"I told you before about how he didn't really seem to give a damn whether Dickie was alive or dead. Right?"

"Yeah…"

"Well I found out that Dickie cut him out of his will a while back."

"So what? Maybe they had an argument. Doesn't mean he'd kill him. Maybe he'd kill him to keep him from changing the will, but after it's already done? I don't see it."

He had a point. It hardly seemed likely that Robert would travel fifteen hundred miles to kill his brother as punishment for changing his will. "So maybe he's not a suspect. Hell, I don't know. Any news on who that was we found out at the beach yesterday."

"Nah. No ID on him. Looks like it was him who got it in Dickie's truck, though- he was shot in the head. We're running his prints, should hear back later today."

"Could you let me know what comes back?"

"Why?"

"I'm curious. Hell, I found the guy. I'd like to know who it was."

"We found him together."

"Well, you wouldn't have if I hadn't started the ball rolling."

"I'll think about it."

"Thanks."

The Chief stood, his chair scraping loudly on the floor, and then said, "I gotta get goin'. Thanks for the coffee."

"You're welcome."

"Mind what I told you, now."

"Yeah, yeah."

He looked at me long and hard, shook his head, sighed deeply and then left. I don't know what was going through his mind, but I know what was on mine: no way. There was more going on here than met the eye, and there was plenty that met the eye, too. No way was I going to sit around the house and wait for Robert to come and try to evict me. What would be the fun in that?

Fourteen

Two hours later I was straightening my – okay, Dickie's - tie in the one of the plate-glass windows that flanked the front door to the building in which the Save Our Shores Foundation headquarters was located in Annapolis. The building was not what I had imagined. Rather than a quaint brownstone downtown by the water, it was a modern five-story building, a soulless pile of concrete and glass hard by Route 50, not far from the Annapolis Mall. Several hundred cars baked in the sun in the expansive parking lot, harsh reflections glinting off windshields as shimmering heat rose into the late-morning sky.

I took a deep breath and stepped into a marble-floored lobby. The only person there was a security guard behind a short counter, an elderly black man with ramrod-straight posture who greeted me politely if formally, and who directed me to reception on the third floor. I walked across the room, self-conscious about the noise of my footsteps on the stone floor, pushed the button and waited for one of the two elevators to arrive.

I rode the elevator to the third floor alone. At least there was no music. The doors opened into a small carpeted hallway that led, apparently, to offices on my right and, obviously, to reception on my left. The reception area was behind a floor-to-ceiling glass wall that was etched with "Save Our Shores" above a double doorway and with large views of the two hemispheres on either side. The etchings were at least three feet in circumference and highlighted the oceans, major lakes and rivers of the world in bold relief. Quite impressive, really. I walked through the doors and was greeted by a pretty plastic blonde with a pasted-on thousand-watt smile. She was wearing one of those headsets with the little microphone that arches around in front of the mouth, but it didn't hide her expensive dental work .

"May I help you, Sir?" she said smoothly.

"I'd like to see Rob Feingold."

"Is he expecting you?"

"No."

The smile faltered a bit but came back just as quickly. "Let em see if he's available. May I tell him who's here?"

I wanted to say, "No," but said, "Steve, um, Bill Flaherty" He already knew my last name, there was no sense in playing games. The blonde looked a little confused. "Bill Flaherty. Tell him we spoke on the phone yesterday evening."

"Certainly, Sir. Have a seat, please."

I'd been sitting on my butt the whole way up from the beach but this seemed like an order so I sat in the chair she indicated with a Vanna White flourish. She murmured into her mouthpiece but I couldn't hear what she was saying because of the burbling of a small waterfall that was built into the corner near the chair. Shortly she turned her attention, and her high-beam smile, back on me and announced that Mr. Feingold would be out shortly. I thanked her and thumbed through the various SOS literature that was tastefully spread out on an end table to my side. Apparently they kept busy here at SOS. There were research projects, and legislative appeals and new properties highlighted in the pamphlets, all of which, of course, had been printed on 100% post-consumer recycled paper with non-toxic soy based inks. I know this because it said it on every piece.

A few minutes later, just as I was getting sick of the self-congratulatory tone of the pamphlets, a harried-looking man came charging into the reception area wringing his hands. He was about forty, fairly short, with short brown curly hair that was thinning on top. Hie shirt was open at the collar and his tie had been loosened, and he wore no jacket. His movements were quick and athletic. He looked like he might have been a good college shortstop or maybe a competitive tennis player who still played a good game. He quickly came over to me, extending a hand as I rose. We shook.

"Mr. Flaherty?"

"That's me."

"What can I do for you? I must say I'm a little surprised."

"Well, it was kind of spur of the moment. Is there somewhere we an talk?"

"Of course. Right this way. Would you like something to drink? Coffee? Soda?"

He didn't mention a double Absolut screwdriver, so I passed. I followed him through a maze of offices to a large office in the back corner of the building. The halls hummed with activity. The average age of the staff seemed to be about twenty-three and the dress was casual. I got the impression that the staff liked it here, that they felt like they were on the good guys' team.

Feingold ushered me into his office, gestured at a chair, then went around the desk and sat down. The view from the large window behind his desk was spectacular, a broad vista that included the distinctive dome of the State Capital, a large slice of the bay, and in the distance the twin arches of the Bay Bridge. "Nice view."

"What? Oh, thanks. To tell you the truth I hardly notice it anymore, I'm so damn busy. Well." He straightened in his chair and clasped his hands before him on the desk. "And what can I do for you today?"

I hesitated, unsure of how to proceed. What I wanted to do was figure out if SOS had any connection with Dickie's death. How to do that was the question.

Feingold asked, as if reading my mind, "Have you come to a decision?"

How did he...? "A decision?"

"About your property."

"Oh. No." I plunged ahead. That's generally my style. "No," I repeated. "Do you...does the name Dickie Harrington mean anything to you?"

There was a glint of recognition. "Oh, the place down on the Delaware shore. Kind of a shame, really."

"Yeah, well, Dickie was a friend of mine."

"He was?"

"Yeah. I'd been living with him - I'm still living in his house, at least for now, but everything's in a state of flux."

"I'm sorry, you're losing me."

"Well, since Dickie was killed, I..."

"Killed? That's terrible."

"I thought you knew."

"No, this is the first I heard."

"Then what were you saying was a shame?"

"That he changed his mind about donating the property."

"Oh, you knew about that?"

"Well, sure. He told me himself. He was sitting right where you are now."

"When was that?"

"A couple of weeks ago. Maybe three weeks."

"Did he say why he was changing his mind?"

Feingold nodded, then leaned back in his chair. "Well, I guess it's not a secret that it's a valuable piece of property."

"No, it's worth some money."

"Quite a bit of money. And it's not exactly pristine, I mean it's very nice and all, but there's development – quite heavy development – on both sides of it. Mr. Harrington thought that by donating the property it would be protected from development. We, uh, had other plans."

"What plans?"

"Look, that property is worth a lot of money. If we sold it, we could use the money to buy quite a bit more property, and if you'll pardon me, more significant property. Mr. Harrington discovered our plans..."

"How did he discover them?"

"Oh, he just asked. It was just a misunderstanding. He had made an assumption, and we corrected it when we learned about it. We're not some secret organization, after all."

"What was all this stuff about you being in his will?"

"What stuff?"

"First he named you guys as the ones who were to get the property, and then he took you out."

"Oh. There's nothing particularly mysterious about that. When someone arranges to donate property at a future date we generally try to get them to make us the beneficiaries in their wills, just in case something happens. And I would guess that when he changed his mind he changed his will, too." He shrugged. "It happens. We're involved in a lot of transaction and they don't all go the way we might like. Part of the deal."

It made sense. I sort of hated to admit it, though. I had had an idea that the evil SOS had killed Dickie to make sure they got his land. But the idea that an apparently thriving organization would arrange a killing over one piece of beach, however valuable, wasn't looking too good in the light of day.

Feingold spoke. "Do you actually have some property or was that just a ruse to get in here?"

"Dickie named me in his will, so I'll have that eventually, I guess."

"Well, if it works out and you want to donate it to us, let me know. I'll be glad to discuss it." He stood. "Now if you'll excuse me, I have a million things I need to get done..."

I rose. Feingold walked around the desk and extended a hand, which I shook. "Thanks for your time, Mr. Feingold."

"No problem. I really am shocked to hear about Mr. Harrington. How did it happen?"

"He drowned. It might have been an accident."

Feingold digested this for a moment. "But it might not have been?" he asked.

"Exactly."

Feingold shook his head sadly, and I turned to leave. A thought occurred to me and I paused at the door. "Hey, I was just wondering, but…"

"Shoot."

"Well, you said Dickie came in two or three weeks ago and told you he changed his mind about the property, right?"

"Right."

"Well, then why were your surveyors working there this week?"

"Surveyors?"

"You know, the guys who mark property boundaries."

"I know what a surveyor is. I just don't know what you mean by "our" surveyors. We don't have surveyors."

"Then who…?"

"I'm afraid I have no idea. But we would only get a property surveyed at the end of the donation process, and this hadn't gotten nearly that far. And we use commercial surveyors. It wouldn't pay us to keep them on staff."

I believed him. The question was, who was Jerry the surveyor? And the answer was, who the hell knows? But I think I had found what we in the trade refer to as a "clue."

Fifteen

It was hot in the car even though I had left the windows cracked. I tore off the tie and threw it into the back seat along with the jacket I had been wearing, rolled down the windows, turned on the air conditioner, and climbed back out to wait while things cooled down. The car is a piece of junk but the AC works great as long as you're not stuck in traffic, in which case you can't run it at all or the car will overheat.

When it was bearable in the car I got back in and drove out of the lot and onto the service road that parallels Route 50. The on-ramp for 50 East, which would take me back to the beach, was about a quarter-mile ahead. But before that was an overpass that would take me to 50 West. That's the way I went, without really thinking about it, without getting into an extended internal debate, which is something I often do. Sometimes I'll get so hung up thinking about both sides of an issue that I end up unable to make a decision. But not this time. The sign said, "To Rte. 50 West – Washington," and I twitched the wheel and away we went.

I piloted the aging pile of Detroit metal around the long curving ramp, the struggle against inertia and the interesting handling characteristics of worn-out shocks giving me enough to think about until I got out on the highway. But once I had managed to get out on the flat pavement and settle in, I began wondering about a couple of things. The first was Jerry the mystery surveyor. Who was he? And why had he said that he was with the SOS foundation? He had certainly seemed plausible enough when we met. Unlikable, but plausible. And without being an expert on surveying, it had certainly seemed as though he knew what he was doing. So I was just going to assume that he was a real surveyor, and that he was either doing the work on his own or that he had been hired. Either way he had lied, and he had known he was lying, when he said he was with SOS. Someone could have contacted him saying that they were with SOS and they would like him to do the work, but then he would have said that he was working for SOS, or that he was doing the work on their behalf, not that he was with them.

It was all quite interesting. Which, while true, didn't get me very far. Who else might have an interest in getting Dickie's property surveyed? The name Lou Nickerson jumped to mind. Nickerson's property was landlocked by Dickie's – and it would be very valuable property if he could get an easement. Perhaps Nickerson had heard that Dickie was getting ready to give his land to SOS and hoped to get an easement from the foundation. Maybe he even knew that SOS wouldn't keep the property, that they would sell it to a developer, in which case his essentially worthless property would suddenly be worth a small fortune. Or not so small. A couple of million dollars doesn't go as far as it used to, but it's still a nice chunk of change.

Why would Nickerson –assuming it was him – need to get the property surveyed? His property was surrounded on three sides by Dickie's and on the fourth side was the ocean. A surveyor would have to find the boundaries of Dickie's property in order to establish the boundaries of Nickerson's. It seemed to fit. Obviously Nickerson would need to have his land surveyed if he was going to sell it. Or maybe he was trying to get a loan based on the new value, and the bank was requiring the survey. That was an avenue to pursue. There aren't all that many banks on the Delaware shore and one, Wilmington Trust, seems to do about ninety percent of the business if the number of branches is any indication. Perhaps the bank had some central database of loan applications. Maybe I could convince them to tell me if Nickerson had applied for a loan. If not, I was sure that Hartner would have more luck. If it came down to it the Chief could get a court order and they bank would have to tell him. Of course for that to happen I would have to tell Hartner what I had been up to. I decided to postpone that course of action.

It occurred to me that if Nickerson had been able to find out that Dickie planned to give his property to SOS it stood to reason that he might be able to find out that Dickie had changed his mind. And that might upset somebody a bit, waving a check with a lot of zeroes on it in front of their face and then pulling it away, like Charlie Brown and Lucy with the football. A turnaround like that, a turnaround of a couple million dollars, might be enough to get someone to kill. People have killed for a lot less, we all know that.

I wondered how Nickerson – or anybody, for that matter – might have discovered Dickie's intentions, his plan to donate the property and his change of heart. There was only one person outside of SOS that I knew of who had been aware of what was going on, and that was Dickie's lawyer, Daniel Morgan. And Morgan was a local, and I had to assume he was well known. He knew Chief Hartner. He had been in politics. Nickerson was also a local and he was on the Dewey town council. There was every reason to believe that they might know each other. It could be investigated, at least. Hell, it might not need to be investigated: Hartner might know offhand. I decided that I needed to talk to him. Soon. Just not yet.

I was building castles in the air but at least I was building something. And since I was already at it I continued. Why would Morgan tell Nickerson about Dickie's will? The word that jumped to mind was money. Morgan is a lawyer and was a politician, and he wanted to get back into office. As such he'd have to have connections to developers – it seems that all politicians do. And if he could broker a deal between a wealthy developer and Nickerson, he'd probably be able to cut himself a nice slice off the top while making the developer happy enough that he might be willing to make some serious campaign contributions. Money in his pocket, money in his political coffers: Morgan definitely had motives for contacting Nickerson. I really needed to get back to Dewey and start talking to some people. So why was I driving away from the beach and towards D.C.?

Good question.

Annapolis was the closest I had been to D.C. all summer. I had seen the sign that said "Washington," and I took the exit. Now, nearing the Beltway, crawling along in the sclerotic traffic, with the air conditioner off and the hazy Washington air flowing heavily through the open car windows, I had time to wonder why. And to wonder where the heck I was going. I couldn't go to my place for another couple of weeks yet. And Ted wasn't around, as far as I knew, so I couldn't go to his place. And everybody else I knew would be at work. I crossed under the Beltway, staying on Route 50 as it turned into New York Avenue heading for downtown. Nothing had changed. The warehouses and rundown rowhouses and ratty motels and fast-food joints were all still there. There were a couple of abandoned cars that I could almost swear I recognized from months ago. The road was under construction as usual, with the same guys leaning on the same shovels. New York Avenue is a shame, really. It's the principal entrance to the city from the north and it looks like hell. Has always looked like hell despite oft-repeated vows from the city fathers to clean it up. My personal theory is that they – whoever they are – they saw that the road was called New York Avenue so they decided it should look like New York, which it does. Or New Jersey, at least, like Patterson or Bayonne without the charm. Which is saying something.

I took New York Ave. all the way downtown. My brain may not have wanted to acknowledge where we were going but my body knew. As I got closer and closer to the center of the city I felt more and more edgy and uptight. I could barely sit still, jiggling my leg nervously as I drove, drumming on the steering wheel, feeling my heart pound in my chest. My destination might be obvious to you but for some reason it wasn't to me, at least not until I got to Fourth Street, Northeast. I put on my turn signal like I had done a thousand times before and when the light changed I took the left. Just a few blocks ahead was Judiciary Square, home to the U.S. and the D.C. courts, Police Headquarters, and my office. And in the office I would probably find Bunny. Bonita Lopes. The Fall River Fireball herself. I hoped that she was there while hoping she was out. Our last conversation hadn't gone very well and she had cheated on me with Ted – twice!-since the last time I had seen her, but I still wanted to see her again. Maybe that's love, I don't know. The thought of her being with Ted really bothered me, but I figured I didn't have much right to complain. If you want someone to stay faithful to you, you should probably call at least once a month.

I got a pretty good parking spot just down the block from the office and a couple of minutes later I took a deep breath, squared my shoulders, and pulled open the heavy wood front door. No one was at the desk that Mary the receptionist-cum-CEO uses as her command station. No one was in any of the offices downstairs at all. There was no one in the little law library in the back by the bathrooms, either. It was getting kind of spooky. There were always people around in the PDS offices. Always phones ringing, doors slamming, the normal hustle and bustle of a busy office. I climbed the stairs to the second floor and there was again no one in the front offices, the ones that the paralegals generally use but which sometimes are occupied by lawyers just out of school and new to the staff. Most of them don't stay long so there's no point in shuffling everybody around just because they've signed on. I walked the short hallway that led to the cavernous loft where my desk –if it was still mine -was located along with the rest of the investigators, some paralegals, a bunch of file cabinets and whatever else can't find a home elsewhere in the building. The door to the room was closed. I'd never seen that before. I didn't even remember seeing a door there before. I opened the door warily. The room was dark. Heavy shades had been drawn across the high windows and the lights were out. I reached around the corner and flicked the switch. A moment later there was a shout of "Surprise!" and people jumped up from behind desks cabinets and tables where they had been hiding I've never had a heart attack, but now I have a pretty good idea of how one must feel. The clamor of voices and noisemakers died away like the dying gasp of a bagpipe and all of us looked at each other. Actually, they all looked at me and I looked at them. Lenny, my friend Lenny, who's been an attorney at PDS for nearly thirty years, stepped forward and said, with a smile, "You're not Bunny."

"Umm, no, I'm not. Sorry about that."

"What's going on here?" asked voice from behind me. Bunny.

Lenny said, "We just threw a surprise party for Bill."

I turned and gave Bunny a sheepish little half-wave. "Hi, Bunny."

The girl has ice in her veins, I swear. Appearing perfectly at ease she said, "Hi, Bill. Nice to see you." To Lenny she said, "I don't get it."

"It was supposed to be for you. Bill kind of walked in and we thought it was you and so he got the surprise instead."

"And, boy, was I surprised."

Bunny shook her head slightly, whether in annoyance or amusement I couldn't tell. "I can imagine."

Everyone was standing around awkwardly, shifting from foot to foot, looking at the floor or the ceiling. Lenny turned to face the gathered throng and said, "Well, we got a little mixed up, but we're here to have a party, so let's party, dammit!"

A cheer went up and soon there was cake and ice cream and a rousing version of "Happy Birthday" for Bunny. When we got a moment to talk Bunny said, "Thanks for coming up for my birthday."

Now, I cannot tell a lie. I mean, I can, I just don't like to, it's too hard to remember what you said. I don't like to lie, but I'm not stupid. I said, "You're welcome,"

Which I thought pretty much covered it. I was going to have to get a present, though. I asked her if she had heard from Ted and she pursed her lips and shook her head, obviously still upset at his absence. I found myself hoping that she was mad because of his failure to post in court rather than because she missed him. But I didn't ask.

After a while everyone went back to work. I asked Bunny if it would be all right if I picked her up after work and she assented. There was a moment's awkwardness when I left her, a moment we normally would have kissed but this time did not and ended up clasping hands briefly instead. Bunny had work to do so I went and found Lenny, who was in his office, rather improbably practicing his putting. He needed the practice. I sat on the corner of his desk to keep my feet out of the way as Lenny sprayed putts and the odd accidental chip shot around the room. His target was a plastic drinking cup lying on its side in the middle of the room. It was in no danger whatsoever.

"What's with the golf, Lenny?" Lenny is no golfer. He's more of the anti-golfer. Thin, unathletic, urban, Lenny was at home in a deli or at a chess board or in a bookstore, but you would never imagine him lining tee shots down the fairway.

"I don't know. Thought I might try it, see what all the fuss is about."

"But Lenny, you're a communist. Commies don't golf."

"I am not a communist. I'm a progressive socialist. There's a big difference."

"Progressive socialists golf?"

"Not as a rule, no."

"So what gives?"

"It's just something I wanted to try. Enough about the damn golf, already. What's up with the great Flaherty? You ever coming back? If you're not, I need to hire someone, and quick."

"Any word from Ted?"

"No, and I don't care. He's fired."

"Really?"

"Hey, you can't just not show up in court. People have rights, and they have lives. That just wasn't right."

"Suppose there was an explanation."

"It'd have to be a pretty damn good one. That was a major screw-up on Mr. Lynam's part. A major screw-up.

I note that you've changed the topic of conversation. I hereby change it back. What are your plans, Bill?"

"I don't know."

"Well, that clears that up," Lenny said as he stroked the ball perfectly into the cup, causing the cup to stand up."

"Nice shot," I said.

"You sound amazed."

"I am, a little."

"Why?"

"I don't know. It just doesn't seem like something you'd do."

His eyes flashed as he rose from retrieving his ball and turned to address to me. I'd seen that look many times. Usually it was reserved for antagonists in court; a lying witness, a dissembling police officer, an obstructionist judge. But this time it was all mine. "What –what the hell- do you know about me and what I would do or why I would do it? What makes you think you know me so well that you can say anything about me or my motivations?"

Whoa. "Um. Well, Lenny, we've worked together almost thirteen years. We've probably worked together on, I don't know, five hundred cases. I've been to dinner with you and Naomi what, call it thirty times. I've stayed at your house. We've had drinks. We've spent a lot of late nights. I've played with your kids. I was there when you got mugged and nearly killed last year, and I was with Naomi at your bedside at the hospital. I know you as well as I know anyone, I like you and admire you and I think you're a hell of a person. So I guess the answer is nothing gives me the right to judge you. But I wasn't. I was asking why you were taking up golf, which just seemed pretty damn unlikely for the Lenny I thought I knew. But hey, I guess it's none of my damn business. Sorry. Look, I got to get going. See ya. "

I slid from the desktop to the floor and started to leave. I had my hand on the doorknob before Lenny spoke. "Stop," he said. "I'm sorry. Come back."

I turned and looked back at him. He wasn't looking very well, ghostly pale but for splotches of color high on his cheeks. His hands fluttered on the shaft of the golf club he nervously twirled like some sort of middle-aged male majorette with bright orange hair. It almost looked like he might cry. "Lenny," I said. "If you don't want to tell me what's going on that's fine."

"No, no. Come back and sit. I have something I want to tell you."

I hoped he wasn't dying and that Naomi was all right. I sat, and he sat behind the desk, across form me. He folded his wandering hands together on the desktop, looked down at them as if to make sure they couldn't escape, then looked up and said simply, "I'm leaving PDS. I'm joining a firm in Fairfax County that specializes in real estate law. They need a litigator. And I need the money."

I would have been less surprised if he had said that he had just discovered that he was becoming a Buddhist monk and was planning to move to Tibet in the morning.

All I could think to say was, "What?" so that's what I said.

"I'm leaving PDS to join a firm in Fairfax." He repeated unnecessarily.

"I heard you. I was just surprised. Am surprised. Wow. I guess that explains the golf."

"I thought it might be necessary if I wanted to fit in."

"Oh, don't worry about that."

He appeared heartened. "So you think I'll fit in?"

I hated to do it to him, but I had to. He needed to hear the truth. "Not in a million frigging years. For God's sake, Lenny, you? Sucking up to developers and real estate agents, slapping them on the back over a three-martini lunch? And defending them in court when they get sued for raping the landscape or for tearing down low-income housing so they can build more McMansions? I don't know, Lenny. I hate to rain on your parade, but I don't see it. Not you. Sorry."

"Look, Bill, I understand what you're saying, okay? It doesn't quite fit my image, but…"

"If it was your image I wouldn't care. But it's not your image, man, it's you. You're a progressive whatever it was you just you said…"

"Socialist."

"A progressive socialist. You couldn't be more of a liberal. You're anti-greed, anti-capitalism, anti-everything that has to do with money and social injustice, for Christ's sake, you've spent twenty-something years here trying to help the poor and the dispossessed, and now you're going to work for developers? Man, you're making my head hurt. What does Naomi think?"

"She doesn't know yet."

"Oh, good. That's real good. She's going to kill you. Or divorce you. Or both, for God's sake. Why are you doing this?"

"I need to make some money. I have kids now. I could afford to be, well, not poor but you know, not wealthy before, but now we got the two little guys and they need stuff. We can't keep living in the apartment. We need a car, a dependable car, a minivan or something. And the kids are going to need to go to school, college will be coming up before you know it..."

"How old are the kids now?"

"Seven and eight." The year before Lenny and Naomi had adopted an orphaned brother and sister from Kosovo. That was a very Lenny thing to do. This was not.

"I still don't understand. Naomi makes good money. If you guys just cut back on the charitable stuff, you should be fine." Naomi was a lawyer for the EPA. She'd never get rich, but they could certainly get by.

"She quit her job. Said she needed more time with the kids."

"She's not working?"

"No. She's doing some volunteer legal services work for Habitat for Humanity. You know, Jimmy Carter's outfit, they build homes for the poor?"

"Oh, that's good. She's helping the homeless and you're helping the developers. Gee, maybe you guys can try a case against each other. That would be fun."

Lenny didn't respond for a moment, instead studying his hands intently. He looked up and said, "Well, what about you?"

"What about me?"

"What are you doing with yourself?"

"I don't really know."

"Are you coming back to work?"

"I'm not sure."

"Are you going to marry Bunny?"

"Marry her? I kind of doubt it, I mean…well, never mind. But marriage is quite unlikely at this point, I can assure you."

"I…see."

"What's that supposed to mean?"

"What?"

"That comment. The way you said, 'I…see' like you're some kind of a damn psychiatrist or something."

"I'm not a psychiatrist."

"No shit. But what's your point?"

"Nothing really."

"Nothing really," I mimicked in a teasing child's singsong voice. Clearly this conversation, or at least my end of it, was not being conducted at the highest of intellectual levels. Lenny looked irked, and in retrospect I guess he had a right to be.

"Look," he said. "I'm doing what I think I have to do. Do you really think that I want to spend the rest of my career rubbing shoulders with fat idiots in greasy polyester suits? Do you? Do you really think I want to spend my time and my energy researching ways to help these guys pave the planet? Do you? Or do you think that maybe I'm doing what I have to do, that maybe, just maybe, I'm doing what a grown-up does when he has to take care of his family? We've known each other a long time now, Billy, and we've been through a lot. Give me some credit, okay? And before you shoot your mouth off any more, how about trying to figure out what it is that you're doing. Your criticisms would carry a lot more weight if you weren't acting like such a damn dilettante."

"Dilettante? Moi?"

"Yeah, toi."

I leaned back in my chair and laced my fingers behind my head. "Well, okay. Duly noted. I guess I don't have a leg to stand on, really. But it just seems so out of character..."

"It is. That makes it hard. And it will be hard. Hell, the partners at my new firm know it'll be hard for me. But they also know I'm good at what I do, and that if I accept their money I'll do my best."

I knew he would, too. Lenny's always been a stand-up guy. "Well, we'll miss you."

"'We'?' So you're coming back?"

"I still don't know. I'm thinking about it. I'll let you know."

"Do that." Lenny stood, and then so did I. We shook hands. Strangely, I don't think we ever shook hands before. Or at least not since the day we met. I looked at my watch. It was almost five. I'd been in Lenny's office for a long time. I decided to go see if Bunny might be ready to leave. Lenny and I said our goodbyes, and I left him still standing there at his desk, his shoulders slumped, his hands thrust deep into his pockets. He was a man with a lot on his mind.

I walked out to the reception area. Mary was at her desk, talking on the phone and she held a hand up for me to wait. I did as she said.. But I always do what she says. Everyone does. Though she's just the receptionist, Mary holds the reins at PDS and she knows it. In another world she'd be the president of a large company – hell, maybe of a country. But the world she came up in didn't hold those kind of opportunities for black women. But she made the most of what she had and she kept her chin up and that's something, I guess.

She hung up the phone and looked at me with a raised eyebrow. "Something you need, Mr. Flaherty?"

"No, not right this minute."

"When you gonna get up and get back to work?"

"Well, now that I'm independently wealthy, maybe never."

She snorted. "You get hungry enough, you'll come back. Only questions are when, and if your job is still here waiting."

"I guess we'll see."

"I guess we will."

I looked around, hoping to catch a glimpse of Bunny. Mary said, "You sure you don't need anything?"

"I was just looking for Bunny."

"She's gone. Ran out of here about twenty minutes ago."

"Did she say when she'd be back?"

"Yup."

"Do you mind telling me what she said?"

"Nope." She was smiling now, playing with me and liking it.

"What did she say, please?"

"She said, 'see you in the morning'."

"Huh. That's weird. We were going to go out."

"Well, you're not now. Sorry about that, Mr. Flaherty. "'Course if you treated her better she'd probably be on your arm right now."

"Thanks, Mary. But I don't need any lectures, if you don't mind."

A Deadly Kind of Paradise

"You need lectures more than anybody I know, Mr. Flaherty. Sooner you realize that, the better."

"Whatever. I'll see you later." I turned to leave, my mind already far away. Why would she just run out on me like that? It wasn't the most mature thing she'd ever done, not that I was the maturity poster child. Had she just forgotten? Or maybe she just had to run out and she'd be back. I didn't want to sit around the office like an idiot waiting for her, but I didn't want to leave if she was coming back, either. That would be great, if I was gone and she came back to look for me. I was at the door when Mary called out, "Why don't you just call her?"

I looked back and said, "I would, but I don't have any idea where she is."

"You ever heard of a cell phone?"

Oh, yeah. "I don't know the number."

Mary shook her head and clucked. "You know, you are just Mister Negativity today, you know that, right?" She scribbled on a piece of paper and held it out to me. I walked over and took it from her outstretched hand. She grabbed me by the wrist before I could move. She was quick. Very quick. And extremely strong. She held me there for a moment, looking into my eyes. "You do right by her, Mr. Flaherty. I'm warning you. You two belong together."

I extricated myself from her grip, no easy task. "Thanks for the advice, Mary. But you know, there's more going on here than you know."

"What, you worried 'bout that little fling with Ted?"

"Jesus! What, was it posted on the internet or what?"

"People tell me things. You know that, William. Must be my sweet personality." She paused and smiled, then continued, "But if you're worried about that little thing with Ted, you shouldn't. It was your own damn fault."

"Don't you think I know that?"

"Sometimes I wonder if you know anything at all."

"Well, gee, thanks for the vote of confidence. I feel a lot better now."

"Only time you're gonna feel a lot better is when you get your life straight."

"Who are you, Ann Landers?"

"That dried up old lady don't know a thing. You listen to me and you'll get somewhere, boy. Now go call Bunny. And be nice. And buy some damn flowers and a card around the corner before you meet her. And take her out to dinner. And tell her you're sorry."

"Jesus. Anything else?"

"You can thank me later."

I folded the paper with Bunny's number on it and put it in my pocket. No way was I going to call her when I was within earshot of Mary. She'd probably be coaching me from the next room. But I was smiling despite myself as I walked back toward the door. I pulled the door open and looked back at Mary. She had the phone cradled on her shoulder and she was dialing a number. I said, "Hey, Mary?"

She stopped dialing, finger suspended in midair. "Yes, darling?"

"Thanks."

She just nodded and made a little shooing gesture, sending me on my way. I walked out and down the stairs.

I stopped by a mailbox and dialed Bunny's number on my own cell phone. Bunny's number was busy. And I had a good idea who was calling her. I had half a mind to run back to the office and catch her at it but I let it go. I had to get over to the florist before they closed.

Sixteen

It doesn't happen all that often, but once in a while Mary is wrong. And it wasn't easy, no matter how she had made it sound. Actually, strictly speaking, it was more of a disaster. What happened was I made another call and Bunny answered this time. After some initial awkwardness she agreed to meet me for a drink and we settled on J. Paul's in Georgetown. J. Paul's is sort of an overblown fern bar, with lots of brass and wood and a couple of bars that are generally packed, and a bunch of picture windows overlooking M Street near the intersection with Wisconsin Avenue. It's not the sort of place I generally frequent, my taste in bars generally running to dives with country music on the jukebox and cheap beer, but at least the throng might prevent a scene from developing, which I thought might otherwise be a distinct possibility.

Maybe things would have gone more smoothly if I had taken Mary's advice about the flowers, but when I was standing there in the florist's I had wondered what kind of flowers say "It's okay that you cheated on me" and the answer of course was none so that's what I bought.

Sitting there at the bar waiting for Bunny to arrive I had had some time to think. Okay, I thought, I felt bad that Bunny had slept with Ted. That was a starting point. Why did I feel bad? Because your girlfriend and your best friend aren't supposed to do things like that. But did my girlfriend and best friend do that – in other words, were Bunny and Ted my girlfriend and my best friend? Certainly at one point they had been. But now there was the question of what they had done. If a woman is sleeping with another man, can she be your girlfriend? Does that make sense? Clearly if she's not sleeping with you and she is sleeping with someone else you're probably a little confused if you think she's your girlfriend. By the same token if your best friend is sleeping with your girlfriend you need a new best friend because you don't have one. So maybe I was worrying about the wrong thing, maybe I should just move on, say the hell with both of them. And as regards Bunny at least, hadn't I already done that? Apparently Bunny slept with Ted because she was distraught and lonely. Why was she distraught and lonely? Because I had left town, I hadn't given any indication when or if I was returning, and for well over a month I hadn't even called her. Now, if you move away from someone, don't tell them what you're doing, and don't even communicate with them for an extended period of time, do you have any right to consider that person yours in any sense? I mean, I hadn't even picked up the damn phone, and that's just common courtesy. On the other hand Bunny hadn't called me either and she knows how to use a telephone. So the question comes down to this: Was there any reason for me to be upset or was I just being petty and selfish? Or maybe a better question was, what do I want to happen now?

Hmmm. No idea.

That's about how far I had gotten when Bunny showed up. She looked beautiful as usual, still wearing the stylish suit that she had worn to work, but now she had let her long dark hair down , framing her face in gentle curls, setting off her slightly olive complexion. Mine wasn't the only head she turned as she strode purposefully across the room. She wasn't smiling, but she didn't look like she was going to bite my head off either. I decided to take this as a positive sign. Not that I was really all that dead set on everything being positive. But we just went over all of that.

I stood and she saw me and a moment later she was standing there a few feet away, looking up at me rather inscrutably. "Hi, Bunny," I said cleverly.

"Hello, Bill," she parried incisively.

"Let's take that table." I indicated an empty table across the rooom, she nodded, and we walked over. We stood there for a moment until I said, "Won't you sit down? Let me get you something to drink." She sat. So far so good, I guessed.

She said she'd love a glass of Chardonnay and sat and I went and fetched hers and another Absolut on the rocks for myself. I t was a little strange, standing there at the bar with her at the little table across the way looking off into the distance, a tableau of great familiarity that was at the same time completely different from all the other times we'd been in similar situations. I managed to get the bartender's attention with surprising speed and it was only a couple of minutes later that I was setting the drinks on the table and sitting down across from her. "So," I said when I was settled. "How are you?"

This is where things began to go downhill.

"Fine," she replied. "Why do you ask?"

No, no, no, I thought. The correct response is, "Fine, and you?"

"Ummm…well. I asked because I was interested?" I hadn't intended to turn the statement into a question, it just came out that way.

"Oh," she said, letting it hang there. After a while she took a sip of her drink.

I was very aware of the need to say pretty much anything that came to mind. Unfortunately, nothing came to mind for a while, and when it did, it wasn't worth the wait. "Heard from Ted?" I asked. I was just trying to make conversation, I swear.

Bunny's dark eyes predictably flashed. "I don't know what possible business it is of yours, but no, the little bastard is still missing."

"Ted's not that little," I said. I was trying to be funny. I've heard that humor can be useful in breaking up tension. Either that is not true or I was not humorous. I prefer to believe the former.

"I beg to differ," she said flatly. Even a hint of a smile would have made her reply funny, but there was no smile evident. And poor Ted. Poor "little" Ted. I almost felt for him. But at least I wasn't the "little" one. Me da man.

But anyways.

Bunny focused her dark eyes on me. "You wanted to see me?"

"Well, yeah, sorta."

"Sorta?"

"I mean, yeah, but, well, I was kinda hoping you wanted to see me, to."

That hung there for a while. This conversation, in case you hadn't noticed, wasn't going too well. The Absolut, on the other hand was going great. In fact it was gone. I longed for another, considered going for one, but Bunny's wine glass was still almost full. Finally I said, "Well, do you?"

"Do I what?"

"Want to see me, dammit!"

"Don't raise your voice at me, Bill."

"How about this: You try to help me have a normal conversation, nothing strenuous, just normal conversation, and I won't raise my voice. That work for you?"

"I really don't need your sarcasm right now."

Me? Sarcastic? Nah. "Look. I know all about what happened. I'm prepared to move on if you are. Shit happens. I forgive you."

I don't speak Portuguese, and right then I was glad that I didn't. There were a few phrases in there that might have been damaging to my self-esteem. When she switched back to English she said, "I don't need your misplaced forgiveness, William." It's always William when she's mad. "What I need," she continued, "is to have my head examined for seeing you in the first place. If you ever grow up give me a call. Until then, goodbye." She got up and stormed off while I sat there with my mouth open. She went about ten steps and turned on her heel and came marching back. For a moment I thought that she had either changed her mind or that she was going to slug me but instead she threw a five-dollar bill on the table, saying, "That's for the wine." Then she turned again and left.

Well, I thought. What an interesting development.

A college boy in khakis and a white button-down shirt was sitting at the next table by himself, apparently waiting for someone. He said, "Dude, whatever you did, you better try to undo it before she gets a gun."

"Thanks for the advice, genius." I said. " Now shut the fuck up." Then I got up and left. Bunny was nowhere in sight. Right now, I thought, was a perfect time to go back to the beach.

I jaywalked across M Street, walked up the hill to O Street, then took a left to the block between 35th and 36th where I had parked the car. I was just outside the front entrance to Georgetown University, dear old Alma Mater, and for a moment I considered walking around the campus. I hadn't been on campus for a long time, but somehow right then the thought of being surrounded by a bunch of fresh-faced kids with their whole lives in front of them was very depressing. It was also kind of depressing that I had a parking ticket. I took the ticket out from under my wiper blade and let it flutter to the ground. They couldn't do anything to me if I didn't come back to DC and right then I had no intention of coming back.

On the other hand I'm not a litterbug.

I sighed, bent and retrieved the ticket from the gutter and stuck it in the glove compartment where it could hang out with its friends. A few minutes later I was on Pennsylvania Avenue heading downtown and a few minutes after that I was outbound on New York Avenue with home, and I definitely thought of it as home, just a couple of hours away.

Or it would have been a couple of hours away if I hadn't stopped at the 404. Remember what I said about the kind of bars I like? Cohee's 404 (named for the fact that Cohee owns it and it's on Route 404 – get it?) is just that kind of place. Good country music – Johnny Cash and Merle Haggard and Hank Williams and Patsy Cline and Dwight Yoakum on the juke, a couple of pool tables, frosty Bud drafts in tall thin pilsner glasses for less than two bucks, it all works. It's the kind of place where you'll never find a Mercedes in the dirt parking lot hard by the highway but there's sure to be plenty of dusty pickup trucks and maybe a couple of Harleys. It's not that I'm a redneck or that I only like country music – I'm nowhere near the first and country's just one of many kinds of music I like. And there's a hell of a lot of country music (including just about anything you might hear on the radio) that I can't stand. But if you want a cold beer and no bullshit, the 404 is the right kind of place. The 404 is about two-thirds of the way to the beach from DC, so it's a natural stopping place. And they have the best crab balls around, served just right with cocktail sauce and saltines. Crab balls are small crabcakes, not some sort of microscopic crustacean anatomical feature. And at the 404 they're good, and they're cheap.

Seven or eight beers, a couple orders of crab balls, about half a bottle of Tabasco, two winning and one losing game of pool, some no-shit conversation and two shots of Jim Beam later I was feeling much better. I still felt fine to drive but I knew I'd fail a breathalyzer so I just eased on down the road at the speed limit after closing time, and forty minutes later I pulled into the driveway at Dickie's place. There was a grey Chevy Lumina with Ohio tags parked out front and I sat there for a minute looking at it until I realized that it must be Robert's rental car, which made me pretty unhappy because I had completely forgotten about Robert coming. And now he was here and I supposed he intended to try to keep his word and kick me out of the house. I guess we'll see about that, I said before realizing I was talking to myself.

For the first time in memory the front door was locked but I had a key and let myself in. There was no sign of Robert on the first floor. Actually there were plenty of signs, just no Robert. There was what must have been a case's worth of empty Old Milwaukee Light Cans scattered around. Livin' the high life, that Robert. Old Milwaukee Light. Shit. You might as well just piss right in your mouth. Although how you would manage that is a good question but not one I'm going to spend any time thinking about. In addition to the beer cans there was an empty pint of peppermint schnapps, half a giant bag of "B-B-Q" flavored pork rinds and the remains of a Domino's pizza. Which appeared to have anchovies and artichoke hearts on it. I swear the boy must have had a tastebudectomy.

There was also a plastic bag half full of dope. I pinched a fair amount and put it in a film canister I found in a drawer. You snooze, you lose. Speaking of snoozing, I thought, if Robert had eaten and drank all of this crap by himself there was no danger of him waking up any time soon. And I could use some sack time myself. I went upstairs and into my room and there was Robert fully clothed right down to his cowboy boots sound asleep in my bed. Call me picky but that was too much. "Hey, Robert," I yelled, "get the hell up and get outta my bed." There was no reaction from Robert except an amazingly long and loud fart. Aromatic, too. But what would you expect after the crap he'd eaten?

"Jesus H...." I gagged as I stumbled across the room to open the window. He could have the damn room, but I had to let the poison gas out of the house before it killed us both. Mission accomplished, I hurried out of the room and across the hall to Dickie's room. I didn't feel like waking up in the morning with Robert in my face so I pushed a chair under the doorknob, and then I went to bed.

I woke up confused. More confused than usual, even. It took me a minute to get my bearings, and when I did, I had a real sinking feeling in my chest. Maybe it was my stomach. Maybe it was a hangover. Robert, I thought. The fuck am I going to do about Robert? At least he hadn't woken me up. I got up and got dressed, removed the chair from the door and went out to face the day. Robert wasn't in my room, so I went downstairs and found him on the back deck eating from a box of Dunkin' Donuts and sipping coffee and looking a bit peaked but generally well – deeply tanned despite the morning-after pallor, hair longish and tied back in pony tail. He certainly looked better than I would have imagined from the picture Dickie had shown me. He motioned to a chair a few feet away and pointed to a large coffee on the table in front of him as he chewed and swallowed. I took the coffee and sat. Coffee had cream and sugar in it, but any port in a storm.

"Mornin' Bill," Robert said when his mouth was empty, sounding like it had been a couple of days since we'd seen each other rather than the close to twenty years that had in fact passed.

"Robert," I said.

"Time'd you get in? Must have been late."

"Yeah. It was maybe three, three-thirty."

"Hmm." He took a sip of coffee and another bite of his donut. Powdered sugar drifted down onto his lap. Robert was seeming pretty relaxed and I wasn't looking for a fight, so I said, "Got any glazed in there?"

Robert nodded and said through a mouthful of food, "Help y'self." A little puff of powdered sugar accompanied the words. The breeze blew it away like smoke before it could settle. I got up and sure enough there were six glazed donuts in there along with four or five others. I took one of the glazed and sat back down. I like glazed donuts. Maybe I was a cop in another life.

"So," said Robert after he had washed the donut down with some coffee. "You're still here."

"Yup."

"Huh."

It wasn't exactly scintillating conversation. But it was still early. Maybe things would get more lively with a good dose of sugar and caffeine. There was only one way to find out, so I ate my donuts and drank my coffee and watched people walk by on the beach. Most of them stayed down by the water, maybe seventy-five yards off. A leggy blond in a bikini jogged by with a Rottweiler on a leash. That kept my attention for a while. Robert's, too. When she had gone Robert said, "Thought you said you were moving out."

"Nope. You told me to move out. I didn't agree to it."

"Huh." He thought about that for a while. "Too short a notice, I guess, right? I can understand that, I guess."

I didn't say anything.

"So, what, I guess you'll be out today, though, right?"

"Robert, I'm not going anywhere. I live here. Dickie invited me to stay as long as I want. I plan on staying a long while."

"Huh. But Dickie's dead now, of course."

"Yeah."

"So don't you think maybe the invitation has, well, lapsed? Or am I missing something here?"

"Can I ask you something, Robert?"

"What?"

"What happened to your Southern accent?"

"Don't have one."

"You did, on the phone."

"Well, I put one on, sometimes, mostly when I'm entertaining the shitkickers."

"Shitkickers?"

"Good ole boys. Fishermen –half-assed fishermen I should say. You know, my clients."

Robert had clients. This was not something I had envisioned. "What line of work are you in, Robert?"

"I run a charter fishing service out of Key West. Doing all right. Get mostly southerners, and man, them boys, they like to fish but they don't come down to Key West just to fish, and that's no lie."

"Your Southern accent just came back."

"Sorry. Sometimes I slip."

"So…how long have you been in the fishing business?"

"Quite a while. Just got a new boat. Want to see a picture?" He didn't wait for an answer, pulling out his wallet, extracting a folded photo and flipping it to me.

I looked at the picture. "Sweet."

"Damn right. Forty-three feet. Two Volvo diesels - five hundred horses each. Sleeps six but we use it mostly for day trips. Do over thirty knots if you got money for the fuel."

"If you don't mind me asking, what's a boat like this go for?"

"Oh, way we got her set up, a little north of nine."

"Hundred grand?"

"Well, yeah. Not million."

"Nine hundred thousand dollars? That's a lot of money to have tied up in a boat."

"Yeah, but I got a lot more than that, all told. She's just the newest. I got three others, too. Got a couple million dollars worth of boat sitting at the dock every night."

"Jesus."

"Another donut?"

"Uh, yeah, sure." I got up and got myself a donut then sat back down and ate it while I sipped my rapidly-cooling coffee. Things were not making sense. As far as I had known, Robert was a deadbeat layabout. But here he was, apparently a successful businessman. Maybe he was a drug smuggler or something. Or maybe he was what he looked like and seemed like, which was an outdoorsy type with a pretty sweet lifestyle who was in no particular need of funds. I needed some more coffee.

"So , when are you moving out?"

Back to that. "I told you, I'm not. It's not your house. It's my house, and I'm staying put."

"Your house? What are you talking about?"

I wondered if I had blown Morgan's confidence. Probably. Oh well. "Dickie willed it to me."

"What?"

"It's true. He told me so himself. And it's been confirmed."

"Confirmed how?"

"I don't think I can tell you that. But wait until they read the will and you'll see."

Robert shook his head. "You gotta be shittin' me. Well, congratulations, I guess. Shoulda known the little prick would screw me again if he got half a chance. Shit. But it figures. It friggin' figures." He shook his head and slumped in his chair. We sat there in silence for a few minutes. Finally Robert said, "Well, If that doesn't call for a joint, I don't know what does. Join me?"

"Nah. Kinda early for me."

"Suit yourself."

"I'll do that." He rose and took a couple of steps toward the house, then stopped and turned. "I feel kinda funny askin', but seein' as how thing's seem to have changed... you don't mind me staying in your house a few days, do you?"

"No, whatever, that's fine. Just move across the hall to Dickie's room, okay?"

"Was that your bed I slept in last night?"

"Yeah."

"Sorry, bro'."

"Don't sweat it."

Robert went inside and I sat on the deck, looking at the ocean. I was very confused. But there was one thing I was pretty sure about: I was minus one suspect.

Seventeen

Hartner didn't take his boots off his desk or his eyes off the piece of paper he was reading.

"So you're back."

"Looks that way."

"Thought you might've run off."

"Nope."

"Wishful thinkin', I guess."

"Watch it, now"

Hartner sighed and put his feet on the floor. He glanced at the paper one more time, wrote something that I guessed was his signature at the bottom, and looked up at me. "What can I do you for?"

"Just wondering if you got an ID on the guy we found out at the beach."

"Oh. Yeah, I guess there's no harm in sharing that. Let's see…" he fumbled through a pile of paper on the corner of the desk. "Here we go…deceased is one Jerry Kavanagh. Late of Henlopen Acres just north of Rehoboth, surveyor by trade, death was…"

"Surveyor?" I interrupted. Guy's name was Jerry?"

"Right twice. Why?"

"There was a guy doing some surveying out at Dickie's place by the name of Jerry. But that was only, well, today's Wednesday, that was Saturday, only five days ago. That can't be right."

Hartner was looking a bit bewildered. "What can't be right?"

"How long had the guy been dead? Did they give you any idea?"

"A couple of days was the initial finding. But that was more or less just based on appearances. There'll be a report later that should nail it down at least a little better. You mind me asking what you're getting at?"

"Look. Dickie's been dead, what, about two weeks? If this is the same guy who was out at Dickie's on Saturday – hell even if it isn't – and he's only been dead a couple days, how does he end up wrapped in Dickie's sail on the beach? It doesn't make sense."

Hartner's response to this was to put his feet back up on his desk. He folded his hands behind his head and leaned back. He needed to get a better brand of antiperspirant.

While he mused I said, "There's another dead guy out there somewhere."

"The material in Dickie's truck."

"Exactly. If this guy's been dead two days his brains haven't been in Dickie's truck for two weeks."

"That would seem to follow."

"Anybody else missing that you know of?"

Hartner glared at me. He was upset, but not upset enough to take his feet off the desk. "Gee, you think I ought to check?"

"Sorry. Just thinking out loud."

"Apology accepted. That was the first thing we did. Nobody seems to be missing locally. No reports filed, no calls logged."

There was knock on the half-open door and Hartner said, "Come."

Young Officer Riley entered, holding a sheaf of papers. He looked haggard, as if he were sick or he'd been up partying all night, which upon reflection was probably the case. "Paperwork, Chief," he mumbled, setting the papers on the desk. "Nothing urgent." He turned to go but Hartner stopped him. "You feeling all right, Riley?"

"Yes, sir. Just haven't been sleeping well last couple of nights. I'll be fine soon's I get some rest." Hartner nodded, dismissing him. As he turned to go Riley caught my eye. His back was to Hartner, so I don't think the Chief noticed. Riley mouthed a couple of syllables but I've never been a lip reader so I don't know what they were. But the message was clear enough, that he wanted to speak to me, so I nodded as imperceptibly as possible and looked away.

Hartner seemed oblivious. He was looking through the papers that Riley had brought in and he didn't look up until Riley had left the room. When he did look up it was to shout, "Riley!" and for a moment I thought he had detected our little exchange. But when Riley stuck his head back in the door the Chief said, "Riley, I know you're tired, but I've already signed all these. Do us a both a favor and wake the hell up, okay? Get some coffee or something." He held the stack of papers out and Riley came and got them, mumbling, "Yes, sir. Sorry, Sir." Riley didn't repeat his effort at communication as he left.

"That boy," said Hartner, shaking his head. "Is a piece of work."

"Seems a little out there sometimes," I agreed for the sake of being agreeable and because it was true.

"A little, my ass. Where were we?"

"Nowhere, pretty much. You were saying that nobody's gone missing lately." Something about that was bothering me, but I couldn't put my finger on what it was. I was also wondering what Riley could want and why he felt it was important enough to go through what I was sure was a ruse with the papers he brought in. Maybe the surf's up, I thought.

"What's so funny?" demanded the Chief.

"Huh? Nothing, sorry."

The Chief looked at me suspiciously, as though he thought I had been laughing at him for some reason. He kept looking at me so I said, "I was just thinking about Riley bringing in a bunch of papers that were already signed. Kid's out there."

"You got that right," grumbled the Chief. "Fact that he thinks he should carry a gun scares the life out of me. He ought to be selling slurpees." In one motion he took his feet from the desk and almost sprang to his feet without using his hands on the armrests. He was in better shape than it appeared. He looked at his watch and said, "Anything else?"

No, I replied. The chief pulled on his jacket, adjusted his holster and said, "I got to get moving. You stay out of trouble. And stay out of the way. I still don't want you messing around in police business."

"Yes, sir," I replied a bit too enthusiastically for the Chief's liking. He looked at me long and hard from beneath his beetled brow, shook his head, and said, "I mean it, dammit."

I bit my tongue and followed the Chief down the short hallway and through the reception area and out into the parking lot. He climbed in his Bronco and drove away without a word. I stood there, blinking against the bright sunshine, then climbed into my car. Another day in paradise, I thought. A deadly kind of paradise.

Eighteen

The first thing I did after Hartner left was climb back out of my car and walk back into the station to look for Riley. He was in a little file room off the reception area. I called his name and he popped his head out like a prairie dog scanning the horizon, almost comically, for danger. Deciding the coast was clear, he stepped out of the file room and up to the counter where I stood. He still looked tired and haggard but now there was an additional component to his demeanor: fear. Riley was obviously scared of someone or something. He opened and closed his mouth soundlessly a few times like a mackerel stranded on the beach. He quickly looked around again, grabbed a scrap of paper from the counter and jotted down "Fager's Island, O.C. 11:00 tonite" turned it so I could read it and looked at me silently, eyebrows raised in question. I nodded, and without a word he turned and walked back to the file room, taking the scrap of paper with him and tearing it methodically into tiny pieces as he went. I watched him for a second, then turned to leave. Fager's Island is a popular bar and restaurant on the bay in Ocean City, Maryland. Fager's is known for its ritual at sunset, when they play the 1812 Overture as the sun sinks into the waters of the western bay. They usually have live bands there every night and it has a reputation as something of a pick-up joint. I hoped Riley wasn't going to try to pick me up but somehow I doubted it. Maybe he was going to ask me for hints on how to pick up girls. Somehow I doubted that, too.

As I went out the door I almost ran into Hartner. "Forgot my cell phone," he said. "What are you still doing here?"

"I had to use the bathroom." It was the best I could come up with on short notice.

"Riley," Hartner bellowed. Riley popped back out of the file room, looking even more alarmed than before. "Riley, you know we don't have a public rest room here."

"Yessir, sorry sir, but...but he asked and, well, it seemed since he was meeting with you...that..."

"Never mind. Just remember the policy. Understood?"

Riley nodded, all but gasping for air, beads of sweat standing out on his forehead. He was one nervous little surfer. For a moment I thought he might faint but before he could topple Hartner said, "Good," and stomped off towards his office. I shrugged at Riley, winked and left. I was hoping that the wink might buck him up a little.

I drove north through Dewey, and stayed right to follow Bayard Avenue, or 1B, or whatever you want to call it, and few blocks further down took a left onto Chesapeake Street. A glance at the phone book before I had left the house this morning had given me the address for Lou Nickerson. Nickerson was still the only one I knew of who stood to benefit if Dickie's property changed hands, the only person I knew of who might have an actual motive for killing Dickie. I had only spoken to him the one time when we met on the beach, and thought it was time to have a chat and get better acquainted. I stopped in front of 127, which looked like a large house but which turned out to be a small apartment building, just four units, two up an two down. The building was built into a slope, so the upstairs units front doors' faced the street and the downstairs units were accessed from around back where they faced Lake Comegys, a body of water for which "lake" was perhaps a bit too grand an appellation.

All I had was the street number, so I walked around the building in the vain hope that Nickerson's name might be posted by one of the doors. I was finishing my circumperambulation, walking up the narrow pathway that runs along the left side of the building, when I was nearly run down by a man carrying two large plastic trash barrels, one above the other. I leaned against the overgrown chain-link fence to get out of the way, hoping fervently that none of the lush vegetation was poison ivy. I didn't realize that the man was Nickerson until he had passed me, and only then because I got a glimpse of his clean-shaven head. "Mr. Nickerson," I called out inventively.

"Yes? Who's that?" He turned toward the sound of my voice, nearly clocking me with one of the cans.

"Me, Bill Flaherty. We met at the beach a few days back, when the surveyors came?"

"Oh, yes, Bill. How are you? Look, let me put these cans away. Why don't you follow me?

"Will do. Here, let me carry one for you."

"Nah, no thanks. I'm not ready for the home just yet."

By the way he hefted the cans it was clear that he wasn't going to be ready for the home anytime soon. I followed him around the back of the building. He set the cans inside a fenced enclosure, closed the gates, wiped his hands on his pants and stuck out a hand, which I shook. I wasn't getting suspect vibes, I was getting gruff good old guy vibes. He struck me as retired military, maybe ex-Marine vibes, probably an officer. He was rather short but wide and he could have crushed walnuts with his handshake. He looked me directly and unblinkingly in the eye as we shook. "How about a cup of coffee, young man?" he asked.

"Well, I don't want to put…"

"Nonsense. Just made it. Come on." He turned on his heel and I followed as ordered. The door to his apartment was only a few yards off. There were flowers in profusion both in planters and in beds around the door, and a couple of green metal garden chairs sat beneath a lilac bower just off to the side. The place showed a woman's touch and I was unsurprised when we came upon a woman in the house. Nickerson introduced his wife June, a trim pleasant white-haired woman of maybe sixty who I immediately felt as though I had known for years. Within a couple of minutes Mr. Nickerson and I were seated in the garden outside the door with steaming cups of coffee and a plate of pastries, all brought out to us on a tray by Mrs. Nickerson. She declined her husband's invitation to join us and withdrew into the house. "So," said Nickerson after she had gone. "I was sorry to hear about Dickie. Why didn't you tell me what happened when we met? Or do I have the timing wrong?"

"No, you got it right. Dickie was already gone when we met. I just…well, I guess I just wasn't up t talking about it right then. I was feeling pretty bad about it all."

"Any particular reason?"

"What do you mean?"

"I mean, was it any of your fault?"

"No, not at all."

"And how are you now? Bearing up?"

"Yeah, I'm fine. " And I was fine, if a little curious about how I had ended up answering questions when I had come to ask them.

"Good. Keep your chin up. Danish?"

"Uh, no thanks."

"Oh, come on. You need to keep your strength up."

Upon reconsideration the lemon Danish looked pretty good, so I took one. "Thanks."

I took a bite and Nickerson said. "So am I your prime suspect?"

I nearly choked on the Danish. Literally. Nickerson jumped up and whacked me on the back a couple times and when I was able to breath again I looked up and he was grinning at me. "Sorry," he said, still grinning.

"Jesus, what are you trying to do, kill me?"

Nickerson sat back down across from me, the ghost of a smile still on his lips. "Nah. If I was tying to kill you, I would have killed you."

"That's comforting. I guess. How'd you know that I thought you might be a suspect?"

"Oh, it was merely my superior intellect and intuition working in sync. That and the fact that the Chief told me that you'd probably come around."

"Oh."

I guess I must have sounded a little downhearted because Nickerson said, "Hey, don't take it so hard. Just because the Chief tipped me off doesn't make it a bad idea for you to come here and ask me. In fact I admire it."

"Why's that?"

"Hey, your friend got himself killed. You're trying to do what you can to catch the killer. I call that loyalty, and in the Marines we value loyalty above all else. Semper Fidelis is our motto, after all. 'Always Faithful'. Faithful to the corps, but also to your friends, especially when they're in need. I'd say Dickie needs somebody to stick up for him. He sure can't do it himself."

"In that case, did you kill Dickie?"

Nickerson's eyes widened for a moment. "Well you're direct, I'll give you that, too. Bravo."

I took a bite of my Danish. Carefully and without incident. When I had swallowed I said, "Well, did you?"

"Absolutely not." The twinkle I had noticed in Nickerson's eye was gone.

"Would you agree that you have a motive for wanting Dickie dead?"

"No."

"Really? What about the money your land would be worth if you could get an easement?"

"It's a non-issue. I don't need it. Besides I'm not so sure I want to see houses on that land. It's nice the way it is. Don't get me wrong – a million or two wouldn't hurt anything and I wouldn't throw it in the ocean. But we've got a pretty good life here, a place we like that's paid for, I run a profitable little business, I've got my pension, we've got good insurance, no real debt. I'm on the town council, which gives me a little say in how things go around here, which is nice. I'm doing all right, thanks very much. So I guess you can take me off your little list."

It sure sounded like it. "I don't really have a list, Mr. Nickerson."

"Lou."

"There's no list, Lou. You were pretty much it. And that was only because I knew you owned that land – you were the only one I could think of that might have had a motive, and I can see that I was wrong."

"Well, no hard feelings, son, but yeah, you were definitely wrong. The way I feel about that property is this: It's going to get developed someday, there's no way around that. And when it does it's going to be worth quite a bit of money. After all, they're not making any more beachfront property. But I've got two grown kids, and both of them have kids. My grandkids could probably use the money a lot more than I can. Until then, it's in the bank; it's just sitting there getting more valuable every day. But in the meantime I can walk my dog down there, or I can have a cookout or a picnic, and nobody can say anything to me, and to me that's worth a lot. Worth more than some damn mutual fund that might lose half its value tomorrow. My grandfather bought that land over fifty years ago for a song. Whatever we get out of it eventually, whenever we get it, it's just gravy."

End of story, I thought. I believed him completely. "You're on the town council, huh?"

Nickerson leaned back in his chair and smiled. "Yeah. I guess it's more of a hobby than anything, we don't have all that much to do in a place as small as Dewey. But I get a say in zoning issues, and if I call because some kids are having a rowdy party I can pretty much count on the police showing up right away."

"Do you know a guy named Daniel Morgan?"

Nickerson shot me a look that I couldn't interpret. It was somewhere between surprise and distaste with maybe a little anger in the mix. There was certainly nothing positive there. "Yeah, I know Dan."

No details. That threw it into my court. "Can you tell me anything about him?"

"Why?"

Suddenly the warmth had gone out of the air like when the sun goes behind a cloud on a breezy day. "No real reason. I met him. I had a kind of a meeting with him, and I don't know…I got a bit of a strange feeling, especially afterwards."

"Left a bad taste in your mouth? Dan can do that to people."

"Well, something happened and it seemed like he was the only one who could have made it happen, and I was just wondering about him."

"What happened?"

"Ah, it was nothing, really. I met with Morgan, and I told him I was looking into things a little. An hour later I get pulled over for speeding and the officer lets it slide that he knows I'm looking into things. I'd been pretty careful to keep a low profile, so I was wondering how he knew about it. It just struck me as odd."

Nickerson was silent for a few moments. Still leaning back in his chair, he contemplated his hands, which were folded over his stomach. He looked up and said, "Look. I don't want to get into any specifics. Dan Morgan has some pull around here, and I live here. I don't need any excess bullshit in my life, if you follow me. But I wouldn't turn my back on Dan Morgan, and I recommend that you adhere to the same strategy." He rose. "And now I'm afraid I'll have to let you go. Got a lot to do today."

I stood as well, and we shook. "Thanks for your time, Mr. Nickerson."

"You're welcome. Stop by again."

"Thanks. Say goodbye to Mrs. Nickerson for me."

"I'll do that." With that he turned and retreated into the house. Rather quickly, I thought. I stood there for a moment looking after him. I couldn't have been dismissed more quickly or effectively if he had set the hounds on me. Probably didn't have any hounds handy.

I walked back around the building, reaching the street just as a jackbooted thug placed a parking ticket beneath my wiper blade. Actually it was an attractive dark-haired young lady in navy shorts and a powder blue short-sleeved shirt with the logo of the Dewey police on the shoulder. But hey, she was still a minion of the guvmint, dammit. I'm being oppressed, I thought, and smiled. Monty Python still cracks me up. I placed the ticket in the glove compartment. It was getting crowded in there. I was only a half-mile or so from home –from Dickie's house, that is – and it was getting close to lunchtime if the empty feeling in my stomach was any indication, so I decided to swing by the house and see if Robert was still there. There were a few things I wanted to talk with him about, and lunch seemed like it would be as good a time as any.

But Robert's rental car wasn't in the driveway when I pulled in so I didn't stop and go inside. I don't know much, but one thing I knew for certain is that there was no food in that house. If you don't count pork rinds, and I don't. I turned the car around in time to see a police car cruise past the end of the drive but when I got back to the street it was no longer fin sight. I thought it had been a Dewey cruiser but I had only gotten a brief glimpse so I wasn't sure. And, I told myself, there was no reason a cruiser couldn't drive past the driveway, even though the house wasn't officially in Dewey. And for all I really knew, it could have been a damn taxi.

I drove out to Route One, with the idea of grabbing a couple of slices of pizza at the Grotto just over the line in Rehoboth. Grotto Pizza is a fair-sized chain of restaurants and something of a Delaware shore tradition. It's not great, in my book, but it's not bad. It didn't take long for my slices to be ready and as I ate I wondered what to do next. I was in a booth by the front of the restaurant, looking out at the steady stream of traffic on the highway, so I could hardly miss the car with the large "Dewey Beach Police" logo on the door and the lights on top when it turned into the lot. I was in Rehoboth, but there's no law that says cops can't cross town lines for a piece of pizza. After all, cops get hungry, too. And it was getting a little late in the day for donuts. The cruiser stopped just behind my car and idled there for a minute or two as I watched through the window wondering what the hell he was doing. I couldn't see into the car from where I sat, so I couldn't tell who was behind the wheel. Certainly he wasn't being very secretive. I wasn't in any hurry to run out and confront the officer, but when I had finished my pizza and my coke was down to ice I couldn't see any real reason I should stay inside and hide either so I walked out into the sunshine.

As soon as I came around the corner the cruiser pulled slowly away, easing around the other side of the building just a bit faster than I was walking toward it. By the time I reached the Impala the cruiser was out of sight. I stood there for a few seconds and saw the cruiser reappear as it turned on to Route One and then pulled away smoothly with traffic. Shielding my eyes against the sun I watched until I lost him in the distance. I wondered if it was the same car that had cruised by the Dickie's driveway but there was no way to tell . I wondered if Hartner was trying to send me a message. Maybe the message was that I was being watched. Maybe he was trying to intimidate me. If that was it, it wasn't working. Last time I checked, pizza was still legal.

"So what are we looking for?" came a female voice from beside me. Startled, I jumped about ten feet in the air. When I landed I saw that it was Denise, mimicking me, looking off into the distance and shielding her eyes from the sun with her hand. It reminded me of a scene from the Marx bothers, and I think it was supposed to. Either that or the Three Stooges. "Sorry," she said when I had composed myself. "Are we a bit jumpy today?"

"I don't know if we are," I said, "but I guess I am, yeah. Where'd you come from?"

"I was over at the drug store," she jerked her head towards the large Ames pharmacy that's behind the Grotto but on the other side of the access road. "I pulled out and I saw you standing there looking off to the horizon like a cigar store Indian and I thought I'd have some fun with you."

"Did you?"

"Did I what?"

"Have some fun?"

She smiled fleetingly and looked down at her bare feet. "Yeah," she said. "Yeah, I did."

I surprised myself by asking, "Do you think maybe we could go out sometime? For a drink or something?" A moment before I said it I couldn't have told you what I was about to say. I guess my mouth just sort of took charge and left my brain out of the decision. But that's happened before.

"Ummm," she said.

"We don't have to," I said quickly. I hate rejection. It makes me feel so...rejected. Besides, even though I was on the outs with Bunny, wasn't I still...?

Shut up, I told my brain.

"No, that's not it," she said quickly. "I'd love to. But I've been off work for the last few days while my sister and her family are in town – I traded shifts with everybody – and today's my last day off for like two weeks. I don't know when we could go. Except tonight, I guess."

"Tonight works for me," I said, hoping that I didn't sound too eager even though I was. "Wait. I have to be in Ocean City at eleven tonight to meet somebody at Fager's. I could bring you back early, or if you wanted, we could go down there together. I just have to see this guy for a few minutes."

"Well, how about we play it by ear."

An eminently reasonable suggestion. One I might have come up with myself if my brain was working. "Okay. Can I pick you up? Do you want to eat dinner? Where do you want to go?"

"Whoa. Whoa, Cowboy." At least she was still smiling. I, on the other hand, was for some reason suddenly sweating. I think I may be a bit out of practice at this dating business. "I have to eat dinner with my sister and the kids," she said. "It's their last night here. How does eight o'clock sound?"

"Perfect. I'll pick you up at eight. See you then." I turned towards my car.

"Hey," she said.

"Yeah?"

"Don't you want to know where I live?"

Nineteen

On Route One in traffic a few minutes later, I realized that I was smiling. I hadn't been doing a lot of smiling lately, and it felt a little strange. But it felt good, and I didn't want to lose the feeling. I turned the car radio on and for the millionth time I wished that WRNR's signal was strong enough to reach the beach, but I wasn't going to let a small thing like the abysmal commercial dreck that passes for radio at this and every beach resort I've ever visited bother me. No, nor the horrible crawling traffic, the squeal of worn-out brakes, the smoke of ill-tuned engines, the mind-numbing stop and go and stop, the heat and the smells and the blaring rap coming from the rusty dented red Mustang with one grey quarter panel in the next lane, no, that wasn't going to bother me either, not today. Because suddenly I was feeling a bit different about things, about everything, and it felt good, felt like a weight had been removed from my chest, a weight that I hadn't even known was there but whose absence made it possible to breathe again, to breathe some fresh air and clear the cobwebs out of my mind.

Even if there was no fresh air, out here on Highway One.

And it wasn't just the lovely Denise, the thought of the date this evening, the anticipation of what might – or of course might not – happen. That was part of it, I knew that. But what I was feeling was more in the vein of that horrible hackneyed term, "closure". It had taken a while but now I realized I wasn't going back to D.C., to PDS, to any of that. For a while I had been feeling that I was more at home here at the shore than I was back in Washington. Back there there had been friends, and a job, and an apartment, and a whole web, a chain, a universe of things that constituted my life for a long time. And now they were gone. Reynard was dead. Big Eddie Jones had retired from the police and moved to L.A. to be near his daughter, who was chasing stardom. Bunny wanted nothing to do with me and the feeling was at last mutual. Lenny was moving to the suburbs and taking up golf, for God's sake. Ted, despite the fact that it turned out to be something of a favor, had slept with Bunny behind my back and I need more from a friend than that. Besides he had left, so the question, as Reverend Jesse might say, is moot. I guess I could have felt lost, cut off from the things and people I had come to care about. I didn't. It was good riddance to it all. Time to start over. And now there was a house, and maybe a girl, and a place that's pretty nice, pretty nice except for the goddamn road I was on while thinking about all of this, and here was where it was going to be, this new life. And this is where he was going to live, at least for a while, this new William Flaherty.

And I owed it all to one person, who unfortunately was dead. Truth be told I had been feeling a little burned out about trying to figure out what had happened to poor Dickie. I wasn't getting anywhere with it. I was pussyfooting around trying to keep from getting in trouble with Hartner. I just wasn't doing much that was particularly constructive or effective. But that, I decided, was just about to change. And the hell with the consequences. If I couldn't lay it on the line for Dickie, then I didn't deserve the gift he had given me, the gift of a chance for a new life, and I might as well slink back to D.C. with my tail between my legs and go back to work.

It was time, past time, to get this done. Traffic broke up a bit as I crossed the bridge over the Intracoastal and I turned off onto Bay Road, right by the liquor store and the Captain's Table restaurant, and cut through the private streets of the condominium neighborhood that lines most of the north side of Lake Comegys, ignoring as usual the strident "No Thru Traffic – Private – Residents Only" signs. Nobody's stopped me yet and I've gone through there a hundred times. A couple of minutes later I was back at the house and this time Robert's car was there, so I parked and went in.

Robert was on the phone when I walked into the kitchen, and he raised an eyebrow in greeting, and did one of those "talkie hand" gestures that indicate that the person on the other end of the line won't shut up. Robert's end of the conversation was a series of attempts to get a word in edgewise: "But…yeah, but….but…look, I…I know, but…yeah, I ….well, I….but…". This went on for some time. After a while it was pretty amusing. Finally, he said, "Okay. I'll call you later," and then he hung up. He heaved a huge sigh and asked, "What's up?"

"Not much. I came by to see if you could use any help."

He looked at me strangely. "With what?"

"Whatever. Arrangements for the funeral, anything."

"Oh. Ummm…I don't know. I've got to make some phone calls, I guess. If there's something I need, I'll let you know, okay?"

"Yeah, sure. Is it going to be here? Or do you know?"

"I dunno. Look, I only got here last night, and I've been running around. I'll let you know when I know more, okay?"

"Yeah, sure. Just trying to help."

"I get it," he snapped. "Message received, okay?" He looked at his watch and said, "Shit. I'm late. I gotta go. See ya."

"See ya."

He strode out the kitchen door and a moment later I heard his car door slam and then the sound of an engine. I was still sitting at the counter as the car crunched down the drive and away. I wondered what he could possibly be late for - he'd been here one day, and so far he wasn't even dealing with the funeral. I decided that there was no sense in worrying about it. It could be anything at all. Frankly, I wasn't all that concerned about it.

I rummaged around in the cabinets until I found the phone books. I looked under Kavanagh and there was only one in Henlopen Acres. The first initial was "J". Bingo. I picked up the phone to call but thought better of it considering I had no idea what to say. Instead I wrote down the address and the phone number, went out and hopped in the car and rode up there.

Henlopen Acres is more like a wealthy suburb than a beach resort, with large homes set well back from the winding roads on large heavily treed lots. The beach is moments away but you'd never know it. Tucked away north of Rehoboth and south of the undeveloped expanse of Cape Henlopen state park, Henlopen Acres is a quiet little world of its own. I hadn't been up there much, and it took me a while to find the address. When I did find it, I parked on the street in front of the house and sat in the car for a moment. The house was one of the largest in a neighborhood of large homes. It was constructed of fieldstone with a slate roof and the front yard was bountifully and carefully landscaped, with masses of rhododendrons and azaleas clustered beneath soaring oaks and maples. A woman was working in a flower bed and after I had been there a few seconds she stood and began walking towards where I was parked. I climbed out of the car.

"May I help you?" she inquired evenly. She was perhaps sixty but still quite beautiful, even dressed in dirt-stained work clothes. She was trim and tan, and her hair, though greying, was long and straight, tied back from her face and falling down her back.

"Um, yes, I hope so. I was looking for Jerry Kavanagh's home."

"Jerry lived here," she replied. "I'm Maureen Kavanagh. He was my son." I noted the past tense.

"My name is Bill Flaherty. Would it be possible for me to ask you a couple of questions about Jerry?"

"Questions? Are you with the police, or the press?"

"Neither, Ma'am."

"Then what's your interest? If you're here to talk about Jerry you must know this is a difficult time."

"I do, and I'm sorry. But you see, a friend of mine was killed a couple of weeks ago, and Jerry was involved…"

Her eyebrows shop up at that one and I quickly added, "I don't mean to say that Jerry killed anybody. I really have no idea about that. But…well, do you have a couple of minutes? I could tell you what I know, and then maybe you wouldn't mind answering my questions."

"Isn't this a police matter?"

"It is, ma'am. But they don't seem to be doing anything that I can tell about my friend's death, and I'm trying to take the bull by the horns. And I have a strong feeling –really I'm positive – that Jerry's, uh, demise is tied in with Dickie's."

"Did you say Dickie? Dickie Harrington?"

"Yea, ma'am, that's, that was my friend who died."

"How terrible. I've known Dickie since he was a boy. We went to parties in that house years ago, when his grandfather was still alive, and I remember little Dickie running around…it was such a shock to hear that he had passed. And now Jerry." She shook her head wearily, looking down at the ground. For a moment I thought she was going to cry, but she rallied. "Why don't you come in and have a glass of lemonade, and we'll see what we can figure out together."

"That would be great."

"Follow me, then."

Inside the house it was deliciously cool. We entered through the side door into a mud room that was about as big as my apartment back in D.C. and I followed Mrs. Kavanagh into a spotless kitchen with dozens of cherry cabinets and acres of light marble countertops. There was a breakfast nook off the kitchen and she indicated a chair at the table in the nook. "Have a seat, won't you? I'll get the lemonade."

I sat and fished a notebook and a pen out of my pack and set them on the table. As I waited for Mrs. Kavanagh to join me I looked around. There was a partial view of a living furnished in dark wood and oriental carpets visible though an arched doorway, and that was all I could see of the rest of house from my vantage point. Somewhere deep in the house someone was running a vacuum cleaner. The breakfast nook had large windows that looked out onto the back yard, which was at least as lush as the front, if less formal. There was a wooden playground set off to one side that appeared to be of relatively recent vintage. I was still looking out the window when Mrs. Kavanagh returned. She set a Waterford crystal glass filled with lemonade and ice on the table before me and sat down opposite me.

"Do you have little ones?" I asked.

"Oh, no. My children are grown. But why…?" She followed my gaze and saw the playground set. "Oh, that. That's for the grandkids when they visit. Jerry's kids, mostly. They stay here – or they did, I don't know what's going to happen now - every other weekend."

"Jerry was married?"

"Divorced. It didn't work out, like a lot of things in his life."

"What do you mean? Do you mind if I take a few notes?"

"No, go ahead, I don't mind." She took a sip of lemonade and shifted uneasily in chair. "I loved Jerry," she said. "He was my son. Of course I loved him. But he was…I want to say star-crossed, but that's not it. Things never worked out for Jerry because he was always looking for a shortcut, an easy way to make it big. He always had schemes and plans, and they never seemed to pan out."

"Surveying seems an odd way to go about making it big."

"He got into that because of my husband. John was quite a successful real estate developer, and he wanted Jerry to join the firm, but he made Jerry start at the bottom. Thank goodness he did, too. At least Jerry had a trade to fall back on. Not that it matters much now, I suppose."

"How did Jerry get involved with the environmental movement?"

"To the extent that he did, and he wasn't all that gung-ho about it, it was a reaction against his father, I think. Jerry's Dad let him go from the firm. Jerry deserved it, more than deserved it – he'd skip work for days at a time, he fudged his expenses, he wouldn't finish his work – and it reflected badly on his father. Other employees were talking, morale was bad, the firm lost a couple of good employees, and finally his father fired him. After that, Jerry decided that his Dad was an evil developer, raping Mother Earth for profit. I don't think he really believed it, but that's what he would say."

"But Jerry lived here, with you and his Dad?"

"Mr. Kavanagh passed away six years ago. After Jerry got divorced I let him live here. I didn't mind, I could use the company, and there's plenty of space."

"Who would you say his close friends and associates were?"

"Well, that's a little hard to say. He didn't hang around with anyone in particular all that much that I knew of. There were a couple of boys – men, now, I guess – that he went to school with that he would mention from time to time. Lee Swift, Derrick Hamilton, maybe one or two others, but it wasn't like they palled around, he never brought them by the house. Jerry knew Dickie, of course, since he was a child, since we socialized with his grandparents, but I haven't heard him mention his name for years."

"I never heard Dickie mention him."

She sighed. "It doesn't surprise me."

"Was there a girlfriend. And what about his ex? Did he see her much?"

"He hardly ever saw Cindy. Just when he'd pick up the kids and drop them off, perhaps once in a while around town. They weren't close at all any more. As far as a girlfriend, he mentioned a young lady once or twice – I think her name was Marla, Carla, something like that – but he didn't seem all that interested. He really wasn't all that interested in very much, I'm afraid. Just in getting rich without working at it."

"Hey, it's the American Dream."

She shook her head. "I'm afraid you're right, God help us."

Twenty

I left Mrs. Kavanagh at the table and showed myself out. She had been brutally honest about her son and it had worn on her. What parent would want to admit to a stranger that their own child, their prematurely dead child, had been a failure? She had put on a brave front – maybe she was just brave and it wasn't a front – but before I left she was crying quietly. I wasn't feeling too good about things as I drove away.

But at least I had a plan. Well, maybe a plan is an exaggeration. But it was obvious to me that Jerry's death and Dickie's were connected. And if I didn't have much to go on regarding Dickie, at least I had some names and numbers to follow up on with Jerry. I called directory assistance on my cell phone and got the numbers and addresses for Lee Swift and Derrick Hamilton. It took me two calls, the phone company clearly thinking I wasn't paying enough for the service already. Lee Swift's address was closer so I went there first. The house was in Rehoboth just off Route One behind the Company Store, a grocery market known for low prices and a somewhat primitive ambiance. The Company Store occupies a group of interconnected building that have been cobbled together haphazardly and which would seem destined to collapse in the next windstorm. Or strong breeze. The neighborhood behind the store, tucked between the highway and the canal and closed off from the rest of the town by an electrical substation, the trash and recycling transfer station and a water purification plant, is one of the more modest in the area and that's putting it mildly. Small bungalows with peeling paint and overgrown yards crowd each other and the street. Rusty ragged waist high chain link fence lines many of the yards, and there's a serious littering problem among the residents. Small dirty kids of every hue rode junky bikes aimlessly in the street or chased each other past old cars that sat up on blocks. The contrast with Henlopen Acres could hardly have been more complete. I found the address I was looking for and parked out front. For a moment I considered locking my car, and I never lock my car, not even in Washington. Generally my philosophy is that there's nothing to steal in the vehicle, so why lock it? It just makes it harder for someone to get in and they might wreck something trying to gain entry. Leave the car open and they can open the door and see there's nothing there.

I walked up the short path, stepping over broken toys and rusted tools, and knocked on the front door. A small dog began yapping inside, followed quickly by a muffled curse and what sounded like something being thrown. The barking stopped and the door opened a crack, revealing a tall thin hollow-cheeked white man of about thirty in a sleeveless tee shirt and dirty jeans. His hair was long and looked like it hadn't been washed in weeks, and a drooping mustache that badly needed a trim covered much of his face. He was holding a can of

Bud, from which he took a healthy slug before saying, "Choo want?"

"Are you Lee Smith?"

"Zaskin'?

"Zaskin?"

"Ah said, who's askin'?"

"Oh. Sorry." I took a mental note to brush up on my redneckese. Looked like it might come in handy. "My names Bill Flaherty. I was hoping to ask you a few questions about Jerry Kavanagh."

"Yew po-lice?"

"No, I'm…"

The door slammed in my face. Wrong answer, I guess. But I'm nothing if not intrepid, so I knocked again. This time the door opened wide, to reveal Mr. Swift, if indeed it was he, with a shotgun under his arm. I took a step back. I can take a hint. A dog, apparently the one that had been barking, came charging out of the house between the man's legs. It looked like some sort of Jack Russell mix, small and sturdy with short legs. It was angry. Probably it didn't have a fulfilling home life. It went for my ankle and somehow I managed to grab it by the scruff of its neck as it charged, lifting the little ball of fury high above the floor. The dog struggled for a moment, then went limp, apparently not eager to fall onto the cement walkway. "This yours?" I asked Swift. He was laughing so hard he could barely breathe, the barrel of his shotgun bobbing alarmingly as he bent over and slapped his knees.

"Serve that li'l sonofabitch right if you dropkicked his ass," he said, still laughing. "Man, you all right. Here, hand 'im over." I handed the calm but indignant beast to its owner, who flung it into the house, where it landed with a crash and a yipe. Swift closed the door before the dog could gather its senses for another charge, then he indicated the top step of the stoop. "Have a seat," he said, and considering he was still holding the shotgun, I did so. He sat next to me, leaned the shotgun against a rusted wrought-iron railing, then stuck his hand out. "Lee Swift," he said. "Pleased to meet ya."

"Bill Flaherty," I said, shaking his callused hand.

"Jerry's dead, you know that, right?"

"Yeah, I was the one who found him, actually."

"Zat right?"

"Yeah. Me and Chief Hartner, from Dewey."

At the mention of Hartner Swift's eyes narrowed. "That sonofabitch."

"Don't like him, huh?"

"Shithead's been after my ass for years. What'd you say you were doin' here?"

"I just wanted to ask you a few questions, see if maybe I could help figure out who killed Jerry."

"Shit, I'll save you some time. Jerry killed Jerry."

"You think it was suicide?"

"I say that? Nope. Jerry was such an asshole, was bound to catch up with him, and finally it did. Boy screwed one too many people. It's his own fault. Boy needed killin'. Why you care about Jerry anyway? You family?"

"Uh, no. It's kind of a long story."

"Shit, I got all day. Want a beer?"

"Sure, if you can keep that killer dog under control. I don't think I could be that lucky twice."

"You know," he said, rising, "I get the feeling you're selling yourself short."

Twenty-One

Less than an hour later I was back in my car, heading for Derrick Hamilton's house. My visit with Lee Swift had been less than completely successful. Lee and Jerry had met in high school, and they had kept in touch mainly because Lee was a small-time pot dealer and Jerry was a world-class pothead. Jerry would stop by Lee's house every couple of weeks, at least once a month, and they would hang out for a while sometimes, drink a beer, smoke a joint, shoot the breeze. "But he was a drag, man," Lee had said. "Always bitchin' about bein' broke, or about something his ex did to piss him off, or about how his mom wouldn't give him any money." Jerry would ramble on about his latest plot, which was sure to launch him into the big time, but there was never any evidence that it was anything but talk.

Lee had last seen Jerry about ten days earlier, and he remarked that Jerry had seemed more upbeat than usual, but that he didn't know what the reason was because Jerry had only stayed a few minutes. And that had been more or less it. As I had walked out the door a Police cruiser was turning the corner down the block, but it was out of sight before I reached the curb. I didn't worry about it. It was easy to imagine that the police spent a fair amount of time in that neighborhood.

Derrick Hamilton lived in a tenant house on a large farm off Route One north of Lewes. It took me some time to find the lane that led to the house and when I did I drove over a mile back off the highway on a narrow crushed-shell road – more like a path - with tall corn arching over from both sides and nearly meeting in the middle. It was like driving in a green tunnel, with just a sliver of sky visible above. Just when I was sure I was lost I came into a clearing with a couple of sheds, a patch of lawn, several large trees and a house. A huge green John Deere tractor was parked under one of the trees, and a classic black Pontiac GTO, maybe a '69 or a '70, was parked under another, an assortment of tools scattered around it on the ground. The house itself was tidy, a simple square two-story affair painted barn red, with a large front porch and a metal roof that glinted in the afternoon sun. A couple of large dogs of undetermined breed emerged from under the front porch as I pulled up, and they came running over to my car. They seemed friendly enough but I stayed in the car to give them a chance to get used to my presence. Before I got out of the car a stocky blond man of about thirty came out of the house, stood on the porch and called the dogs off. He was wearing well-worn jeans and had no shirt on. He held a large crescent wrench in one hand, but loosely and not in a threatening fashion, so I climbed out.

"I'm looking for Derrick Hamilton," I called.

"Well, you found him," he replied. "Who're you?"

"Bill Flaherty. I'd like to ask you a few questions."

"You selling something?"

"Nope. Not a thing. It's about Jerry Kavanagh."

"What'd that asshole do this time?"

"Got himself killed."

There was a pause while he absorbed this information. Then he shook his head and said, "Well, I can't say that that comes as a complete surprise. Come on up."

I walked over and climbed the three steps up to the porch with the dogs underfoot sniffing me the whole way. I nearly tripped over one of them on the top stair, and Hamilton shooed them away. "Don't mind them," he said. "They're friendly. Just curious as all hell. Don't get a lot of company out here." He scratched one of the dogs behind the ear. "You're not with the police," he said.

"No."

"Then why would you want to ask me questions? Were you a friend of Jerry's?"

"No. I only met the man once, for about five minutes. A good friend of mine got killed, and then Jerry got killed. It seems like the two things are connected – in fact I'm sure of it. I haven't been able to figure out what happened to my friend so I'm trying to figure out what happened to Jerry. I'm kinda looking for a back door."

"Huh. Have a seat."

We both sat. A dog came over and stuck his head in my lap, waiting to be patted. "G'wan outta there," said my host. "Leave the man alone."

"Oh, I like dogs," I said truthfully. I'm not crazy about tripping over them, or having them stick their faces in my groin, but I like them in general.

"You do, huh?"

"Yeah."

"Well we got some puppies, if you're interested."

"Uh…" I couldn't think of anything else to say. I certainly hadn't been planning on getting a dog.

"Come on," he said. "I'll show 'em to you." He jumped down off the side of the porch and waved for me to join him. "They're over in the shed here with their mommy."

I followed him. I couldn't think of an excuse not to. And believe me, I tried. We walked over to the smallest of the sheds and Derrick pulled the door open. In an instant half a dozen or more tiny bundles of fluff and energy tumbled through the doorway followed by their mother, who looked on tolerantly as her pups played. This was getting serious. The one real rule if you like dogs but don't want one right at the moment is stay away from puppies. They have a way of getting to you.

The puppies were rolling around, jumping over each other and on me and on Derrick, yipping, yapping and nipping and I almost did it. I almost picked one of them up. That's the second rule: Don't pick the puppy up. It's a slippery slope from there. Actually, looking at them, I actually considered it for a moment. I like dogs. But today wasn't the day. I was on a mission, I reminded myself, and it wasn't a mission to get a pet.

After a while I stood and shook my head at Derrick, who was standing off to the side with his arms crossed and an amused look on his face. "I can't do it. Not right now at least."

"Well, that's okay," he said with the ease of a polished salesman. "They're not weaned yet anyway. Be a couple weeks before they're ready to go. All I'm asking is fifty bucks, and that's just to cover their shots and worming. I won't make any money off them, but I need them to go to good homes. Which one do you like?"

"What kind of dogs are they?"

"Mutts," he said unapologetically. "Half German Shepherd, half everything else. Their Mommy got a visit from a traveling man. So which one do you like?"

"I don't know," I said. I nodded at a jet-black female with white paws, a white blaze on her chest and a tail which ended in a white tip. "This black one seems nice."

"She's yours, then," he said before I could sputter my objections. "Come back in a couple of weeks and she'll be ready to go."

It was easier to go along than argue. Besides, a couple of weeks was a long time. Maybe I could get out of it somehow. Derrick shooed the dogs back into the shed, closed the door, and then turned to face me. "So," he said, obviously and justifiably pleased with his salesmanship. "What was it you wanted to know about Jerry?"

"Do you know anybody who might have reason to kill him?"

"Not really, I guess. I mean, he was always scamming, always trying to get over, and he was a real pain sometimes too. He pissed people off. A lot of people didn't like him. He owed people money. But kill him? I guess I can't think of anybody who'd do that, not offhand. Doesn't mean there wasn't somebody, though."

"Well, he is dead."

He nodded. "There's that."

"How'd you meet Jerry?"

"He was doing some surveying out here. My dad was thinking about selling off some of the farm, up by the highway."

"This is your Dad's farm?"

"Yup. Be mine someday, I guess, if things go according to plan."

"Where does your dad live?"

"In the big house. Here on the farm. You might have seen it from the highway if you came from the north, but you came from Dewey, right?"

"How'd you know that?"

"Got a call."

"Lee Swift?"

"Yup."

"Lee a friend of yours?"

"That's putting it a little strong. I known Lee a long time. He used to work here on the farm. Hell of a mechanic, when he's sober, which isn't often."

We stood there in silence for a moment. There was the sound of a tractor in the distance somewhere. A crow yelled insults at us from the safety of a high tree limb. Otherwise it was very quiet. I couldn't hear the highway at all. "How big is the farm, if you don't mind me asking?" I asked.

"Hell, I don't mind. About twenty-six hundred acres. Plus we lease about another thousand. Pretty fair sized."

"Jesus. I guess." I did some math. They owned about four square miles. Nice spread.

"Yeah, I guess that's what got Jerry onto me in the first place. Farm this size is worth a fair amount of money. And Jerry never saw money he didn't like, as long as it came easy. And his Dad was some big developer, and he thought he could broker a deal and get a cut."

"What kind of deal?"

"Oh, golf courses, houses, every damn thing. My Dad went along, at first, but he didn't really want to sell, and

I didn't want him to either, so nothing came of it. Funny thing was that Jerry still came around after, and we got to be friends after a while. He wasn't such a bad guy when he'd relax a little. And out here he was able to unwind, maybe let go, more than it seemed like he could other places." He looked around. "It is sorta peaceful."

It was, although the tractor that I had heard was getting closer, and a few seconds later it rumbled around the last bend in the road and into sight. It was a giant eight-wheeled John Deere with an air-conditioned cab, pulling a trailer with a large plastic tank containing some kind of liquid. Behind the wheel was a man who looked very familiar. It took me a second, but I realized it was the short round-faced man who had been assisting Jerry the day I saw him surveying at Dickie's place. Derrick waved and the man waved back, continuing past us and on up the road without giving me a second look. When quiet returned I said, "Who was that driving that tractor?"

"Hired hand. George Shaw. Why?"

"I've seen him somewhere before. I was just trying to place him." I wasn't sure why I lied, I just did it. "Does he live in Rehoboth?"

"Nah, he lives here on the farm, in a little tenant house up by the highway. Been here forever. Harmless guy. Good worker."

I debated asking more about the guy but let it go. "Who else do you think I should talk to about Jerry?"

"What do you mean?"

"Who else knew him, who might have hated him, liked him, whatever."

"Well, you could talk to his ex, Cindy. I think she's up in Wilmington or somewhere. And he was seeing that little girl Darla, you might talk to her."

When Mrs. Kavanagh had mentioned the girlfriend she hadn't gotten the name right. But Derrick had, and it rung a bell. "This Darla, does she work for the state parks?"

"You know, I think she does in the summer. Parking attendant or something at one of the parks. She lives somewhere down by Bethany, far's I know. Never been to her place. Jerry brought her out here one time when we had a bull roast. Fourth of July weekend." Nice little thing. Kinda plain. Kinda quiet. But nice."

I nodded. "Look, I can use any help I can get. Why don't I give you my number, and if you think of anything useful, give me a call, okay?"

"Sure. I don't know what it would be, though. Spend most of my time right here on the farm."

"Well, just in case." I got a piece of paper from the car, scribbled down the number at Dickie's place, and gave it to him. "Hey, you wouldn't mind if I talked to Mr. Shaw, would you? I'd like to figure out where I've seen him before."

"No, it doesn't bother me any. Best thing to do would be to ride on over to his place and wait for him. He must be about done for the day. Here, I'll draw you a map through the farm. Shorter than goin' all the way back out to the highway." I gave him a piece of paper and he drew the map. When he gave it to me I thanked him and we shook hands. As I was walking back to the car he called, "Two weeks."

I turned back, puzzled. "Two weeks what?"

"Your puppy. Better start thinking about a name for her. Come on out and see her anytime you want."

"Uh, okay," I said. "Thanks."

As I drove away Derrick was leaning over the open hood of the GTO, wrench in hand. It didn't seem like a bad way to live. I followed the map Derrick had given me through endless fields, past a pond and a complex with silos and barns and eventually came out to the verge of the highway, where the farm road turned to parallel the roadway. A couple of hundred yards down there were three small houses, the middle one of which, Derrick had told me, was occupied by Shaw. I parked out in front and went up and knocked. There was no answer so I knocked again, more insistently. Still there was no answer. The house was close enough to the highway that I could feel the breeze when large trucks swept past. I had just decided to leave when the door opened. Shaw stood there, buckling his belt and grumbling, "Can't a man use the bathroom around here, for God's sake?" He paused looked at me without a hint of recognition and said, "I ain't buying anything today, Mister."

I was starting to think I must look like some sort of door-to-door salesman. "I'm not selling anything, Mr. Shaw. I just wanted to ask you a few questions."

"What about?"

"Jerry Kavanagh."

"What about him?"

"He's dead."

"Huh."

"You don't seem all that interested."

"Nope, can't say that I am."

"But you worked for him, didn't you?"

"Gave him a hand a few times when Derrick told me to, that's about it."

"Do you remember meeting me?"

"Yup. Damn near to give me a heart attack."

"What can you tell me about that day?"

"Not much. Jerry he came by in the mornin', asked Derrick if he could borrow me, things here was pretty slow, so Derrick he said all right."

"Then what happened?"

"Drove over there, surveyed that place, ran into you, got yelled at about ten times by Jerry, went home."

"Jerry didn't tell you who hired him, did he?"

"Nope."

"Anything else happen, anything unusual, out of the ordinary at all."

"Nope. Was late for my dinner cause that damn Jerry kept talking so long."

"Talking to who? Me?"

"Nope, to that police fella. And that other fella. Three of 'em must've argued for a damn hour."

"Which police fella?"

"Don't know his name. I seen him in Dewey, though."

"What's he look like?"

"Like he's half dead. Skinny, tired looking guy. Maybe sixty."

That sounded like Bellegarde. He'd been looking into Dickie's murder, I knew that, so it seemed reasonable that he'd come by the house and ask questions. "Who was the other guy?"

"Don't know. Never saw him before. Maybe forty, forty-five. Dark hair."

"That could be a lot of people."

"Yeah. Yeah, I reckon it could. I can't help that."

I waited in hopes that he might come up with more details but none wee forthcoming. "Could you hear what they were talking about?"

"Nope. Not a word. They went off walking together a ways, then stood there talking. Looked like Jerry wasn't none too happy when he come back, but he didn't tell me nothin' an' I didn't ask."

"Okay, thanks. Was there anything else? Did Jerry make any stops, or talk to anyone else? Say anything else?"

"Nope. Look, I got to get some chow on. We done?"

"Yeah, I guess so. Thanks."

Shaw just nodded, turned and went inside and closed the door without a word. Loquacious fellow. But the one thing he had told me was interesting. Might not mean anything, probably didn't mean anything, but it was still interesting. Jerry had had a heated discussion with a police officer and another man. The police officer might be Bellegarde. The other man might be just about anybody. I looked at my watch and saw that it was after five. I thought about paying Bellegarde a visit. But considering I wasn't supposed to be investigating it was hard to think how I could go about asking him questions. I looked at my watch and saw that it was well past five. Any questioning was going to have to wait for tomorrow. It was time to go home and get washed up. It wouldn't do to pick up Denise stinking like sweat and yesterday's beer.

Twenty-Two

Robert's rental car was in the driveway when I pulled in, but when I went inside and called his name there was no answer. I looked around and found that he wasn't in the house, so I went upstairs and took a shower. When I got out of the shower I heard voices downstairs. I got dressed and went down, but by the time I got downstairs Robert was alone, sitting on the couch with a beer in his hand and a magazine spread open on his lap. He looked bloated and tired, as though the pork rinds-and-beer diet wasn't doing him any good.

"What's up?" he said without any real interest in his voice.

"Not much. Was somebody here?"

"Yeah. Chief Hartner. He just left."

"What'd he want?"

"He was just asking some questions."

"About what?"

"This and that. Dickie. Et cetera."

"Made any headway on the funeral?"

"Some. Got a funeral home. Service is Saturday, ten o'clock. Don't know what we're gonna do with the ashes yet. My folks are coming in tomorrow. I'll talk it over with them." He paused, then added, "They're staying in a hotel."

"They could stay here. There's plenty of room."

Robert took a long swig of his beer, belched, and said, "Oh no. I don't need that on top of everything else, thank you very much."

"Suit yourself."

"Thanks, I will." He eyed me suspiciously. "What are you all dressed up for?"

"Got a date."

"Hey, all right. Li'l Billy gonna get him some."

"I doubt that. It's not a priority, at least."

He mocked me, mouthing my words back at me, then said "Well, even a blind squirrel finds a nut once in a while, my man."

"Yeah, well, screw you, too."

"Aw, lighten up, I'm jes' funnin' ya."

"Man, that's one sorry Southern accent you got there, Robert."

"Works on the good ole boys."

"It would."

"What's that supposed to mean?"

"Nothing. Look, I gotta go. See ya."

"All right."

I picked my keys up off the counter and left. I was a couple of minutes down the road when I realized I didn't have my wallet. I'm not too proud to go Dutch, but it wouldn't do to go out on a first date and make her pay for everything, so I pulled a U-turn, and went back. I went in the kitchen door, grabbed my wallet from the counter where I had left it, and turned to go. From the living room I heard Robert's voice. He was on the phone and although I couldn't make out what he was saying, I could tell he wasn't happy. I eased over to the door and eavesdropped. Whoever he was talking to was giving him a hard time, and he sputtered as he tried to get a word in. Finally he said, "Fine. If that's how it has to be, then I guess that's how it has to be. But then we'll be square. Two days. Fine. I'll call you." With that he hung up the phone and cursed. I took my wallet from my pocket, quietly went back to the kitchen door, opened it and then slammed it, staying inside and pretending that I had just come in.

"Who the hell's that?" called Robert from the living room. A moment later he strode into the kitchen, eyes ablaze, obviously an angry man.

I held out my wallet and said "Just me. I forgot my wallet. Now I'm late. See ya."

He nodded and mumbled "Okay, see ya," and I went out the door. I glanced in the rearview mirror as I pulled out of the driveway. Robert was standing in the doorway watching me drive off, his face an unreadable mask.

"What the hell was all that about?" I asked myself as I drove off. Two days. Something was going to happen in two days. And I didn't know what. But it didn't sound like it was going to be a good thing.

I was still thinking about Robert when I parked in front of the address that Denise had given me. Two days wasn't much time, and it didn't feel right going on a date while the clock was ticking. Felt a bit like Nero, in fact, fiddling around when I should be doing something constructive. But my mind cleared – or was it fogged? – as soon as the door opened and Denise was standing there in front of me. I stammered out a greeting and she invited me in. She had let her hair down, and it spread across her shoulders like a silken cape, shining softly in the light. "Uh, where're the kids?"

"My Sis took them over to the Royal Treat for ice cream. They just left."

"Oh." Pitiably, that was all I could think of to say. The silence grew as I searched the databanks for some clue as to what I should say. The databanks have taken some abuse over the years. Nothing came up on the screen. Denise saved the day.

"Can I get you something to drink?" she asked and I nodded.

"Well, what?" she said sensibly.

"Oh, whatever. Maybe a beer? Or a glass of wine?" I still had to meet Riley later so I didn't want to drink too much. On the other hand I was unaccountably nervous, and something to settle me down seemed like it would be a good idea. A triple shot of Absolut would be just the ticket, I thought, immediately cursing myself silently for the very idea. I like to drink too much. And I don't like that I do. The circular nature of these sentiments often upsets me, at least until I've had a couple of drinks.

"What's the matter?" Denise asked as she handed me a bottle of Sam Adams and a glass. "I didn't know if you wanted a glass."

"I do, thanks. Nothing's the matter. Actually everything's the matter, but no more so than usual for lately."

She sat on the couch right in the first-date zone – not all the way at the opposite end from me, but not right next to me, either. "What do you mean?"

"Ahh, it's nothing. Just obsesssing about what happened to Dickie."

"Still?"

"Well, yeah. It's only been a couple of weeks. The cops haven't come up with a damn thing as far as I can tell, and I've been trying to make sense out of things on my own. With very little success."

"Which police have been investigating? Rehoboth?"

"No. Dewey. And apparently the Delaware Bureau of Investigations, though you wouldn't know it. As far as I can tell they came out one day, yelled at me, and never came back."

"Yelled at you?"

"Yeah, the guy – Smith was his name – seemed to think that Dickie and I were gay lovers and that I killed him in some sort of spat. He as much as said it straight out. It wasn't too cool."

"I bet it wasn't. You weren't, were you?"

"Weren't what?"

"Lovers?"

"Uh, no. I'm emphatically heterosexual. Enthusiastically, too. Dickie and I were just friends. What made you ask that?"

"Well, there's a lot of gay people around here."

"Yeah…but what would I be doing sitting here if I was gay?"

"Well, you could be bi."

"Oh no I couldn't. Man. You got some ideas floating around in your head, you know that?"

She smiled and put a hand on my thigh. It felt like a jolt of electricity shot through my entire body. "I was just checking," she said. She removed her hand from my thigh. I wished that she hadn't. "So, where do you want to go?" she asked.

I couldn't tell her the real answer, no on our first date. "I don't know. I thought we might just grab a drink somewhere. I've got to be in Ocean City at eleven. If you want to come along, we could head that way. If not, we could go somewhere closer, so I can get you back here."

"Where do you have to be in Ocean City? Didn't you say Fager's Island?"

"Yeah."

"Well, why don't we just go there, then? It's a pretty good place, and we would definitely be on time to meet your friend."

"Sounds like a plan," I said. "You ready?"

"Give me a minute. I'll be right back."

"I'll be right here."

She left the room and I watched her go. The girl was in shape, there was no question about that. I stood and walked around the small, room, finishing my beer. On the mantle over the brick fireplace were a number of framed photographs, mostly somewhat yellowing, of kids and dogs and slim clean-shaven men with crew-cut hair and women in skirts. There was one of a group, twelve or fourteen people, a couple of families, standing on a long porch in front of a house that looked familiar. Denise came back into the room with a sweater draped loosely around her shoulders and I asked her where it had been taken.

"Right out front," she replied. "On the porch."

No wonder it had looked familiar. "Is that your family?"

"Our family and our cousins. They used to come and stay a few weeks every summer."

"Does your family own this place?"

"I do, now. My mom sold it to me after my Dad died. I should be done paying her off in about a hundred and ten years."

"Do you live here year-round?"

"For five years now."

"Must be nice."

"It doesn't suck completely. You ready to go?"

"Yup. You?"

"Ready."

"Then let's do it."

And we did.

Twenty-Three

In winter Ocean City is a small town, a seaside village of less than ten thousand souls. But on a big summer weekend there can be over three hundred thousand sun- and fun-seekers shoehorned into the hotels and condos that crowd the narrow barrier beach that separates the shallow waters of the bay and the wide Atlantic beyond. Washington, the politicians and the technocrats and the consultants and the lawyers, goes to the Delaware shore, to Rehoboth and Dewey and the self-named "Quiet Resorts" of Bethany and Fenwick Island. Baltimore goes to Ocean City. Or not to Ocean City – to O.C.. There's a big difference between Baltimore and Washington, and nowhere is it more apparent than in the two cities' choice of summer resort. Ocean City may be the Camaro cap- itol of the world, although Mustangs and Firebirds are certainly well-represented too. And Ocean City – sorry, O.C. – could quite possibly be the world tattoo capitol as well. But despite the crowds and the traffic and the somewhat scary looks of much of the younger crowd, O.C. can be a lot of fun, too. There are hundreds of bars and restaurants, the beach is white and wide, and there's a palpable atmosphere of good cheer, of just-plain-folks out for a good time at the beach. Of all the bars and restaurants, Fager's Island is one of the most well-known. It's a big place, a large restaurant by the water on the bay side, with several bars and live music almost every night. Every day they play The 1812 Overture as the sun sets, concluding as the sun slips into the waters of the bay. It's a fun place, and it was a good choice if you wanted to meet someone and make it look accidental, because so many people go there. Riley had been thinking.

The trip down from Dewey took longer than I had expected and it was almost nine-thirty by the time Denise and I found seats at a small bar outside on the deck overlooking the bay. The place was jammed with revelers, and the dance floor inside was pretty much cheek to cheek, so to speak. Labor Day was fast approaching, and the pasty city dwellers were determined to grab some summer before it got away. If that meant partying all night and sleeping on the beach all day while turning themselves lobster-red, well, so be it. There was a quasi-reggae band playing inside, a bunch of white guys with short hair and Hawaiian shirts playing up-tempo tunes with an island lilt, and they weren't bad. The band was clearly but not painfully audible from our seats, and barely had to yell to ask Denise what she'd like to drink. "Absolut Citron and soda with a piece of lemon," she replied. That sounded good, so I ordered two when the bartender made his way over to where we sat. While he made the drinks I looked around on the off chance that Riley had arrived early. I saw a bunch of people, many of them obviously having a fabulous time, but no Riley.

"Who are we looking for?" asked Denise.

"A tall skinny surfer-type guy with sort of dirty-blond hair. He's a cop in Dewey."

"Riley?"

"Uh, yeah. I guess you know him?"

"Oh, I've known Riley for years."

"I should have known. Well, if you see him, let me know."

The bartender showed up with our drinks before she could reply. I gave him a credit card to hold so we could open a tab, and when he was gone, I took a sip of my libation. It was pretty damn good and I said as much to Denise. "Hey, I'm a bartender," she replied. "I should know a good drink."

She had a point. "You know," I said, "I think we're perfect for each other."

Her eyes widened a bit, but she didn't choke on her drink or laugh out loud, both positive developments from my point of view. She swallowed and asked, "Why's that?"

"Well, you make drinks, and I drink them. It's a match made in heaven."

She laughed, obviously glad I was kidding around. I was confident that she liked me. I was also confident she wasn't ready for any life-altering experiences just at the moment. We talked and had a few laughs, and soon it was eleven. There was no sign of Riley. I walked around the place a couple of times looking for him but had no luck. Finally, a little after twelve, we gave up and headed home.

"That was odd," I said as we headed north out of Fager's parking lot.

"Yeah. Yeah it was. Riley's kind of a flake, but he's a good kid. Something must have happened."

"Yeah, like he forgot. Or got a date. Or the surf's up."

"It's midnight, Bill. Nobody surfs at midnight."

"Riley might. But I doubt that's it. He seemed like he was worried, maybe scared, by something he wanted to tell me. That's why he set it up for way down here. I doubt he just blew the whole thing off. It's more likely that he got even more scared and decided against coming. Something like that."

"I agree. He's a wacky kid, but he's got a good heart, I think. He tries. I really think that something must have happened. Let's go by his place."

"I don't know where he lives."

"I do. We can just swing by and see if the light's on."

"If it would make you feel better, sure."

"It would."

"Okay, then." I switched the radio on and punched the button for WRNR, sure I wouldn't get it. But it was a clear night with some high thin clouds and I'm not a radio engineer but I guess the signal was reflecting off the clouds somehow and it came in clearly. Dr. John was singing about how it was such a night, such a night, sweet confusion under the moonlight, and despite Riley's no-show I was feeling all right as we made our way out of Ocean City and to the open road beyond. We rode in companionable near-silence, both of us more or less talked out for the time being, and that was fine with me. It gets wearing trying to be on, trying to be witty, after a while. I mean, I'm always witty, but trying to be impressively so can be hard. The view from the top of the Indian River Inlet bridge was glorious, the white line of waves breaking on the beach clearly visible, stretching off into the distance. There was no traffic visible in either direction so I stopped the car at the top of the bridge. Denise shot me an alarmed look. "What are you doing?"

"Just taking in the view for a second. Why, did you think I was getting ready to jump or something?"

She laughed a little nervously. "No…no. I don't know what I thought. Never mind. It's beautiful, isn't it?"

"Yeah. I just wish I could have seen it when it was all like this."

"Well, at least there's been some saved, like this."

"And like Dickie's place."

"And that."

Headlights were approaching from behind, still quite a ways off, but close enough that it was time to get moving. A few minutes later we were rolling up Route One through Dewey. There were a lot of people on the street but traffic was light. Denise directed me to Old Bay Road, which is about a mile north of the center of Dewey and which runs back off Route One towards, appropriately, the bay. "This is the one," she said, and I pulled over in front of a somewhat run-down bungalow with asbestos-shingle siding in some indeterminate pastel. There were no lights on inside, but a single bulb burned by the front door. There were a couple of partially disassembled mountain bikes on the porch, along with an old sofa and a couple of green plastic trashcans. The small front yard hadn't seen a mower for some time. There were no cars in the short gravel driveway. I looked over at Denise. "What now?"

"I don't know," she whispered. "Maybe we should knock."

"We?"

"Okay, you."

"Why are you whispering?" I whispered.

"I don't know. It seemed like the right thing to do. I have a bad feeling."

I generally believe in feelings, especially when they come from smart women. So I began whispering too. "How do you know Riley, anyway?"

"He dated a friend of mine for a while. Why?"

"Just wondering," I said. I really didn't know why I had asked, but I knew I was glad that the answer hadn't been that she had dated him. "I'll go knock. Stay put." I climbed out of the car and walked up the uneven concrete walkway and up the stairs to the door. There was no sound from the house. There was no sound in general, except for a vague whooshing that might have been cars out on Route One or just a breeze in the leaves. I knocked, and there was no reply, so I knocked again. Nothing. I tried the door and it was unlocked, so I pushed it open and called Riley's name into the dark interior of the house. It was hard to see, but the light on the porch provided a little illumination through the open door. The place was messy, but not outrageously so. There was a couch, a couple of chairs, a TV. A couple of pizza boxes were on the coffee table. There were some clothes draped over the couch. A surfboard leaned against one wall. There was a doorway that led back further into the house but it was to dark to see anything that far inside. I called Riley's name again and when there was no answer I looked back at Denise and shrugged, closed the door and walked back down to the car. "Nobody home," I said when I reached her open window.

"Maybe you should check inside."

"Oh, c'mon…oh, all right." It's amazing what we'll do when attractive members of the opposite sex are involved. I walked backup to the house and went in. A switch just inside the door turned on a lamp in the far corner of the room, and with light the place didn't look any worse than it had in the dark. Or any better, either. I went toward the back of the house, turning on lights as I went. It would be my luck to wake Riley from a deep sleep and get shot for my trouble. But he wasn't there, so I escaped intact. There was nothing that suggested anything bad had happened except that Riley's mother should have taught him the value of doing your laundry and your dishes more frequently than once a month. I switched lights off as I made my way back out and closed the door behind me before going back to the car. "Nobody home," I said when I was back behind the wheel. "Doesn't look like anything bad happened, as far as I can tell. Looks pretty normal for a young guy's place. You happy?"

She looked hurt. "I'm sorry for making you go in there. It didn't make me happy."

"No, I just mean, are you satisfied? Or should we look for Riley somewhere else?"

"I'm satisfied, I guess. I just thought…"

"Don't worry. I was a little worried, too. But I'm sure something just came up. Maybe he had to work an extra shift at the last minute, who knows?"

"That must be it," she said in a voice that, translated, said "no way."

"Look, I'll do whatever you want. But you have to tell me what that is. I'm not a mind reader."

She smiled a thin little smile. "I know. I'm sorry. Maybe I should just go home."

"Do you want to come over for a drink first?

"No, no thanks. It's late. And my sister's kids will be up early, and it's their last day here. I better get going."

"Your wish is my command," I said.

"Thanks," she replied. "I know."

Twenty-Four

There had been a brief and somewhat unsatisfying good-night kiss, nothing more than a quick brush of lips. On the other hand, I thought as I drove away, at least there had been a kiss. And after all, it was on the lips. Could have been worse.

I pulled into the drive at Dickie's house – I couldn't think of it as mine, and wasn't sure if I ever would – and noted that Robert was out. Or at least his car was. I parked and got out and paused to look at the house, which was ablaze with light. "Figures," I said aloud. "That asshole doesn't have to pay the electric bill."

"Which asshole?" said a voice right behind me.

After a moment, when I was pretty sure I wasn't having a heart attack, I turned around and saw Riley's smiling face. "Some other asshole, Riley. Jesus. Don't sneak up on people like that. You're lucky I didn't have a heart attack."

"Seems like you're the lucky one."

"You're lucky because If I had died I would have come back to haunt you. Where the hell were you tonight, anyways? We waited for you."

"Sorry. I couldn't make it."

"Yeah. I noticed. Why not?"

"Couldn't get away. I was being watched."

"By who?"

"Don't know. I got a look at him, but I didn't know him. I ditched him and I circled back around here. I figured you'd be back sooner or later."

"Why would somebody be watching you?"

"'Cause they suspect me."

"Who suspects you of what?"

"I don't know."

"You don't what? Which part don't you know?"

"Either part."

"Well, that narrows things down. Why don't you try to give me some clue as to what you're talking about. Even a hint might help."

"I heard something."

"Okay, I give. What?"

"You know that little file room down at the station? Just off the reception area? Where I was working before?"

"Yeah. What about it?"

"Well, the Chief's been a little pissed at me lately. He's been making me do all the filing. And there's a shitload of it, you couldn't believe it. I mean, there's maybe a dozen cardboard boxes full of stuff, and not little boxes, either, and there's always more…"

I cut him off. "There's a lot of filing. I get it. What about it?"

"Well, there's a big tropical storm off the coast down south. It might bump up to a hurricane. And the tide turned at about five o'clock this morning. I thought maybe with the storm and the tide there might be some waves this morning, so I got up early to go surfing."

"Does this relate to anything I'd be interested in at all?"

"I'm getting to it. Hold on. So I got up early and rode down to the inlet at Indian River, sometimes there's a good break there off the jetty, but man, this morning it was flat, nothing at all. Maybe the waves will get here tomorrow. Anyways, I was up, you know? And dressed. And I didn't have to be at work 'til nine, but what I figured is I'd go in, get the damn filing done, make the Chief happy for a while, and I'd get to do something else, you know?"

"Okay…"

"So I'm in the filing room, minding my own business, and I hear voices out in the reception area. I'm not worried about it, there's always people in and out, It's a police station, you know?"

"Yeah, I know. Would you mind getting to the point sometime today?"

"So I hear voices. At least two, but I think it was three people, the third guy didn't say anything I could hear. But it's kind of tucked back in there, where I was, and it was kinda hard to hear, so I'm not positive. I could hear the other two pretty well, but I didn't recognize either of their voices. That's one reason why I think there had to be at least three people."

"I'm not following."

"Well, it's a police station, right? And I know all the cops, I think I'd recognize their voices, and I didn't recognize any voices, so there must have been someone there, who either talked really softly or maybe didn't say anything, you know? I mean there must have been a cop there. Why would two people go to a police station to have an argument? Like, 'Dude, I want to argue with you, but let's go to the cop shop first'? I don't think so."

"Maybe they just ran into each other."

"Maybe, man. But here it is, like six o'clock in the morning, and these two dudes happen to run into each other? And like, it's when there just happens to be no one on the desk? And how do they get in? I let myself in with my key, and I locked the door behind me. I think I did. I'm pretty sure, at least."

"How come there was no one on the desk?"

"Early like that, there's no one there a lot of times. It's just a little force, man. Most early mornings there's only one guy on. If the guy has to go out he'll just forward calls to his cell phone. Works pretty good, mostly."

"Do you know who was supposed to be working this morning?"

"No, but I can find out."

"Do that. And let me know. Now, what were the people arguing about?"

"You, dude. Mainly, at least."

"Me? What about me?"

"Whether they should kill you."

"Huh. And…?"

"And what?"

"And what did they decide, dammit?"

"Oh. Sorry. The decision seemed to be, not yet. That too much had already happened, and another person dying would call too much attention. But I got to say, the one dude, he was rooting to snuff you, at first."

"Did he say why?"

"Just that you were poking around too much, that you were trouble, that they were better off just doing you and hiding the body, maybe dumping it offshore, instead of taking the risk that you'd figure things out. The other guy didn't think you were smart enough to figure anything out, so it wasn't worth the trouble to kill you when there was so much downside."

"I'm not sure which one I like better."

"I'd go with the one who thinks you're dumb. At least he doesn't want you dead."

"I guess. They give any hint about what they don't want me to find out?"

"The murders, dude."

"No, I know that. But what I'm trying to figure out is why anyone got murdered in the first place."

"Oh. No, not that I heard at least."

"Too bad. Why did you think that someone was watching you?"

"Maybe I was imagining things, I don't know. But after the voices stopped I stayed in the file room in case they were still around somewhere. After a few minutes, maybe ten or fifteen, the Chief came in, calling my name. I didn't know what else to do so I answered him."

"What did he say?"

"Said he'd seen my car out back. And asked me what I was doing, and how long I had been there. Seemed a little surprised to see me there, I'll say that."

"That doesn't prove anything. What was it, maybe seven? And you're in there doing filing and you're not due in for another two hours? Hell, I'd be surprised too."

"Yeah, I guess. But maybe you're wrong. Could be he was there the whole time and now he figured out I was there and I heard all this stuff. In which case I would be in deep shit, brother. Deep doggy do. And remember, that wasn't all. There was the dude following me around. What about that?"

"I don't know what about it. How do you know he was following you?"

"I just kept seeing him. I must've seen the dude five times, including when I was getting ready to come down to O.C.. That's when I ditched him and circled back."

"Why didn't you just stop him and ask him what he wanted. You're a cop, after all."

"I...I guess I was scared. I mean, people been getting killed, man. What if he shot me?"

"No one's going to shoot a cop just for pulling him over. Almost no one, at least. Besides, you've got a gun, too."

Riley looked a little embarrassed. "Uh, no I don't, dude."

"You don't have a gun? Why not? How can you be a cop without a gun?"

"I'm, uh, not really a cop. I mean, I will be, if I can pass the test, and I get the training and all, but I haven't yet. First I got to get out of school, though."

"You're in school?"

"Yeah, U.D. – University of Delaware, up in Newark. I should finish this year, though. Probably, at least. Hopefully."

"How old are you?"

"Twenty-six. "

"And you're still in college?"

"Well, I mean, I took a few years off. Went out to Cali. Did some surfin', but it got kinda old. I was starvin', bro. And my Mom said if I came back and went to school she'd pay for it and help me out a little. She owns my house, so I don't pay rent"

"So what is this, a summer job?"

"Well, yeah. I mean, I've done it three years now. It's not like I'm a rookie or anything."

"You're a rent-a-cop."

"We don't say that, dude. We're associate officers."

"What about when you pulled me over?"

"We can give tickets. The Chief puts me in one of the cruisers sometimes. Once in a while. Really, it's more like a deterrent. To scare people, you know? You sit there in the car and people go slower when they see you. You're not supposed to pull anyone over unless they're being a real idiot, and even then you're supposed to call for backup right away, even before you pull them over."

"Why'd you pull me over, then?"

"'Cause I knew you, dude. And you were kinda cruisin', you know. I just figured I'd let you know to take it easy before you ran into a, uh, real cop."

"Gee, thanks."

"No prob."

Apparently Riley was immune to sarcasm. "How come you've been pulling all this desk and filing duty? Most of the rent-a-cops are out patrolling the beach or walking around town."

"I been sorta gettin' punished."

"For what?"

"I was sorta surfin' on the clock." At least he looked sheepish about it.

"Sorta?"

"Well, I got busted before I actually caught a wave. So, you know, technically I wasn't really surfing."

"That's pretty technical."

"Yeah, I was lucky I didn't get fired. Probably would have if my Mom and the Chief weren't so tight."

"Your Mom and the Chief are tight?"

"Oh, yeah. They've been dating for a couple years now."

Out on the street there was the sound of a car slowing down, and then headlights swung across the drive as the car turned into the drive. It was Robert's rental car. I turned to Riley, but he was gone. The kid wasn't all that bright, but he was fast. I turned back and, shielding my eyes from the lights, waited as Robert pulled up to a stop.

He turned the car off and got out. "Whatcha doin' there, li'l Billy?" he asked. "Lose your key?"

"No, I , uh, I just got home a second ago."

"Huh. Oh yeah, , you went out on a date. Didn't get any, huh?"

He was slurring noticeably and his eyes seemed slightly out of focus. He probably shouldn't have been driving. I should sic Riley on him, I thought. "Uh, no. But we had a nice time."

"Oh, well, then," he said, sarcasm dripping from every syllable. "That's fine, then. That's very very important. Ain't as important as gettin' laid, but it's important." He stretched and yawned. "Well," he drawled, "been a long day, and tomorrow's gonna be another, so I'm goin' to bed. You comin' in, or you just gonna hang out here in the driveway all night?"

I couldn't think of a reason to give him for staying outside. "I'm coming in," I said. I quickly looked around for Riley but didn't see him, and then I went inside. Inside, Robert said goodnight and went upstairs almost immediately. I stayed downstairs and turned on the tube in the den, which is at the end of the house and overlooks the deck. There's no door to the deck from the den but the windows are right there. I figured I'd give Robert a little while to fall asleep and then go out and see if Riley was still around. For all I knew he had left. I was watching a rerun of the old Bob Newhart show on Nick at Nite when there was a faint rapping on the glass of the window to my left. I went over and saw Riley's face, wide-eyed with excitement or perhaps fear, on the other side of the glass. I motioned for him to go to the sliding door in the living room, but he violently shook his head no and motioned for me to open the window. I sighed and did so. "What is it, Riley?"

"Shhh. Where is he?"

"Who, Robert?"

"I don't know his name," he whispered urgently. "The guy who came in here with you. Where is he?"

"He went upstairs, he's probably asleep by now, why?"

"Will you keep it down? It's him."

"It's who, Riley? Try to make sense."

With a visible effort, Riley calmed down. He took a deep breath, exhaled slowly, and said. That's the guy who was following me."

"You're positive."

"Hell yeah, I'm positive."

"It's not the only grey car in the world."

"Yeah, but the Ohio tags, I noticed them before. And he looks like the guy who was behind the wheel. And I think he was one of the guys down at the station house this morning, too. I could be wrong, but I think he was the one who kept wanting to whack you."

I probably wouldn't trust Riley on a lot of things, but for some reason I trusted him on this. And here I'd been sleeping in the same house with Robert. The hair on the back of my neck stood up at the thought of what might have happened. Of course it made sense. I'd thought Robert was involved from the beginning but had allowed myself to become convinced otherwise. As usual I should have stayed with my first instinct but I had over-analyzed things to the point that I had come to doubt myself. Stupid, stupid, stupid. "Wait right there Riley. I'll be right out." Riley nodded and I went around to the sliding door and let myself out.

Shortly I was with Riley on the deck. "What now, dude?" he asked as I joined him.

"I don't know. You really think it was him at the station?"

"I'm almost positive, man." Riley sounded a little exasperated. "That "redneck way he talks. It's got to be him. And if it is, man, he must have said that they should whack you about ten times. You need to get out of there. You can't stay in that house with him."

"Why not? He's not going to just shoot me."

"How the hell do you know that?" Riley demanded. "I wouldn't do it, man. Stay at my place. You'll have to take the couch, but you won't get whacked in the middle of the night."

"I guess you're right. Let's get out of here."

We turned to leave. From the shadows a voice drawled, "Goin' somewhere, fellas?" It was Robert, of course. He stepped into the light and I saw that he was wearing flip-flops and a blue terry bathrobe. And he held a gun.

Damn, I hate guns. Especially when they're pointed at me.

"Hey, Robert," I said as calmly as I could manage. "What are you doing up?"

He shook his head and smiled thinly. "Could ask you the same question. What are you doing out here?"

"My friend Riley here stopped by. We were just talking. Would you mind putting that gun away?" To my amazement he did so, sliding the weapon into a pocket in the robe.

"Sorry," he said. "I heard voices out here and I came to see who it was."

"No problem," I said in what I hoped was an even tone. "What do you have a gun for, Robert?"

"I always have a gun. Why?"

"I'm not too crazy about having a gun in the house. Those things can hurt people, you know."

He smiled again, but there was no mirth in it. "Yeah. I know."

Riley spoke up, surprising me. "I hope you have a license for that thing."

"What are you, a cop?"

"Yes, I am." He paused and added lamely, "Sorta."

Robert looked puzzled, which wasn't surprising. Riley has that effect on people. But he said only, "Well, it's late. See you in the morning."

"G'night, Robert," I said to his back. When he was gone, I breathed for what seemed like the first time in five minutes, and then said to Riley, "You think he heard us?"

"I dunno, dude. Must not have, I guess. Let's get out of here."

"I'm going to stick around. You go ahead and take off."

"What? Why? Dude has a gun, and he wants to kill you. Are you crazy?"

"Yeah, probably. But it'd seem too weird if I disappeared. He'd figure out something's up. It's better to make things seem as normal as possible."

Riley looked down and scuffed a toe on the wooden deck. "You sure?"

"Positive. Take off. I'll call you in the morning."

"Okay then. See ya." He walked off, giving me a little wave over his shoulder. I almost called to tell him to wait, but bit my tongue. I'll be fine, I told myself. Robert wouldn't dare shoot me after Riley had seen him with the gun. "I'll be fine," I said aloud. I only wished that I believed myself.

Twenty-Five

Somehow I lived through the night. I had propped a chair against the door, but it still took me a long time to fall asleep, every creak and squeak sounding to my straining ears like stealthy footfalls. But sleep finally came and when I opened my eyes it was full morning, sunny, cloudless, the birds chirping merrily away, just another day in paradise. I looked at my watch and was amazed to see that it was already past nine o'clock. Time to move. I got up and checked across the hall. Robert wasn't there, and he wasn't downstairs either, so I grabbed a Pop-tart, made some coffee and took a quick shower.

For a long time I had felt almost powerless to accomplish anything, the combined weight of my own inability to figure out what was going on and Hartner's prohibition against getting involved acting as an anchor. But suddenly everything had changed. For one thing I was sick to death of all this crap. I wanted it over, and now. For another thing I was now convinced that Robert was at least involved in Dickie's death – and wouldn't have been surprised to find that he was the murderer.

But hard evidence was problematic: Apart from what Riley had overheard, there wasn't much to point to. There was the fact that Robert had a gun – who would bring a gun to what was essentially a funeral? And there was Robert's telephone conversation that I had overheard. Two days, he had said. He'd have it in two days. To me it sounded like he owed money to someone and they were pressing him for it. If that was the case, killing Dickie to get the house would at least make some sense if Robert hadn't known about Dickie changing his will. But it didn't make complete sense because everybody knows that wills and probate and all the rest of the details surrounding estates take time to resolve. And certainly nothing would be resolved in two days. And now it was only one day. Whatever he had said he would have, he was supposed to have it tomorrow. It was possible that it was an innocent exchange, of course – for all I really knew he could have been talking about flowers for the funeral or a plot for Dickie to be buried in, but I doubted it. His tone, the way he had sputtered and objected and then finally, resignedly, acquiesced told me that there was more to the conversation than flowers.

What the case needed was police work – fingerprints and search warrants and computer checks and all the stuff that police can do better than any individual, even one as brilliant as me. I flirted with the idea of going to Hartner but decided against it. For one thing he wouldn't be happy about my involvement. For another, there was the question of who the third person Riley had overheard might be. It could be Hartner himself. That was doubtful, I supposed, but possible. It would explain a lot if it was true, like why the Chief didn't want me looking into things and why it seemed that no progress was being made in their investigation. Despite everything

I liked the Chief, and I didn't want to suspect him, but I couldn't simply rule it out either.

So what did I have? A plot in which at least three people were implicated, Robert and the two other people he was talking to at the police station. I knew nothing about the second person except that Riley didn't recognize his voice. And nothing about the third person except that he was probably a cop and that he didn't talk loudly or often, at least within the context of that particular conversation.. This wasn't exactly narrowing things down much. Really, the only thing I was sure about was that Robert was involved. So it was time to take on Robert. I checked to make sure he wasn't pulling into the driveway and then went up to Dickie's old room, where Robert had been staying. I don't know what I hoped to find, but it was a place to start. The room was a mess. Clothes were strewn about, his half-unpacked bags were in the middle of the floor, and the bed was unmade. The shades were down and there was a musty fetid smell of perspiration and dirty socks in the air. I left the shades down and began looking around. I checked the pockets of the pants on the floor for any wayward scraps of paper, looked under the mattress and in the chest of drawers, searched the closet, even picked up the throw rugs to see if anything was there, all to no avail. Every couple of minutes I went out into the hall and checked to make sure Robert hadn't come back.

I was standing in the middle of the room, turning around slowly, trying to get an idea of where else to look when I noticed that a large Monet print from a museum show was slightly askew on the far wall near the bed. I went over and idly pulled it out to glance behind it, and there was paydirt. Someone, and I would have to guess that it had been Robert, had created a hiding place behind the picture by cutting away the drywall behind it, and then making a shelf in the cavity with a length of two-by-four which had been toenailed to the studs. It was a neat job. The cavity created was sixteen inches wide by about a foot or so high, and it was impossible to tell it was there as long as the picture remained undisturbed. I wondered when Robert had made it. The work didn't look particularly new, but that was based only on the lack of dust and the somewhat yellowed state of the piece of wood that served as the shelf, and he might have just used an old piece of wood he'd found lying around. Or it was possible that the niche had been there for years and that he had known about it. Astutely, I decided it was immaterial.

What was material was the contents of the hidey-hole. To wit: one pistol, a sub-nosed thirty-eight which was loaded and which I promptly unloaded, putting the bullets in my pocket. Also: Eleven hundred and forty-six dollars in cash, all hundreds except for the forty-six. A passport in Robert's name, from which I with some difficulty tore his picture, rendering it useless. There was an airplane ticket to London, with the date two days hence, but no return ticket. It looked like Robert wasn't planning on attending his brother's funeral. There was a wad of traveler's checks, several thousand dollars worth, more than I cared to take the time to count. I put it all back as I had found it, leaving the gun for last. I held the weapon and looked at it. Dickie had drowned, but Jerry Kavanagh had been shot. Was this gun, I wondered, the one that had killed him? Had Robert held this in his hand, hefted it, before squeezing the trigger and snuffing out his Kavanagh's life? I don't know why, exactly, but I was sure that it was. The metal felt colder than it should have, the gun itself heavier than it could possibly have been, as though the weight of death and sin and evil had somehow become attached to it. I shivered and put it back, then carefully slid the picture back over the secret cavity. I was almost to the door when I stopped and went back. I retrieved the gun from its niche and carefully wiped it down with the corner of my shirt. I didn't need my fingerprints on there.

Back downstairs I considered what to do. My deliberations were cut short by the sound of a car in the drive. I stood and looked out the window, and saw that it was Chief Hartner's Bronco, so I went out to greet him. I stood on the stoop, shielding my eyes from the sun with my hand, as he approached. "Mornin' Chief."

"Good morning, " he said flatly and a little heavily. "How's things?"

"Can't complain."

"Wouldn't do any good anyway."

"Exactly."

We stood there in silence for a little while until I asked, "Want to come in?"

He looked up as if he was surprised to see me. "Oh. Sure."

The Chief didn't want coffee but I did, so I poured myself a cup and then went and sat across the table from the Chief. "So, what can I do for you?" I asked.

Hartner leaned back in his chair and fixed me with a weary stare. His eyes were rimmed in red and appeared almost sunken in his head, so deep were the bags beneath them. "Well…" he stopped and cleared his throat. "Look. I've been in law enforcement a long time, and I'm good at what I do. You get me?"

Not really. "Sure."

He nodded. "Good. Because I want it understood –clearly understood- that this is not a question of competence. Okay?"

I nodded. I had no idea what to say, because I had no idea what he was driving at.

"Okay. Good. Since we understand each other, let me ask you a question. When do you think we last had a murder in Dewey Beach?"

"Well…a few days ago."

"No, before that."

"Well, Dickie got killed a little over two weeks ago."

"Jesus. It's like talking to fucking retard. Before Dickie."

"I have no idea."

"Try never."

"Okay…" I still didn't know what he was driving at. Maybe I'm dense.

"Assaults. Robberies. Burglaries. Arson. Vandalism. We've had a couple of drownings, car accidents, stuff like that. That's what we get. And to tell you the truth, not much of most of those."

Chief, look, I'm not trying to be disrespectful here. I'm really not. But what the fuck are you talking about?"

"Any of that coffee left?"

I glanced over at the pot. "Yeah. Want some?"

"Sure. I could use it after all."

I got up and poured him a mug. "How do you take it?"

"Black's fine." That was good , because there wasn't any milk in the house. And I wasn't sure about sugar. I carried the mugs to the table and set one in front of him. The Chief cupped his in both hands and slurped from the steaming surface. "It's good. Thanks."

"You're welcome." I have good manners. I was raised right. "You were saying…?"

"Let me bring you up to date on the investigation. The investigations. This is what we have." He stopped and took another sip of coffee. Set it back on the table and looked me in the eye. Seconds ticked by, their passing made audibly the clock on the wall. "Fucking nothing."

"What about the State guys? What have they come up with?"

"As far as I can tell, they haven't done a damn thing. But they're not telling me anything. That asshole Smith…" The Chief's voice trailed away and he shook his head. "But I guess I'm in no position to talk."

I looked across the table at the Chief and I almost felt sorry for him. Hell, I did feel sorry for him. "So what brings you here?"

Hartner cleared his throat and squared his shoulders. "I know you've been looking into things," he said.

"I…" I tried to interject.

The chief held up a hand. "Don't even try and bullshit me, Flaherty. I don't need it. Like I said, I know you've been looking into things. The way I look at it now, that's okay. It hasn't been your fault I haven't found out what happened. And maybe you found something out that might be useful."

I shrugged.

"What I need," he continued, "is for you to tell me everything you've got. I need to get these cases solved, and obviously I need help. Anything you tell me, I'll keep it in confidence. There will be no repercussions to you. So what have you found out?"

I started to tell him. I got as far as opening my mouth, but then I closed it again. But the thought of the third person at the police station, the silent one, the one who must have been a cop, who had to have been a cop, stopped me. Riley hadn't gotten back to me yet with the name of whoever it was that had been on duty yesterday morning. And for all I knew it had been Hartner himself. And maybe now he was on a fishing expedition, trying to find out what I knew in order to assess the degree of threat I presented. He was a cagey old fart, I knew that. And how likely was it that he hadn't been able to come up with anything at all? Not bloody likely, I thought. Something didn't seem right. "I really haven't come up with anything."

"Oh, come on," the Chief snorted. "I didn't just fall off a Christmas tree."

"Huh?"

"It means I wasn't born yesterday."

"Oh."

"Now c'mon. Level with me. What do you have?"

"I've been going around talking to people. But you knew that." The Chief nodded. "But I haven't been able to figure a damn thing out. Nothing fits."

"Well, do you have a theory? Something I could follow up on?" The Chief looked so eager and puppy-like that I almost gave in. "I need to talk to a couple more people. How about we meet later today" That would give me time to talk to Riley, at least.

The Chief appeared crestfallen. "When later?"

"How about noon?"

Hartner sighed and stood. "I guess I can wait that long. Where do you want to meet?"

"Here's as good as anywhere, I guess."

"All right. I'll be here at noon. And you better be here too. You better not be pulling anything."

"I'm not," I assured him. "I just need a little more time"

As the Chief headed toward the door I called after him, "Hey, if you don't mind me asking, what time did you get into your office yesterday?"

"Yesterday? I don't know. Early. Why?"

"Were you there at six o'clock in the morning?"

The Chief looked at me quizzically. "Six o'clock yesterday? No idea. I might have been . I wasn't in bed, I'll tell you that much."

"Were you the only one working?"

"No. Somebody else was on. Somebody else is always on."

"Do you know who it was?"

"I'd have to check the roster. I don't remember. You want me to call in and find out?"

Probably I shouldn't have said as much as I already had. "Nah, that's okay. I was just curious. It doesn't matter." The Chief studied my face for a moment, shrugged and left. Over his shoulder he called, "Noon."

I sat at the kitchen table until he was gone, waiting for the sound of tires on the rough drive before rising. I called Riley's house. There was no answer, but that didn't mean much. He could be at work, for all I knew. Hell, he could have been surfing. I called down to the station house and asked for him, hoping to complete the call before Hartner got back there.

"Dewey Beach Police," answered a raspy male voice that I didn't recognize.

"May I speak to, uh, Riley?" I asked, realizing that I had no idea whether Riley was his first name or his last."

"He's not in. Take a message?"

"Well, do you know when he'll be there?"

"No idea. Supposed to be here now, so your guess is as good as mine. You wanna leave a message?"

"No, that's okay, I'll try back. Thanks." I hung up without waiting for a response. Maybe Riley had been too paranoid to go to work, I thought. I hoped that was all it was.

Twenty-Six

It took just a few minutes to drive over to Riley's place. It didn't look any better in daylight than it had in the dark. Actually it looked quite a bit worse. The junk on the porch was still there, but now I saw that the railing was splintered and falling away from the house. There were rotted boards on the porch, and something seemed to be destroying the siding where it met the foundation all around the house. A side window was broken, patched with plastic sheeting and duct tape. The roof had a distinct sag to it, and the asphalt shingles were shiny with age and curling. The small yard still needed mowing, and in daylight the siding looked even uglier than it had at night, a pale insipid pastel green. I knocked but there was no answer, and the door was locked. I stood there on the porch for a moment considering my options. I could break in, but that seemed a bit extreme. I could call Hartner but I was going to see him in a couple of hours anyway and, besides, I wanted to talk to Riley before I saw Hartner again. I had only been there a few seconds when an undercover police car came around the corner and turned towards Riley's house. It was "undercover" in the loosest sense of the word, a light brown Ford Crown

Victoria with a searchlight by the rearview mirror on the driver's side, two long buggy-whip antennas, and municipal tags. The car pulled to the curb and idled there for a few seconds, then the driver turned ignition off. It was more seconds until the door opened and still more before the driver climbed out and turned to look at me. It was Lieutenant Bellegarde, the predictable cigarette clamped between his lips, smoke rising around his eyes.

"What are you doing here?" he asked. It was hard to tell whether he was trying to sound tough or if his throat was simply ravaged by the cigarettes.

"Looking for Riley." Duh.

"Why?"

"Because I wanted to talk to him."

"What about?"

"I really don't think that's any of your business. Because I wanted to talk to him."

Bellegarde squared his shoulders. I think he was trying to look intimidating. It wasn't working. He still looked as though a moderate breeze would blow him into the next county. "Don't get smart with me, tough guy."

"Oh, don't worry, I'll talk slowly."

"What?" He began coughing, a racking sound that came from deep in his chest. It nearly doubled him over, and left him ashen and wheezing when it passed. "Jesus," he gasped, then wiped his mouth with the back of his hand. The guy definitely needed to cut back a little. I said as much. "I want shit from you," he said, "I'll squeeze your head."

I laughed out loud. I always liked that line. I think it was in a movie. Or at least it should have been. It would sound good coming from Schwarzenegger. I don't think

Bellegarde liked getting laughed at. "Get the hell off that porch," he growled.

"Why?"

"You're trespassing . Get down off there."

"It's only trespassing if the owner doesn't want you there. Riley's a friend of mine. He wouldn't mind me being here."

"Yeah, and it's attempted Breaking and Entering if I say it is. Get the fuck off the porch."

"All right, all right. Don't have a heart attack, for God's sake." I walked down the short flight of stairs and towards Bellegarde's vehicle. "Keep your distance," he rasped, his right hand darting inside the ratty houndstooth sports jacket he wore.

I stopped and raised my hands. "Whoa, whoa. Take it easy. I'm not coming anywhere near you. I'm not threatening you."

He let his hand fall away from the gun I was sure he wore beneath the jacket. "Better damn well not be," he said.

"I'm not. I'm leaving. But you can bet your ass I'm going to be talking to your Chief about this. You're way out of line. Way, way out of line."

"Do what you want," he sneered. "I don't give a rat's ass."

"Do what I want? If I did what I wanted to, you'd be reaching for that gun again."

Twenty-Seven

As I drove away I glanced in the rearview mirror. Bellegarde was leaning against the trunk of his car, arms crossed, watching me go. What, I wondered, had that been all about? Why would Bellegarde take such a hard line with me when all I was doing was knocking on the damn door? Something definitely didn't add up. And Riley was part of the equation, whatever it was. I pulled around the corner and when I was sure I was out of Bellegarde's sight I stopped the car and sat there for a couple of minutes. When I felt like I had waited long enough I started back up and made my way around the rest of the block, stopping again when I could look down the block to Riley's house. Bellegarde's car was still parked in front of the house, but there was no sign of Bellegarde himself.

Something, I thought astutely, is going on around here.

I backed the car up until I could just barely see the front of Riley's house and Bellegarde's car, shut the motor off, and waited. I must have looked away for a moment, because a couple of minutes later Bellegarde appeared by his car, looking around in what I could only describe as a furtive manner. I hadn't seen him come out of the house but there was little doubt in my mind that that was where he had come from. I slid low in my seat and watched him. He held something – an envelope, maybe a folded piece of paper – in his hand, glanced at it quickly, and then slid it into his inside jacket pocket as he approached his car. It seemed suspicious on the surface, but who the hell knew? It could have been anything at all.

Bellegarde started his car and after a moment pulled away slowly. I thought about following him but decided that that probably worked a lot better in the movies than it would for me. Besides, my junkpile of a car is pretty recognizable. When Bellegarde was out of sight I climbed out of my car and strolled down the block , trying to look as unremarkable as possible, a surprisingly easy task, then turned into Riley's yard and climbed the front steps to the door, which was still locked. There was no sign of a forced entry. I went around the house and nothing seemed particularly amiss.

Back on the porch I stood with my back to the door, looking around to make sure no one was watching. When I was satisfied that I was unobserved I gave the door a sharp backward kick and with a splintering of old dry wood it opened. I looked around quickly, then ducked inside, pulling the door shut behind me. The place was still a mess but not noticeably worse than it had been. There was no sign of a struggle, nothing obvious like a pool of blood on the floor or bullet holes in the walls. Basically it looked like the home of a twenty-six-year-old bachelor. Which it was, of course. The phone rang, briefly startling me. I let it ring and the answering machine picked up. Riley's lazy surfer-boy drawl invited the caller to leave a message, and then there was a beep. "Hi, honey, it's Mom," said the caller. I deduced that it was Riley's mom calling. Hey, I'm a trained investigator. "I called you at work but they said you weren't there. Give me a call when you get this message, okay? It's important. Love you, bye." I was standing there feeling quite melancholy, thinking about the love of a mother for a son, about the tragedy of a mother losing a son, worrying about Riley, when from the front door came a voice. "What the fuck...?" said the voice, and then, "Shit!" It was of course Riley. "Someone in there?" he called. "I've got a gun!"

"Riley it's me," I called. "Bill Flaherty. Don't shoot me for God's sake"

There was a moment of silence. Riley was apparently digesting this new information. Finally the door creaked open and Riley stood there in the doorway, backlit by the sun, a tall thin figure looking strangely like Clint in "A Fistful of Dollars." Or maybe it was "The Good, The Bad, and The Ugly." Whatever.

"What are you doing here?" Riley demanded. "Did you break my door?"

"No, I, um, yeah."

Riley stepped into the room. The resemblance to Clint Eastwood vanished. "Is that a yes or a no, dude?"

"It's a yes. Sorry. I was worried about you."

"You were? Why?"

"When you didn't go to work, and it seemed like no one knew where you were, I was worried something happened. And then I came over here and that dick Bellegarde was poking around...I don't know. It seemed like a good idea at the time."

"Bellegarde was here? What was he doing?"

"I couldn't tell. I was here first, then he came along and basically told me to leave or he was going to arrest me. I ducked around the corner and watched but I couldn't tell what he was up to. He only left a couple of minutes ago. Oh, and your Mom called."

"My Mom? What?"

"She called and your machine picked up. She left a message."

"What'd she want?"

"Didn't say. Said to call her. Said it was important."

Riley considered this, then shrugged. "What are we gonna do about my door, Dude?"

"Got a hammer and some nails? We could nail it shut for now and you could use the back door until you get it fixed. I'll pay to fix it."

He considered this for a moment and then nodded. "That'll work, I guess."

"You don't really have a gun, do you?"

Riley looked startled by the question. "Of course not, man," he stammered. I was just saying that to scare whoever was in here." He paused and added, "Hammer's in the top drawer behind you, man. I'll go get some nails."

He turned and left. I found the hammer and shortly Riley returned with a small handful of nails and a couple of pieces of two-by-four. As we nailed the door shut I asked, "Did you ever find out who was on duty yesterday morning?"

"It was, uh, Bellegarde."

"Huh." I considered this. Bellegarde. The guy was an ass, but I couldn't see him killing anyone or masterminding some conspiracy to kill me. But still…

he kept turning up, he was more hostile than he needed to be, maybe there was something there. Maybe he was involved. He probably knew Robert. Maybe the two of them had cooked something up. I couldn't see his angle, though. Why would he be involved? What did he stand to gain? Maybe Robert had promised him money. It was hard to say. "Maybe that makes sense."

Riley shrugged but didn't respond. We finished nailing the door in place and I put the hammer back where I found it. I looked at my watch and saw that it was after 10:30 already. Another hour and a half and I was supposed to meet Hartner. "Hey, Riley." I said as the thought struck me, "why aren't you at work?"

"Uh, I called in sick, man. After all the excitement last night I couldn't sleep. I felt like shit, so I called in."

"Huh. That's weird, they didn't know where you were."

"They didn't?"

"No. And they were looking for you."

"Well, I'm right here. Somebody must have forgotten to pass the message along."

"I guess that must be it. Look, I got to get going. Maybe you should call in again."

"I'll do that, man. See you later."

"Later."

I left through the back door and walked back to where I had parked. I had a parking ticket. The ticket cited me for parking at an expired meter, but there were no meters anywhere nearby. As far as I knew there were no meters in Dewey. There are thousands of them in Rehoboth – everywhere you turn there's a meter, but none in Dewey. But it was a standard ticket, probably used by every Police department in the state, so there was a box for "expired meter" and it was checked. And when I looked closely, I saw that it was signed "D. Bellegarde". That bastard. Obviously he had come back and knew that it was my car. It was harassment, plain and simple. I almost threw the ticket away but decided to keep it to show Hartner. Maybe I could get Bellegarde in trouble. I sure wasn't going to let him get off any easier than I had to.

I got in the car, started it up, and pulled away. What, I wondered, is going on? We've got two confirmed murders and a possible- damn near definite - third one. A valuable piece of oceanfront property. A man, Robert, who felt that the property was rightly his. And Robert, if I was right about the phone conversation that I had overheard, owed money to somebody scary. We had Riley eavesdropping from the safety of his filing room on a conversation between Robert and two others, one of whom was unknown. The other was apparently or at least possibly Bellegarde.

Could Bellegarde be the murderer? Or could he be protecting the murderer if he wasn't the actual killer? Maybe so on both counts. If so, what was his motivation? From my experience it pretty much always comes down to either sex or money, and I could be wrong but I somehow doubted that Bellegarde was too into sex at this stage in his life. In fact it looked like it would kill him. So, money. And the money in this case was coming, had to be coming, from the value of the Dickie's property. As it stood now, assuming Dickie's will went through, I was the only one who stood to gain from Dickie's death. Me, and maybe Lou Nickerson if I was ever to decide to develop the property. Thinking about

Nickerson and his inholding, I realized that I didn't know for a fact that Nickerson's property was the only inholding, that it was possible that someone else owned part of what I had thought of as Dickie's beach. I thought back to the survey flags that Jerry Kavanagh had placed on the property. But there had been a lot of flags and I couldn't draw any conclusions from what I had seen. For a moment I wondered how else I could determine who if anyone owned part of Dickie's beach, and quickly I decided that I needed to see the land records for the area. I knew the land in question was not part of either Dewey or Rehoboth, so I figured that any records must be held by the county. And the county seat is Georgetown, a half-hour away to the west of Dewey, a straight shot on Route Nine, which intersects Route One just north of Rehoboth. I turned the trusty Impala around and headed toward the highway.

I pulled into the center of Georgetown about twenty-five minutes later. A couple of fairly imposing government edifices were clustered in the center of the small town, surrounded by modest homes and a few shops, with farmland as far as the eye could see just beyond. I parked and asked around until I found out that land records were held at the courthouse. A few minutes later I standing in front of a desk in the courthouse, asking a pleasant middle-aged black woman where I could find the tax maps for unincorporated land in the county. "Doesn't matter whether it's in-cor-por-at-ed," she said, punching out the syllables Jesse Jackson-style, "or un-in-cor-por-at-ed. It's all in the county, and we tax it all. All the records are by area only. Which area you interested in?"

I told her and a few minutes later was seated in a cubicle with a microfilm reader, scrolling down through the plats and subdivisions of coastal lower Delaware. It took me a little while to find what I was looking for, but I found it: a neat little map showing the slender strip of land where Dickie had lived, with the ocean on one side and Silver Lake on the other. Nickerson's land was clearly shown, and there were no other properties within Dickie's land. I stared at the map for a while, willing something to jump out at me. And lo and behold, eventually it did. The north end of Dickie's property abutted Rehoboth, but the map showed that the land there was a conservation easement, apparently granted or taken by the town to ensure beach access. The easement had been partially paved and served as a road, but it was still a dedicated conservation area.

I studied the map further and saw that the southern end of Dickie's property ran right to the Dewey Beach town line, as I had thought. Right across the town line lay a small tract, really a sliver of land, labeled as belonging to a C. Ordner, and just to the south of that was another easement, this one labeled as belonging to the Sussex County Sanitary Commission. I studied this for a while. The Ordner property was deep but very narrow – it was hard to tell from the map but it looked as thought it might be only a dozen feet wide. But it effectively hemmed Dickie's property in. It bordered Dickie's land from the ocean back to the lake. To the north, Dickie's property was hemmed in by the conservation easement. To the east of course was the ocean, and to the west the lake. Dickie's driveway ran across the conservation easement in the north, but was not shown as an easement itself on the map. Probably, though, he had a right-of-way. But would a right-of way be valid for access to additional homes built on the property? I didn't know. It was certainly possible that the residents of other homes might have to get to those homes some other way. And the only other way was across the Ordner property to the south. I looked at the map some more and realized that I was looking at something else important: the sewer was on the other side of the Ordner property, too. There was no way homes could be built on Dickie's land if they didn't have access to the sewer. I knew that Dickie's house was on a septic system, but it had been there for years and years. Laws and regulations had changed a lot in the intervening years. There was no way that type of system would be approved today for low-lying land that was susceptible to flooding and which bordered a beach. Besides, Dickie's house was on a bit of a high spot compared to the rest of the land there.

I looked at my watch. It was almost twelve. I was already going to be late for my meeting at the house with Hartner, so there wasn't any point in rushing back. I went back to the woman at the front desk. She looked up at me over the glasses perched on the end of her nose as I approached. "Something you need, young man?"

Young man. I liked that. I wasn't feeling too young these days. I asked her if it was possible to look up the name and address of a property owner.

"It's all public information," she said, punching out the word "information" as she had the other words earlier. "You bring me liber, folio and plat, and we'll look it up."

I must have looked confused. She smiled. "Book number, page number and lot number. It's all on the microfilm."

"Oh. Okay, I'll be right back."

She looked back down at her work. "And I'll be right here."

Twenty-Eight

Not much more than a half-hour later I was back in Dewey. I was on my way to meet the Chief at the Station – he'd long since left the house. I had C. Ordner's mailing address and copies of the relevant tax maps on the seat beside me. I had called Hartner from the road, and while he had been less than thrilled at my tardiness, at least he hadn't put out an APB for me. I wonder if they still have APB's. I wonder if it matters. Probably not.

I wanted to swing by the Ordner address but thought that keeping the Chief waiting any longer was probably not in my best interest. And when I walked into the Station house I knew that I had been right: Riley was at the front desk – apparently he'd decided to come into work after all – and when I walked in he gave me a wide-eyed look that said "Yikes!" and a nod of the head toward Hartner's office, a message I received loud and clear. I mouthed "thanks," and then said, "I'm here to see the Chief," rather formally. Riley responded just as formally. "He's in his office waiting for you, Sir. You can go back."

Hartner was at his desk, looking none too happy. "You tell someone you're going to be somewhere," he said, "you damn well ought to be there."

JOE GREANEY

"I'm sorry. I told you on the phone that I got caught up. I got here as fast as I could."

"Caught up in what?"

"I was doing some research over in Georgetown."

"Research on what?"

"Land records. I've got something pretty interesting here."

"Yeah?" He raised an eyebrow. "What?"

I spread the maps out on his desktop. "This is a map..." I began, but the Chief cut me off. "I can see that," he snapped.

"Jesus. Do you mind if I talk? I mean, if you're not interested, just tell me."

The Chief grunted. "Go on," he said.

"This is a tax map of Dickie's property and the surrounding properties. I don't want to read too much into it, but it's pretty interesting."

"You said that already. What's interesting about it?"

"Look here," I pointed at the north end of Dickie's property. "This is a conservation easement. Basically guarantees that nothing can be built there."

The Chief took this in. "So?"

"So maybe nothing. But you can't put a driveway on it, and you can't put a sewer through it. Now look at this." I pointed to the south end of Dickie's property, where it abutted the Ordner property. "If you want to put a driveway or a sewer line in from this direction, you have to go across this little strip of land here."

"Huh."

"Exactly. Huh. So you can't go through the lake, obviously, and if you can't go this way, to the north, and

—301—

you can't go this way, to the south, then Dickie's property isn't worth very much, because you can't develop it."

"But if you can get to it it's worth a lot."

"Right. But here's the other thing: Look at this property." I placed a finger on the thin sliver of land labeled "C. Ordner" on the map. "Look how skinny it is . I'd be surprised if it's deep enough to build a house on. So it's not worth much of anything. But if you want to develop Dickie's property, and assuming you can't go the other way, suddenly this little piece of land could be worth a lot of money."

"Like how much?"

"I don't know. But Dickie's land gains maybe five million bucks in value if you can develop it. Hell, maybe ten, the way property values are going. That's got to make this piece worth maybe a million, wouldn't you say?"

The Chief rubbed his chin, thinking it over. "But if Dickie doesn't want his property developed, if he makes sure that the property can't be developed, that makes this piece…"

"Practically worthless. And we know – I know – that Dickie was trying to do just that, trying to preserve his land. "

The Chief stood up. "Sounds pretty much like a motive to me. Let's see if we can find out who C. Ordner is."

"I have the mailing address right here."

"Is it local?"

"Right here in Dewey."

"Then let's take a ride."

We walked out into the reception area. Riley was still at the desk, trying to look as though he was accomplishing something. The Chief gave him a skeptical look, and Riley ducked his head, then picked up the phone when it rang a second later.

"Dewey Beach Police, Riley speaking." He was silent for a moment, and then said, "Hold on, I'll see if he's here." He held the phone against his chest and said, "It's Marge Reston."

"Oh, Jesus," the chief groaned. "That woman's gonna drive me nuts." He looked at me. "Lady lives behind the Bottle and Cork. She calls to bitch almost every day. I'll be a minute." To Riley he said, send it back to my office."

Riley nodded, and said into the phone, "Hold on Ma'am. He'll be right with you." Then he punched a button on the phone and set it back on its cradle. He looked up. "Looks like you calmed him down, at least," he said.

"Yeah, I guess so. I got some information, so I guess he forgives me for being late."

"What'd you find out?"

"Oh, it might not amount to anything, but we're going out to talk to this person who owns some land next to Dickie's place. Might be that they have a motive. Might not be, too. We'll see."

Riley was shuffling some papers. Without looking up he said, "Huh. Who's the person who owns the land?"

"Somebody named Ordner. Don't know if it's a man or a woman. But I got the address from the tax records so we're going to swing by there."

Hartner came back into the room, wearing his sunglasses. "Goddamn woman," he said. "Buys a house next to a bar and then she's surprised when it's noisy. Jesus. Okay, let's go," I followed him out to his truck and we both climbed in. "What's the address?" the Chief asked as we pulled out of the parking lot. I looked at the piece of paper and told him. We rode north on Route One in silence. He turned off by the canal and after a couple of turns slowed in front of a small brick bungalow that could have used a little paint on the trim but which was otherwise neatly kept. The grass in the small front yard was trimmed and there were a couple of healthy pots of flowers on either side of the front door. There was no garage, and no car in the short asphalt driveway. After we had sat there for a few seconds I asked, "Aren't we going to get out?"

"I don't know what the hell we're going to do."

"What do you mean?"

"There's got to be some mistake," he said.

"Mistake about what?"

"About the address you got. You must have written down the wrong number, transposed it or something."

"Why?"

"Because I know whose house this is. I should have recognized the address but I guess I wasn't thinking."

"Whose house is it?"

"A lady friend of mine. A fine woman. Wouldn't have anything to do with anything like all of this in a million years."

"Well, is her last name Ordner?"

"No."

"Well, then maybe I did make a mistake. I mean, it's never happened before but I suppose it's theoretically possible."

Hartner shot me a glance. I don't think he found me amusing just then. "Maybe so," he said and then paused. "First initial is 'c', though. Carol."

"That doesn't prove anything."

"No," he said. "No it doesn't. Makes you wonder, though."

I couldn't argue with him there. But everything had been making me wonder for a while now. This was just one more thing on the list.

"Well," the chief said, shifting in his seat and opening his door. "I'm sure she's at work but I might as well check and make sure."

"You want me to come?"

He shot me a withering look. "I think I can handle it. Sit tight." The chief climbed down from the truck, hitched his holster up, made his way across the sidewalk and yard, mounted the steps and knocked. There was no answer, no telltale twitch of the curtains. The Chief knocked again, turned and shrugged, then walked back across the yard. A vehicle pulled up behind us and I turned to see that it was a battered old silver Toyota pickup. As I looked, Riley climbed out of the truck, a goofy smile on his face. I climbed out to greet him, and Riley the Chief and I all met on the sidewalk in front of the house.

"Hey, Dude," Riley said lightly.

"What's up?" I asked.

Before Riley could answer the Chief said, "What in hell you doing here, Riley?"

"I'm on lunch. My mom asked me to take care of a couple things for her. What are you guys doing here?"

That was when I remembered that the Chief and Riley's mom were seeing each other. "Do a couple things? Like what?" The chief asked. "And how do you figure you get lunch when you came in two hours late, anyways?"

"Chief, I thought it would be okay. It's for my mom."

"Well…make it quick. You don't get any special privileges just because I've been dating your mother."

"Thanks, chief. Hey, if you two could give me a hand I could get this done in about one minute." He looked at me. "Give me a hand, dude?"

I hesitated. Something was seeming very odd here. "Um, okay, I guess."

Riley said, "Chief?"

"Oh, for Christ's sake, okay."

The three of us walked up the path, Riley in the lead. I still had a feeling that all was not well but I couldn't put my finger on it exactly. It just seemed odd that I would get the wrong address for this Ordner person, and that the address would turn out to be Riley's mom, who happened to be dating Hartner, and that Riley would show up when we were there. Riley unlocked the door and we stepped into the narrow hallway. Suddenly Hartner's hand shot down toward his holster, and it was all clear: Everything had been Hartner. That was why he had made no progress on the case. He hadn't wanted to make progress. Ordner must be Riley's mom's maiden name or perhaps it was the name of someone she had inherited the property from. In any event, Hartner had found out about the property and had orchestrated everything in order to make the money off it. The guy was an evil genius. "Riley, look out," I yelled as Hartner's hand, with the gun in it, began to rise.

Twenty-Nine

Things changed in a hurry. Riley spun on his heel. He had a strange look in his eyes. And a very large pistol in his hand. He looked quickly at Hartner. "Drop it, Chief, or I'll put a hole through you so big I could drive through it." Hartner let go of his revolver and it slid back into his holster. Keeping his gun pointed at Hartner, Riley reached out and took the gun from the holster. He took a step backward, then looked at me, still smiling strangely, "Thanks, 'Dude'" he said, the quotation marks clearly audible. "Another second and he might have gotten me. And that would have spoiled everything"

Spoiled everything? What the hell...? Under his breath Hartner mumbled "Asshole". I don't think he was talking about Riley. It suddenly appeared that I had assembled my facts incorrectly.

Riley said, "You two put your hands against the wall, feet back and spread 'em. You know the drill. Do not move. I got to make a call."

We did as instructed, side by side in the narrow hallway. Riley kept the gun pointed at us in one hand and with the other he dialed on his cell phone, looking up at us between numbers. I whispered "sorry" to the

Chief, who just rolled his eyes and shook his head. I wasn't on his good list just then.

Riley held the phone to his ear and apparently whoever he had called answered. He took a few steps away and began muttering into the phone rapidly. It wasn't possible to make out most of what he said, but it was clear what the topic was. After a while my arms began to ache from the strain of leaning against the wall, so I said screw it and stood up straight.

"Hey," Riley snarled, brandishing the pistol, "what do you think you're doing?"

"What does it look like, genius? I'm standing here."

"Hands against the wall or I swear I'll blow you away."

"Oh, go ahead. My bet is you're gonna do it anyway. I might as well be comfortable." The Chief took my lead and stood up as well, rubbing his shoulders. "Gotta go," Riley said into the phone. "Get your ass moving." He pressed the button to end the call, folded the phone and stowed it in his front pants pocket. "You guys are a couple of idiots," he said. "You know that, right? Why the fuck wouldn't I shoot you?"

"Because you like us?" I replied.

Riley's mouth twisted in what might have been a smile. "Jesus," he said. But then he sighed and shook his head and said, "Okay, I guess there's no real reason for you to be standing around holding up the wall. Into the living room." He gestured with the pistol toward a doorway directly in front of us. "And don't try anything funny"

"You have watched way too much TV in your life," I said. But I did as he had said. The living room was small and tidy. It looked like somebody's Mom's living room, which of course it was. Riley gestured to a beige sofa upon which a couple of large light-blue pillows in a floral pattern reposed. "On the couch," he said. "Both of you."

We sat. Riley sat across from us in a navy wing chair. "This thing's a recliner," he said, apropos, apparently, of nothing. Neither the Chief nor I could come up with an appropriate response. "Check it out," Riley said. He pushed back on the armrests and the chair tilted backwards and a footrest folded out from beneath. It was, in fact, a recliner. "Pretty cool, huh?" Riley said as he folded the chair back up.

"Yeah, pretty cool," I said. I thought I should answer him. The guy was obviously a nut, but he was the one with the gun, after all. Riley seemed happy that I concurred with him. And if he was happy, I was happy.

We sat there in silence for a few seconds. Finally the Chief said, "Does your mother know about all this?"

"No way! It'd kill her."

"So you're going to kill us instead."

"Chief, I'm sorry, but there's not a hell of a lot I can do about that. My mom's gonna miss you. Sucks, but there you go."

I said, "Maybe I'm missing something here. Why exactly do you have to kill us?"

Riley looked at me. "'cause we don't wanna get caught, dude. Why do you think?"

"Yeah, but two murders – somebody's going to investigate. You can't kill everybody."

"I dunno. Maybe not. But we've made a pretty good start on it already."

I couldn't argue with that one. He was right. "But… well, if they catch you, you're gonna get executed."

"Look, I don't know why I'm bothering to explain this. But here's the deal, bro. There's already two down. We get caught, we're already gonna get fried. And I don't wanna get fried, man. So, if taking you two out keeps me from gettin' fried I win. And if we take you out and we get caught, well, they can still only fry me once, you know? So I got, like, no choice. Get it?"

Unfortunately this made sense. So I wasn't going to talk him out of it, that much was clear. It was time for plan B. Actually, it was time to think of Plan B, and then it would be time for Plan B.

"Yeah, I get it. But it's three dead, not two"

"Three? No, two. Dickie and the girl."

"What about Kavanagh?"

"Who?"

"The surveyor."

Riley shook his head. "Don't know anything about it."

That was odd. But then there was a lot of odd stuff going on. "What was all that crap about being at the Police station and overhearing Robert talking about killing me?"

"Just tryin' to confuse you, Dude. Like misdirection. Get you chasin' your tail."

"But why bring Robert into it? Why would you put your partner under suspicion?"

"My partner? He's not my partner."

"I could have told you that," the Chief said. I looked over at him and asked, "Why didn't you?"

"I didn't mind you thinking it was him. Gave you something to do."

"Gave me something to do? Dammit, I…"

Riley waved the pistol. "Cut it, fellas. You're giving me a headache. Just sit there and shut up, okay? We'll be leaving soon."

"Where are you taking us?"

"To tell you the truth, I don't know. It'll all be the same to you, though."

Great.

We sat there for over fifteen minutes, the only sounds the ticking of the grandfather clock in the front hall and the low rumble of the central air conditioning. Finally the front door opened. I could hear it but I couldn't see it from where I sat on the couch. Heavy footsteps came down the hall, and a moment later Riley's partner stood in the doorway. "Hey there, Lou," said Chief Hartner.

"George," Lou Nickerson replied. "Sorry we have to meet this way."

"Not as sorry as I am," Hartner replied.

"I guess not." Nickerson sat in an armchair across the coffee table from the couch. He shook his head. "What are we going to do with you two?"

"Let us go?" I asked.. Hey, it never hurts to ask.

Nickerson regarded me coldly. "Shut up or I'll shoot you right now."

Okay, most of the time it doesn't hurt to ask. This might be an exception. I shut my mouth and sat there for a moment. Then something occurred to me. "Look, just let me talk for a minute, okay?"

Nickerson didn't say yes, but he didn't say no. "You two obviously got into this for the money."

Riley said, "Well, duh." Nickerson shot him a look and Riley shut up.

"You got into this for the money, but face it – you're just nibbling at the edges. You, Mr. Nickerson, you stand to make quite a lot of money if that property is developed, and you'll make less, Riley – or your Mom will- but you'll still do pretty well.. But the person who owns Dickie's land will make the most by far. And that person's me. I'll trade you that land for my life and the Chief's life. I'll sign it over to you, and you'll make five times as much as you stand to now. All you have to do is let us go."

Nickerson looked surprised. "That's bullshit. You don't own that land."

"Yes I do. It's true. Dickie willed it to me. I have a copy of the will. Hidden in a very safe place."

"But I've seen the will. It gives the place to Robert."

"That's the old one. Robert did something – I don't know what – that pissed Dickie off. That's when Dickie started talking to SOS. But he didn't like what they had to say, either. And I guess I was handy, so he changed his will and gave it to me."

Nickerson slowly shook his head, looking stunned. "You're not lying?"

"It's gospel."

"But…but it can't be. I saw the will. Morgan showed it to me."

"I just told you. There's another one after that."

Nickerson jumped to his feet. I think I might have cringed. I've never found cringing very attractive. He snarled, "That thieving bastard!"

"Who?"

"Robert, that son of a bitch. Took me for half a million fucking dollars. Every cent I have in the world and then some." He slammed his fist on the arm of his chair. "Shit!

How could I be so fucking stupid?" He sat down heavily and cupped his head in hands.

"How'd he do that, Lou?" asked the Chief.

To my surprise Nickerson answered him. "Oh, he gave me a security interest in the land against a loan. Said he needed it for his boat. Fucking Morgan recommended it. Shit!" He began pacing rapidly. "Shit!" he said again. "Fucker's probably half way to Mexico by now."

I asked, "When'd you give him the money?"

"Yesterday."

"Well he was still here this morning – I talked to him. Said he was here until after the funeral tomorrow." I made the last part up but thought it sounded good. I didn't want Nickerson doing anything rash.

"Where was this?" asked Nickerson.

"The house. Dickie's house."

Nickerson stood again. "Let's go," he said. "Now." He nodded at Riley, who waved the gun at the Chief and myself. We stood. Nickerson said, "My van's outside. Just stay real calm and get in the back seat and nobody gets shot."

"Yet," I said.

"Yet," Nickerson agreed.

We walked outside, Nickerson leading, Riley following. Just a few steps out into the yard Nickerson stopped. "Shit. We can't leave your truck here, George. Okay, change of plan. George, you get behind the wheel of your truck. Riley, you ride in the passenger seat. Keep him covered. You," he nodded at me, "drive my van. I'll ride with you." To Riley he said, "We're going over to that house. Any monkey business, put a hole in him." Riley nodded, looking, I thought, a little glum. Maybe it was because he had to wait for monkey business before plugging Hartner, I don't know.

We were a strange little procession as we headed through the neighborhood and onto Route One, the two cars almost bumper to bumper, the Chief driving with exaggerated caution, using his signals carefully and coming to a complete stop at each stop sign. Nickerson and I didn't speak until we were nearing Dickie's place and I said, "I can't believe you'd kill somebody just to get money. You don't seem like that kind of guy."

Nickerson grimaced. "It didn't start out to be like this. But this is where it is. And there's no way to go back now."

"How'd you decide to kill Dickie?"

"Decide, hell. I didn't even set out to hurt him. I just wanted a chance to talk to him but he'd been ducking me for weeks. I knew he was getting ready to donate his land to that SOS group, and I didn't want him to do it . Riley came and told me that Dickie was down at Keybox, and…". He paused. "One thing led to another."

"How'd you know that Dickie was talking to SOS?"

"They contacted me, asking if I was interested in donating my land since it would never be able to be developed after Dickie donated his to them."

It occurred to me that apparently SOS wasn't above being a bit disingenuous when it suited them. They had told me that they would likely turn around sell the property but they told Nickerson they never would. That way they could get Nickerson's property on the cheap. Buy low, sell high, as they say. I wondered who had told him this – if it was it was the same guy I had met with at SOS, Bob Feingold. "Who from SOS contacted you?"

"No one at SOS. Dan Morgan called me."

"Morgan? Why?"

"He's their attorney."

"That can't be right."

"Why not?"

"Well, I'm sure they have their own attorneys. Lots of them."

Nickerson rolled his eyes. "All I know is what he said. And he said he was acting for SOS." We turned into Dickie's driveway, still right behind the Chief's big Bronco. Robert's rental car wasn't there. The Bronco came to a stop, and Riley opened the passenger door and emerged, pistol leveled back through the door at the Chief. I could see that Hartner had placed his hands on his head. Riley circled the car quickly and pulled the driver's side door open. He was doing a good imitation of a cop. Hartner climbed out of the car, shaking his head in disgust or amusement or both. Riley said something. I could read Hartner's lips – he said, "Shut up" and then he leaned against the side of his truck with his arms crossed, waiting for me and Nickerson. Go Chief. You tell 'em.

"Let me ask you something" I said. "This security interest you gave Robert – how was it done?"

"What's it to you?"

"Humor me. What do you have to lose?""

He sighed, and then said, "Well, he had a document drawn up, and we both signed, and Morgan's secretary witnessed it."

"Morgan drew it up?"

"Yeah. Why?"

"Hold on a sec. Where is that document now?"

"In Morgan's safe. What's all this about?"

"I'm starting to have an idea."

"What, dammit?"

"I think you've been scammed."

"Well, no shit. When I find Robert, I…"

"Not by Robert. Or at least not only by Robert. By Morgan."

"I can't worry about Morgan right now. Get out of the car."

I complied. Riley and Hartner were still standing there looking angry with each other. "In the house," said Nickerson. He turned and walked ahead without a glance back. Hartner and I exchanged a glance and followed, with Riley bringing up the rear.

Nickerson tried the door but found it locked, and turned to me, hand outstretched. I gave him my keys and we went inside, and on into the living room. We stood there looking at each other for a moment. "What now?" Riley asked.

"Hell if I know, Nickerson replied. "Wait and see what happens."

Which we did. And it didn't take long for things to start happening. About five minutes, actually. We were still sitting in the living room looking at each other when the sound of car tires on the crushed shell driveway was clearly audible. To Riley, Nickerson said, "See who it is." Riley rose, went to the window and looked out. "Who is it?" asked Nickerson.

"Dunno. Some dude. He's gettin' out of his car. He's comin' this way. What should I do?"

"Get away from the window, for starters, dipshit." Riley jumped back from the window as though he had been stung. "Now," Nickerson continued, "You take the

Chief here out back. Shoot him if he makes a sound. George, please be quiet. We're still trying to figure a way out of this. I don't want to kill you but I will if I have to. Now go on." Riley and the chief left the room just as a knock came on the door. Quickly, Nickerson said, "Flaherty, you answer the door. Get rid of this person. Do not do anything stupid. I'll be right behind the door listening to every word." I nodded and walked toward the door just as a second, more insistent knock came. Hartner took his position and nodded at me. He held his pistol in both hands, barrel pointing at the ceiling.

I opened the door. "Hello, William," said the dapper fellow standing there.

"Ted! What the hell are you doing here?"

"I wanted to talk to you. May I come in? What are the police doing here?"

"The police?"

"There's a police car in the driveway."

"Oh. Um..." I said, scrambling for something to say, "It had some kind of engine trouble...they're coming back for it."

"Oh. So can I come in?"

"I'm, uh, kinda busy right now." I rolled my eyes and nodded my head toward the door behind which Nickerson stood not two feet away from us. "It's not really a good time." I mouthed the word "help" or tried to. I couldn't be sure Ted understood.

"Is everything okay?" he asked.

"Oh, sure," I said, trying to sound casual while at the same time frantically shaking my head no. "It's just not good right now. I'll call you later, okay?"

"Uh, sure, Billy. Well…I guess I'll …I'll see you in a while"

I pointed at the door quickly and made the shape of a gun with my hand while mouthing the word "gun". Ted nodded quickly and I said, "Well, see you later, okay?"

"Okay, Bill." Ted replied. Then he mouthed "I'll be back," and I nodded.

We said goodbye and I closed the door. Nickerson was there, smiling at me. "Good job," he said. "Who was that?"

"Just a friend of mine, Ted Lynam."

"What'd he want?"

"Man, how do I know? You could hear him as well as I could. I guess he just wanted to say 'hi'".

"Okay." Nickerson looked doubtful, but then appeared to make up his mind about something. "Riley, put the Chief's truck in the garage. We can't have that thing sitting around out there. After you've moved it, wipe it down for fingerprints anywhere you might have touched. And you two sit down and shut up."

Riley did as he was told and the Chief and I did the same. Nickerson sat heavily on a large brown leather club chair across from us. He sighed and shook his head. I might have imagined it, but it seemed like his eyes got a little moist for a second there.

The Chief spoke for the first time in a long while, startling me. "What are you going to do, Lou?" he asked calmly.

Nickerson looked up. "I guess turning back time isn't an option, huh?"

"I guess not. But don't make any more mistakes. This is all going straight to shit on you, you know that, right? Don't make it worse."

With no trace of rancor in his voice Nickerson said, "Shut up, George."

The door opened and Nickerson jumped up, but it was only Riley. He walked quickly into the room and said, "There's too much crap in the garage. The truck won't fit."

"You can't make room?"

"I probably could, but there's a lot of stuff. It'd take a while."

Nickerson looked at me. "Go help him. And remember I've got your buddy in here. Try not to be an idiot. And Riley – pull the truck around back of the garage until you can get it in there. I don't want anyone to see it."

Riley nodded, looking rather glum, then looked down at the floor. He said, "Keep him here for a minute while I move the truck, okay?"

Nickerson nodded and Riley went out. A couple of minutes later he walked back in, looked at me, and said "C'mon." I followed him outside. It was bright out and it took my eyes a minute to adjust. I followed Riley to the garage and together we looked in. I'd been in the garage before, of course, but it hadn't really hit me how full of stuff it was until now. There had to be at least a dozen surfboards and windsurfers in the two-car garage, along with sails stacked like cordwood and a forest of masts and booms . I saw at least three bikes, garden tools, trash cans, old flower pots, piles of newspaper and every type of assorted junk a household might generate. Dicky had obviously been something of a pack rat.

"Might as well get to it, Dude," Riley said. "Any ideas?"

"I guess if we stack all the boards on top of each other on one side, that'd be a start Then we can pile the rest of the crap on top of them. First we have to make some room for the boards, though."

Riley nodded. "What a goddamn pain in the ass," he said. I couldn't argue with him. We began working, me in the back of the garage and Riley up front by the open door, and as we did I wondered what had happened to Ted. Maybe he'd gone to get the police. Riley and I cleared some space on one side of the garage and began piling the boards up, with each of us taking one end. Riley was hampered by the pistol he kept in his hand. Twice he dropped his end of the board we were moving, and the second time the edge of the fin on the board caught me right on the bone in my right shin. Which hurt. "Shit, Riley," I said, "put the gun down or put it in your pocket or something. You can't do this one-handed."

Riley looked at me for a moment, eyes blank, then shrugged and set the gun on a trash can by his side. Immediately, Ted stepped in from around the corner, and hit Riley in the head with a shovel. Riley dropped as if he'd been shot. Ted stood over him like a gladiator, not a hair out of place. He wasn't even breathing hard. "That's one down," he said. "How many more are there?"

"Just one."

"Halfway there, then."

"Are the police coming?"

"I didn't call them."

"Shit, why not?"

"Because of that truck. I thought maybe it was the police that were giving you the trouble."

I picked up the gun from where Riley had set it. "Take this," I said, holding it out.

Ted shook his head. "I don't like guns."

"Well, neither do I."

Ted shrugged. "Leave it, then."

"Nah. I'll keep it, I guess. Right now we need to get this dope tied up."

We looked around, and I found a roll of duct tape on a shelf, which was just the ticket. We taped his feet together, and then taped his hands together, with his arms looped around one of the metal poles that hold up the roof. A piece of tape over his mouth completed the job. By the time we were done, Riley wasn't going anywhere. While we worked, we talked about the situation and tried to come up with a plan. "Look," he said, "there's a nut in there with a gun. Let's just call the cops and stay put. Let them handle it."

"I can't. Go ahead and call the cops, but I can't just sit here. Hartner's in there and it's my fault. I have to do something."

"Always the noble Irishman."

"It's my fault," I repeated.

Ted sighed. "Okay. I'm in. Do you have any ideas?"

"No. Yeah. Sneak around back and try to get in there."

"Hell of a plan."

"It's all I got."

" I'm coming with you."

"No, all we've got is one gun. What's point?"

"I'm coming with you."

"Shit, you're a pain in the ass, you know that, Ted?"

"I like to think so."

I tried to think of a plan. "Okay. How about this? You go to the front and knock again. And be persistent. Just keep on knocking. I don't think you'll get shot for that. If a guy comes to the door it'll either be Chief Hartner or this guy Nickerson. You've met Hartner before. Nickerson's got a gun. If it's Hartner at the door, remember Nickerson's probably right behind the door like he was when I answered the door. Just try to keep whoever it is that comes to the door occupied – keep asking where I am, when I'll be back, what they're doing in the house, whatever you can think of. I'll try to sneak in from the back while you keep them busy. Okay?" Ted nodded. "Okay, then," I said." Let's do it. First let me get to the corner of the house – where's your car, by the way?"

"Down the street."

"Go get it and drive in like you did last time. That way they'll hear you coming and they won't start wondering what's going on quite so fast."

"Got it. Back in two minutes."

"Call the cops, too."

"Will do."

"Now go."

Ted quickly ran off through the low scrub pines that flank the garage. I waited a few seconds to make sure there was no reaction from the house, no shouting or shooting, then scrambled across the grass to the back corner of the house. I sat on the ground with my back to the wall and waited.

It was longer than two minutes before Ted returned. More like three or four, but it seemed like an eternity.

When I heard the crunch of tires in the driveway I stood, staying flat against the wall, pistol clamped in my sweaty white-knuckled hands. I was around the corner from the front door, but close enough, I hoped, to be able to hear what was going on when – if – the door was answered. I could hear Ted's car door close, and a few seconds later I was able to hear him knocking. He knocked softly at first, and then paused. When there was no answer he knocked again, more loudly this time, then paused again. He started a third time, knocked just twice, and stopped. A few seconds later I heard him say, "Hello, I was looking for Bill Flaherty. Aren't you the Police Chief?"

Good ole Ted. He knew that I might not have been able to hear whose voice it was, so he had tipped me off. And I knew that since Hartner was at the door, Nickerson was most likely right behind it. I ran along the side of the house and turned the corner into the back yard, then up the two steps to the door.

I was dizzy and feeling queasy from the adrenaline rush as I stood there for a moment. I took a quick peak through the glass panel in the door. There was no one visible, so I looked again. Definitely no one. I tried the knob, but it was locked. Shit. I couldn't kick it down or break the window, Nickerson would hear me. And shoot me.

Think, think. Think, dammit!

Against all odds, I actually had a thought. I ran over to the window where a lifetime ago I had been talking to Riley. Peaked through. Nobody. Tried it. It was unlocked. I slid the window up as slowly and quietly as I could, boosted myself up and climbed in. I was in the den. The TV was to my left, to my right was a short hallway that led to the living room. I knew that on the far side of the living room was the foyer and the front door. I couldn't see the front door from where I stood, so I edged my way up the hallway, pistol still in hand. What I don't know about guns would fill volumes, but like Riley I've watched too much TV in my life, so I did the SWAT team thing – gun pointed at the ceiling as I neared the corner, then ducked around the corner, ending up on one knee with the gun in both outstretched arms, sweeping it back and forth to cover the room.

There was no one there. I got back on my feet and moved a few steps to my left, to where I knew I would be able to see the front door, but I already knew that something was wrong – I couldn't hear anyone talking. A moment later my suspicions were confirmed. The door stood open, and there was no one in sight. I went to the door but before I got there I heard a car engine start, followed immediately by the sound of tires spinning on the drive. It was Ted's car. The passenger side was to me, and I could see the chief in the passenger seat and Nickerson in the back. That meant Ted was driving, God help them all. Ted's a lot of things, most of them good. But one thing that is not good is his driving.

I ran around to the back of the garage and jumped in the Chief's truck. The keys weren't in it. I climbed back out and ran back around and into the garage. Riley was awake now, struggling against his bonds, his eyes wide with fear and frustration, his face red and sweaty with exertion. I ripped the tape from his mouth. I said, "Where are the keys, asshole?"

He looked at me with dewy eyes, like he was a moment from crying. I didn't care. "The keys to the Chief's truck! Where are they? Now, dammit!"

"In my…in my pocket."

"Which one?"

"But…"

"You got one second before I kick you in the head. Which one?"

"Front…left, but…"

I pushed him on his side, but the tape on his wrists and the pole they were fastened around prevented him from falling all the way over. I held him still with a foot, fished in his pocket for the keys, found and retrieved them. As I ran back out of the garage, Riley called after me, "Wait…stop…you can't…." I ignored him and ran to the truck, jumped in, fired it up, and tore around the garage, the tires spitting chunks of grass and dirt.

Ted's car was nowhere in sight. I went the couple of blocks to Bayard and stopped. Left was Dewey, right Rehoboth. There was no way to be sure. I spun the wheel and went left, almost killing a rollerblader in a black full-body spandex suit and a fluorescent green helmet. How I didn't see him is something of a mystery. I gunned the truck and covered the half-mile to the center of Dewey in seconds. I caught the green light and cruised down Route One, looking down every side street, but with no luck. When I reached the south end of town I pulled a U-turn and went back. When I reached the cut-off for One-A I went right, back towards Rehoboth. There was still no sign of them.

The light was red at the Avenue and I sat there idling in traffic, trying to think where they could have gone. I doubted Nickerson had simply fled with Ted and Hartner as hostages. He was too mad, too unstable to just run. But where would he have gone? And suddenly it hit me: Who was the central figure? Who had been manipulating things behind the scenes? Morgan, of course. If Morgan hadn't been involved, Nickerson would never have killed Dickie, would never have even known that Dickie was thinking of donating his property to SOS. Without Morgan, Nickerson would probably be home, gardening or drinking iced tea in the shade somewhere. That had to be it. Nickerson figured he was out of luck but he wanted to make sure Morgan went down to.

The light was still red but there was no oncoming traffic so I cut into the other lane and charged up to the intersection. I had the radio in hand and was flipping switches on the dashboard as I drove, trying to figure out how to turn on the lights and siren. Somehow I managed to turn on the PA and "Shit!" echoed down the street as people turned and stared. Finally I got the lights working, and a moment after that, the siren.

I quickly glanced to the right, toward the ocean, a didn't see Ted's car. So I went left, toward Route One. All I had to go on was a hunch, but I decided to follow it. I still had the microphone in my hand, so I pressed the button and talked into it. "Dewey Police, Rehoboth, State Troopers! Can anyone hear me?"

I released the button. There were a few seconds of static, then a voice I recognized. "Dewey Beach Police, Bellegarde here. Who's this? And what are you doing on our frequency?"

A Wonder Bread truck pulled out of a side street directly in my path. I swerved to avoid him, the Chief's truck leaning heavily. "This is Bill Flaherty. I'm driving your Chief's truck west on Rehoboth Avenue, heading for Route One and then Lewes, and I need backup!"

"What in the hell are you talking about? This is Flannery?"

"Flaherty. Bill Flaherty. Remember me? Chief Hartner has been kidnapped, along with a friend of mine named Ted Lynam, by Lou Nickerson. I'm guessing but I think Nickerson is going to an attorney's office up in Lewes – Dan Morgan's office. "

"This...you...you're crazy, you know that? You're driving the Chief's truck?"

"Yeah., I had to take it, it's all there was to drive. Get somebody up there to Morgan's office. Nickerson has a gun and I think he'll use it."

There were several long seconds of silence. Finally Bellegarde came back on. "This better not be bullshit, Flaherty."

The road curved to the right, and just ahead was the yield onto Route One. I took the bend at speed and again it felt as though the big truck might tip. Traffic was mercifully light and I accelerated rapidly. Cars moved out of the way as I approached, the siren working wonders.

"Flaherty?"

"Yeah. I'm here, sorry. It's no bullshit. Chief Hartner and Ted Lynam have been kidnapped at gunpoint by Lou Nickerson. I could be wrong but I think he's taking them to Dan Morgan's office in Lewes. That's where I'm heading now – I should be there in five or seven minutes. And I don't feel like taking this guy on alone."

"What's the address?"

"I don't know it. It's on Route Nine, on the right, not far off Route One. In a little shopping center. You might have to look it up. Hell, the Lewes cops should know."

"What kind of car are they in?"

"It's a gold Acura. I don't know the model name. One of the smaller ones, and it's maybe 4 years old. D.C. tags. Three people in it. Nickerson's in the back, or he was."

"Where are you now?"

"Route One, heading north. I'm past the outlets. Just passed the Lowes a minute ago."

"Well, stop and turn around. Come back here."

"No. I'm going up there. I'm in this too far to stop now."

I almost thought I could hear him sigh over the radio. Probably just static. The radio crackled back to life. "Lewes has people on the way. You might beat them there, or they might beat you. Whatever you do, don't go off half-cocked. Let someone with some experience and training handle it. You got it?

A late-model Cadillac wasn't moving out of the way. I braked sharply and laid on the horn. I started to go around it on the right, and the driver put the turn signal on, so I stayed in my lane. Long seconds passed before the car began to move right. I glanced at the driver, an ancient woman with a mound of white hair, and resisted the impulse to give her the finger. With some luck I'd be old someday too. With a lot of luck.

"I said, you got it?"

"Yeah, I got it, sorry. I was dealing with traffic."

"Leave the radio on. We've got Lewes on the other line. I repeat: If you get there first, stay put. We don't need any more hostages, and we don't want anyone shot. You hear me?"

"Yes, sir."

"Good then. What's your twenty?"

"My...? Oh. I passed the exit for Route 24 a minute ago. I'm getting there."

"Keep us posted. And don't kill anyone with that truck."

There didn't seem to be much to say to that one.

Bellegarde came back on the radio. "We've got units on the way. So do the State Troopers. And Lewes. You better be sure about all of this."

I didn't answer. I couldn't be sure at all. If I was wrong, some people were going to be upset with me, there was no way around that. And if I was wrong, Ted and the Chief were in serious trouble. Hell, either way they were in serious trouble.

There was no radio communication for the next couple of minutes. I was left alone with my thoughts and the blaring siren. When I could see the exit for Route Nine I picked up the radio and called in. "Hey, Bellegarde...". This is probably not generally accepted police radio etiquette.

"Yeah? Where are you?" came the response.

"Just turning off on Nine. I'll be there in less than a minute."

"Okay. Don't be a fucking idiot."

This was probably not accepted radio etiquette either.

"I'll do my best."

The response came back garbled. It sounded like "That's what I'm afraid of."

Thirty

I pulled into the lot and drove all the way around the building looking for Ted's car, but it wasn't there. I parked the Chief's truck out of plain sight behind a dumpster in the rear of the building, and got out, taking the pistol with me. I tucked the gun in my waistband in the small of my back, and pulled my shirt out to cover it, then walked around to the front of the building as casually as possible. It didn't look like Nickerson had come after Morgan, after all. And now I was about to catch some serious hell for crying wolf – even though I really hadn't been. And Law Enforcement probably wasn't going to like the fact that I had taken the Chief's car, either. There wasn't much I could do about that now.

I looked around the small crowded parking lot again. Ted's car was still not there. In the distance I could hear the ululation of approaching sirens. I debated going into Morgan's office but decided against it. There wasn't anything else to do, so I stood on the sidewalk in front of his office and waited for the troops to arrive.

I'm not sure how much time went by – a minute, maybe two, but suddenly everything began to happen all at once. The door behind me swung open and Morgan came charging out, carrying a briefcase and with a huge sheaf of paper clutched to his chest.. His white hair was disheveled, his face red and wet with sweat. I managed to say, "Hey, where…" before the gunshots rang out, two of them in quick succession. Just then two cruisers swung into the lot, sirens blaring, tires shrieking in protest. Morgan stopped as if he had walked into an invisible wall, gave me a strange wistful little smile, and toppled backward onto the sidewalk. I dove behind a trash can, clawing at the gun in my belt. A car horn began blowing steadily, and a woman began screaming. I had the gun in my hand and was trying to stay as small as possible behind my tenuous shelter. One of the cruisers skidded to a stop, the driver's side door flew open, and a cop with a gun, his face twisted in fury, shouted "Freeze! Drop it now!"

Inanely, I thought that it was impossible to do both. Sanely, I dropped the gun and put my hands up, still crouched behind the trash can. The car horn stopped, the sirens ground to a halt, the woman stopped screaming, and there was a moment of perfect stillness. I heard the laugh of a gull, apparently amused by the commotion. But the calm was broken almost immediately. The cop from the closest car came running up, his gun trained on me, and kicked the pistol away. Without taking his eyes –or his gun- off me he sidled over to Morgan's inert figure, bent and put a hand to the lawyer's throat, feeling for a pulse. Two other cops ran up, weapons at the ready. "Get an ambulance, Jimmy," said the first cop. "Not that it's going to do any good. And get the Chief up here, and we're gonna need crime scene. Get it all rolling." The cop who was obviously named Jimmy nodded and ran back toward his car.

"I didn't shoot anyone," I said. "The gunshots came from over there."

"Where?"

As if in answer to the question, a voice called out, "Hey, can we get a little help over here? Or is that too much to ask?"

Ted. It was Ted. Thank God, he was alive. He was standing next to a blue Buick maybe thirty-five or forty yards off, waving both arms above his head.

"See what he needs, Rick, but be careful." said the first cop to the third. "You," he added, looking at me, "don't move a fucking muscle."

"I am a statue."

He just shook his head and glared. Some people are so uptight.

I noticed Hartner walking across the lot in our direction. "Ask him," I said. "He'll tell you I didn't do anything.".

Hartner walked up, shaking his head in amusement or disgust. The cop turned and said, "Hey, Chief Hartner. You got here quick. "

"I was already here." The cop looked puzzled but Hartner didn't expand. "You can let him go, Sergeant. He didn't do anything. For once"

"Sir, he had a weapon…"

"I know. I saw the whole thing. He's got things to answer for, but he's no threat."

The Sergeant looked at me. I tried to look eager and harmless, like a puppy. I guess it worked. The cop shrugged and said, "Okay. Put 'em down. But don't go anywhere."

"I won't."

"Hey, Sarge!" It was the cop named Rick. "Come over here, wouldya?"

The Sergeant turned and looked at me. "Stay put."

"Yes, sir."

The sergeant trotted off towards the blue Buick, the gear on his overloaded belt jangling almost musically as he ran. I looked at Hartner and he looked at me. "You're a piece of work," he said.

"Thanks, I think. What happened?"

"Your friend saved your ass. Nickerson put Morgan down, aimed at you, but before he could shoot your buddy got him by the hair and slammed his head into the windshield. Pretty strong for a skinny guy."

"Yeah, he is. Thank God for small favors.. Oh, here he comes."

Ted was walking almost jauntily across the parking lot towards us. For somebody who had knocked a man unconscious with a shovel, been kidnapped, and knocked another man unconscious with his bare hands, he looked pretty chipper. "Hey, guys," he said when he was still a few yards off. "What's up?"

Thirty-One

I stood at the railing on the deck, watching a couple of young lovelies saunter by on the beach. It was late afternoon, a couple of hours since Morgan had been shot – a couple of busy hours of questions and statements and admonishments, but now Ted and I were back at the house, and a warm gentle breeze was blowing, and I had a cold drink in my hand, and the world seemed to be sorting itself out. I heard the sound of ice cubes clinking in a glass as Ted poured himself a drink, and a few seconds later he joined me at the rail. Neither of us spoke for quite a while. Finally Ted sighed and said, "I still don't get what was going on with that fellow Morgan. What was he doing?"

"Comes down to greed."

"A lot of things do, Billy. But what was he trying to accomplish?"

"He was basically playing both ends against the middle. He was in a position to know what was going on with everyone involved, and he tried to turn it all to his advantage."

"But how?"

"He was Dickie's lawyer, and he'd known both Robert and Nickerson for years. He didn't want Dickie to donate the property to the SOS – he figured he could get a slice of the pie for brokering the deal if Dickie was to sell it to a developer. But then Dickie comes in and makes a new will, giving everything to me…"

"And he's screwed."

"Exactly. So Dickie does the new will. I don't know exactly what happened, but I can sort of see it – Morgan goes to file the will away and there's the old will giving everything to Robert, and a light goes off. If nobody knew about the new will, then the old will would still be in effect. And he had them both. All he has to do is get rid of the new will and if something happens to Dickie, Robert gets everything. I assume he got in touch with Robert and they came to an agreement."

"Well, okay…but what about Nickerson? How did he get involved.?"

"The way I see it, Nickerson got involved, and killed Dickie, before Morgan got in touch with Robert. It's the only way things make sense. Morgan gets Nickerson involved simply to try to keep Dickie from going through with his donation to SOS – all Morgan wants at that time is his slice for brokering the property to a developer. I assume Morgan figured out the business about Riley's mother's property and contacted Riley around the same time. Or maybe he told Nickerson and Nickerson contacted Riley– it doesn't matter. Anyways, Nickerson doesn't want SOS involved. He and Riley go to talk to Dickie, one thing leads to another, and then Dickie's dead, and that poor girl Darla, she was the parking lot attendant at Keybox, sees what happened, and they kill her too. I don't know when Morgan found out Dickie was dead. I might have been the one who told him when I went up there, or for all I know Nickerson told him. But once Dickie's dead, and Morgan has the wills, it all clicks for him. He's looking at a big score if he can just get Robert on board. And once he knows, Robert is very much on board. Either I get the place and Robert gets nothing, or he splits the money with Morgan. I don't think Robert had anything to do with Dickie dying, I just think that with Dickie already dead, Robert figured he'd rather get something than nothing and he sure didn't give a damn about me."

"Well, no one does."

"You got that right."

"William, I was joking. A lot of people care about you."

"Name two."

"Well, let's see…there's your Mom, and…" He stopped, a twinkle in his eye. "Nope, I guess you're right."

I took a long sip of my drink and set it on the railing. I knew he was kidding, but it still didn't feel very good. He was closer to the bone than he knew. The sun was getting lower in the sky, and the shadow of the house stretched all the way across the wide beach into the ocean. A kid was throwing a stick into the water for his dog at the water's edge. For some reason I felt very melancholy indeed.

"Billy." Ted said softly.

"What?"

"You know that's not true. I was just joking around with you.. Look, I came back all the way from San Francisco because I didn't like the way things were left."

"Yeah, and because you didn't want to be there."

"Well, there's that, of course, but…"

"Look, stop. Don't worry about it."

"Well, what about Bunny? And Lenny? And everyone else back in D.C.? They all care about you."

"Yeah, I guess so."

"What does that mean, 'you guess so'? It's true and you know it."

"Whatever."

"Again, and I'm sorry if I'm being a prick, but 'whatever'? What do you mean?"

"I mean, whatever. Maybe they do and maybe they don't. It doesn't matter. It's not an issue."

Ted looked out at the ocean, idly swirling the ice around in his glass. Without looking at me he said, "When are you moving back?"

"To D.C.?"

"Yes, of course."

"I'm not." This surprised me almost as much as it did Ted. I hadn't been aware that I had made a decision but I had obviously done so. And suddenly I felt a lot better.

"You're not? What about work? What about Bunny? You can't just stay here."

"Why not? I like it here. I've got a place to stay – a pretty damn nice place that's paid for – and Bunny's over. Very over. And as far as work goes, I've had enough of that job to last me. Especially now that Lenny's leaving, and considering the fact that I would see Bunny every day if I was there, I say the hell with it. I'll find work here. Maybe I'll start a business or something."

"What, selling t-shirts?"

"Hey, why not? As long as it pays the bills."

"I don't think you're thinking this through."

The anger in his voice was unmistakable. "What's the problem, Ted? I don't get it."

He kept staring into the distance. "You're forcing me to make a choice."

"Ted I'm not forcing you to do a damn thing. I'm not even asking you to do anything. What are you talking about?."

"If you're not going back, I don't want to go back either. So what am I going to do? Beg my Dad to get my job at Merck back? Not bloody likely."

"Why don't you move down here?"

"Move down here? And live where?"

"Right here, man. There's plenty of room, and you could help out on the bills, maybe we could even keep the heat on this winter. And still eat."

"I'm not exactly a beach person, William."

"Suit yourself, Ted. But no one says you have to go to the beach, you know."

He opened his mouth to say something, but the sound of footsteps in the gravel walkway stopped him. In a few seconds Chief Hartner came around the corner. He saw us and mounted the steps to the deck, saying, "Don't you answer the door when people knock?"

"Sorry," I replied. "Didn't hear a sound. What's up?"

"Not much. And yes."

"Yes what?"

"Yes I'll have a drink please."

"Oh, sorry. Not used to being the host here, I guess. What can I get you?"

"Got any beer? Or whiskey?"

"Got both. Just stocked up on the way home." It still sounded funny, "home".

"Good. Then that's what I'll have."

"I'm sorry. What?"

"Beer and whiskey, please. It's been a long damn day."

Ted said, "Coming right up. Ice in the whiskey?"

"Whiskey in the whiskey. Bourbon if you got it."

"That's what we have. Be right back."

Ted scurried off like a chastised butler. Now Hartner and I stood by the rail looking out at the ocean. After a few seconds he cleared his throat. "Well," he said.

I looked over at him. He didn't continue. I didn't care. I looked back at the ocean.

"What I mean to say…." He said, and stopped again. I waited. And waited a little more. Finally he continued. "What I mean to say is I might owe you an apology. And a thank you."

Ted came back with the drinks before I could respond. Unbelievably, he had found a small silver serving tray, and he had a crisp linen napkin draped over his arm. Now he was a waiter. A man of many talents, that Ted. He set a bottle of beer and a hefty tumbler of whiskey on the rail in front of Hartner, straightened, and looked quickly from Hartner to me and back. He cleared his throat and said, "I, ummm, need to go powder my nose. Excuse me."

Hartner "Thanks for the drinks."

"You're welcome. Give me a shout if there's anything I can get you." With that he turned on his heel and went back into the house.

Hartner took a big swallow of bourbon, and a few seconds later a healthy swig from the bottle of Beck's that Ted had given him. "Look," he said, "I'm sorry I kept you in the dark. I was never completely convinced that you weren't part of all this. My gut was that you were on the level, but I was never sure. Be that as it may, I'm sorry."

"For what, exactly?"

"For putting you in danger."

"Hell, you were the one in danger. Nickerson might have killed you."

"And you. If it wasn't for your friend, he might have done it. And Riley could have done it too. I knew – in my heart I knew – that he was involved somehow. But I didn't want to believe it because of his mother. I guess I figured that he was involved, so was she, and I didn't want to believe that. But I knew something was very wrong when he showed up at his mom's place. I was going to try to let it play out, and see if I could catch him in the act, but…"

"Yeah, I kind of blew that one."

Hartner chuckled. "Yeah. Kind of." He paused, took another sip of his beer. "You did good, though."

"Me? What the hell did I do?"

"You got Riley out of the picture…"

"I had help."

"So? And you figured out about Morgan, and you got backup up there, and you risked your life…you did good. I might not be alive right now if it wasn't for you. So…thanks."

I shrugged my acceptance. I didn't have much to say, except…"Hey, Waiter!"

Ted showed up at the sliding door after a couple of seconds. "You rang?"

"I'm getting thirsty. Let's have some drinks out here!"

He looked at me and smiled. "Coming right up, anything for my landlord and his guest."

"Your landlord?" I asked.

"I live here, don't I?"

"I guess you do, my man. I guess you do."

www.ingramcontent.com/pod-product-compliance
Lightning Source LLC
Chambersburg PA
CBHW062017170626

46813CB00001B/203